THE ROGUE'S CONFESSION

All people are fictional,

All events are real.

By:

Serge Pospelov

Page left intentionally

Copyright

Acknowledgement

I am deeply indebted to my friends who had the spirit and courage to share with me their stories and information during dark times of total censorship and oversight, which enveloped Russia and prevented me from using their real names.

Dedication

For my friends, alive and dead, maimed and healthy, who like leaves in the autumn storm had been dispersed over the world.

About the Author

Serge R. Pospelov is an accomplished author and former officer of the Russian Army, originally from Astrakhan, USSR. After graduating from Penza Higher Artillery Engineering School and the prestigious St. Petersburg Artillery Academy, Pospelov served during one of the most tumultuous periods in Russian history, the 1990th. His military career, combined with his personal experiences, has shaped his unique perspective on the social and political upheavals of post-Soviet Russia.

Pospelov's writing is rooted in his firsthand experiences, including his failed attempts to leave Russia, his wrongful imprisonment under suspicion of espionage, and his eventual daring escape to Canada while being under FSB surveillance. His memoirs include HISTORY OF DISEASE. ESCAPE and HISTORY OF DISEASE. ARMY offers sharp insights into the complexities of life under an oppressive regime, blending dark humor with poignant sarcasm.

The new book, THE ROGUE'S CONFESSION, is a collection of fictional stories based on real events, describing the lives of Russian mercenaries from the Wagner group in the Central African Republic, sailors from a merchant fleet in the Gulf of Guinea under pirate attack, and the revenge of a Russian defector.

Now residing in Canada, Pospelov continues to write, sharing his compelling stories and offering readers a rare glimpse into the challenges faced by different categories of people caught under unfavorable and peculiar circumstances.

Chapter 1

African Diary

-I was told that they don't really shoot here.

-No, of course not, only if there's a holiday or just for

fun, so as not to offend somebody.

From the conversation in the former residence of Emperor Bokassa

"I am sure," continued Alexander, "you remember that Yuriy always had a certain inclination for what we tried to stay out of – his friends, his habits… You know what I am talking about. He found me here, in the US, through "Odnoklassniki," social network, and that is how I heard his story, which I found quite interesting. At that time, I offered him to meet in Baku, in Azerbaijan, but he started laughing and said that it would take him some time to get there with one leg."

"With one leg?!" I did not get it.

"Yes. Oh, you did not know that? He lost his leg in Central Africa, where he volunteered for the "Wagner' group."

"Hm, it is sad, but it is his style," I nodded after a brief pause, "that is why I am not surprised about it. But tell me about him. I lost track of him a while ago and did not know where he was."

"Well, then, I will tell you what he told me. I assure you that even without one leg, he is still worth hearing about. Just as I said, I talked to him for hours a few times. I cannot promise you that he was sober enough when he told me his story, nor was I, but I can tell you what I remember."

We left Boudreaux's Louisiana restaurant in St. Joseph downtown, took a cab, and left for Alexander's house on Noyes Boulevard, in an exceptionally picturesque and old area of St. Joe, Missouri. His wife was out in New York, and we had plenty of time and wine to continue our reminiscences from the old days.

Spring in the Midwest is not exceptionally warm, so the fireplace enlivened our conversation, and the Chianti from his cellar woke up vague and ghostly images of the old times and people on the other side of the globe, that seemed from another world.

The rest of Alexander's story I will describe using Yuriy's words to make it as close as possible to what I heard.

"At the end of the 90s, there was not too much work available. I used to live with my grandmother then. You remember that apartment on the fifth floor, don't you? I tried different jobs, but without much luck. They were rarely available and did not pay enough, but there were always good people somewhere around – and I stuck with the local group that tried to "control" local convenience stores and small businesses. You know what I mean. Rackets at that time were still a popular business. They accepted me right away. I knew some of the boys from that group, so they took me without any hesitation or probation. Plus, as you remember, I never drank too much and did not like dope at all, so for those bums, I was an asset.

But just as I said, it was 2000, and all areas were already divided between the big boys. It was a bit too late for us to expand our business, and its limits did not provide us with a chance to live the way we wanted, after watching popular gangster movies at that time.

One day, "Vava", who was then our leader, disappeared together with his VW car. Initially, we thought that he ran away with all our money, but a few days later his car, or to be more precise, what was left of it, was found burned out, and a month later dogs of the local villagers dug out his corpse in the river grove not too far away, and not deep enough, from the same area where they had earlier found his wrecked car. By itself, the case was not extraordinary or surprising, but what followed was a bit worse.

Several days later, cops apprehended one of our guys, and a week after, another two were arrested. Not too much left for me to do. I left my grandmother's apartment and landed temporarily in Natasha's house. One time, you, Andrey, and I met there. Remember? It was an old house on Plescheev Street. No? Anyway... Nobody was supposed to know about that place, and everything worked out well for me for a while. I had some money that I had collected from our previous escapades. Our business with extortion, although not long-lived, provided some means for a decent living. Though I knew very well that cops would learn about me, and it would be a matter of time before my buddies would leak information, and cops would find my whereabouts. You know, it is the last thing to trust your buddies; they will sell you out without much ado and too much hesitation, trust me. So, I had enough brains not to have illusions.

Right at the same time, my sister brought me a call-up to the military commissariat for the fall conscription. It was not my cup of tea, and I had no desire to fulfil my civic duty, but there were no other options left for me. Soon my money would be gone, and my girlfriend already cost me enough to stay at her house without attracting much attention from neighbors or interested parties, while my buddies were already in the "White Swan," Astrakhan Interrogation Jail on Lenin's square. I hope you have not forgotten your home city, have you? Sooner or later, the cops would pick me up; it was just a matter of time before it happened. So, I, like an exemplary citizen, went to our commissariat and told them that I am ready to valiantly sacrifice my life for my Homeland.

Unfortunately, those commissariat log heads took my statement literally and sent me directly to Chechnya, where the second Chechen war was in full sway. Well, not right away, to be honest, but after a couple of months of training, but does it really matter?

As you know, I never had any desire to do anything with our Army. It was not my hobby and definitely not the voice of my conscience, but it was the best haven to hide in at that tumultuous time. That is how I thought. It turned out that I was partially right, but only partially. I hid from the prosecutor's office but encountered another enemy that was, maybe, less dangerous but considerably more mortal. At that time, I did not know yet that whatever games you play with the Government, you will lose. Well, what I did not know at that time, I learned a bit later…

I was sent to the Signal Corps to learn how to operate basic radio stations, learn the basics of radio and electronic reconnaissance, put up telephone lines, and all the other crap of that sort. Initially, I liked it – sitting in the warm headquarters, in the command vehicle was not like running around donned in a bullet vest with a submachine gun. I can tell you that's a fool's destiny and a typical cannon fodder's job. Yes, it is a fool's job, but at that time, I did not know yet that very soon I would become one of those fools by my own will. The first few months I spent at the training grounds by Uryupinsk. It looked like everything was quiet, no cops found where I was, or maybe they did not look hard enough, but I felt safe under the wing of our legendary, unbeatable Russian Army. But soon it turned out that our dear Army had certain plans for me that did not match mine. Do not forget that in 2001, the war in Chechnya was in full swing, and that is where our train, loaded with all our vehicles and equipment, was merrily running.

The good side of that story was that it was definitely not the place where they would be looking for me, but the bad side was that I would rather spend five years, the sentence measured for my buddies as jail time in the labor camp, than leave my stupid head somewhere around Gudermes or Samashki. But once again, there was not too much trouble for most of the time. I was attached to the artillery unit, so I should be in the relative rear, still learning my trade. Learning is good and useful, of course, though overly intensive learning might be quite detrimental and not healthy. But I learned this mistake after I had been sent with an artillery spotter to observe and correct the work of our artillery from the very front line.

From what I experienced being a radio operator, I saw almost nothing since I was deep in the MTLB command machine without being able to see what was going on around, though it was quite interesting to see what our artillery could do. To correct its fire was even more interesting. There were some cases that gave me a good perception of how to do it properly. One case I still can clearly see in my mind since I was able to observe the entire battlefield, like from the theater front row.

We positioned our vehicle very smartly on the slope covered with mask nets and branches, dug in the ground where, without thermal imagers, the Chechens would not be able to detect us. To hit us covertly, approaching our position was not easy either. The field in front of us was exposed, and there were no ravines or bushes to approach us without them being detected. About three kilometers ahead, in the village stretching along the road and a steep hill behind, defended a company of rebels. The approach to the village was open, but the bushy hill was also secured by the flank group of guerrillas.

That was a job for us to ensure that resistance was suppressed enough to take it with the frontal attack. Our artillery group included half of an eight-piece battery of 82mm mortars but was reinforced by one battery of BM-21 multi-barrel rocket launchers, two hundred forty barrels of which were sufficient to mix the village with earth.

The first rocket from the main launcher flew beyond the village and hit the hill behind, which could be observed clearly without any optical devices. The range was 3,600 meters plus correction to the landscape elevation, and the wind was negligible. Artillery observer, the senior lieutenant dictated corrections to me, and I radioed them to our artillery commander, periodically observing green terraces ahead of us. The second rocket landed near the first house, closer to the front side of the village, and the third one landed in the central part of the village. That is when all the fun started. The remaining two hundred thirty-seven rockets left the launchers within less than thirty seconds. The entire village was covered with thick layers of dust when a rocket ellipse covered it like a giant umbrella. The elongation of the ellipse of explosions did not coincide with the long side of the village veering for about twenty-five degrees, but most parts of the village were in the fire zone. Earth shook and splashes of explosions were visible only when the first rockets hit the target, then all was covered with smoke and dust, and only flying debris were visible at the windward side. It was a paramount scene of destruction, scary but beautiful at the same time.

Smoke started to dissipate when the first two BMP-1 infantry fighting vehicles cautiously started moving along the road within a hundred meters one after another. They moved slowly. Both vehicles' turrets were directed towards the slope of the hill, partially covered with bush and low trees. It did not help them too much… Not even reaching the outskirts of what was left of the closest houses to us, the first vehicle hit a mine, which blew out its ammunition stock. All its 73mm shells blew up, throwing the turret high in the air. Flame mushroomed ten meters above the ground, and fire started to billow from where the turret once was, rear doors flew open, and a distorted body of a soldier was thrown out. There were no survivors...

The second vehicle briefly stopped as if in hesitation, turning its turret from side to side, and then started moving forward parallel to the road. A few seconds later, it was hit by a rocket grenade launched somewhere from the bush. The vehicle with billowing smoke continued to move for another few meters when its crew and squad of soldiers started to jump out from the hatches and doors. Stunned by the explosion, they staggered from side to side and did not make any attempt to hide or look for any protection on the ground, and had the guerrillas had one machine gun, they would have dispatched the entire squad.

After that, I could not see too much when the lieutenant started to dictate coordinates for the mortar battery.

To correct mortar fire is an absolute pleasure. Mortar is a fine tool. A good mortar commander can put a mine precisely at the target, considering that he has the correct coordinates. The rest will be done by the following mines. Particularly, a 120mm mine would not leave any chances to whoever did not take the time to dig into the trenches. In our case, the half battery of four mortars spews their mines right to the area where we suspected the rocket grenade was launched from, hardly leaving any chance for defenders to retreat or even raise their heads. Still, during the mortar barrage, another five battle vehicles rush at full speed parallel to the road towards the village. We did not see any splashes of fire from the village, though all armored vehicles were moving, firing their guns and machine guns.

There were no more losses on our side. The village was taken over. It was hard to say whether guerrillas were scattered or there was nobody in the village. Actually, nobody would not be the case, because several bodies of the civilians were visible from what left from the house yards. Though it was hard to say whether they were civilians or guerrillas. Such peaceful villagers, who are peaceful in daylight, did not hesitate to shoot at our backs in the darkness. So, no tears were shed while seeing their worn bodies. One man in torn bloody rags without a hand and with a bloody mess in the place where he once had a head, with a still howling dog nearby, lay on the side of the street. Nobody paid attention – we had to move forward.

Poor dogs – innocent victims of the war, which is what caused my pity. Why? Because I like dogs and do not like guerrillas, that is why. Behind me, I heard a short burst of submachine gun fire – some kind soul finished the dog's agony.

The effectiveness of one well-laid salvo was apparent. Destruction was complete. There were no roofs and only damaged or destroyed walls, fire and smoke from where just minutes ago houses had stood, garbage, and debris all over the road was all that was left of what once was a small village. We did a good job, giving correct coordinates, saving enough trouble for the advancing troops. Ruined houses and structures turned into piles of logs, bricks, distorted metal roof sheets and windowless walls, construction garbage, stones, and whole concrete panels covered the main street when we moved through, while somewhere behind were heard single shots when our soldiers finished the wounded guerrillas. In a fast advance, there is no time to take care of the wounded and no desire to get a bullet in the back between your shoulder blades, so do not take your chance and do not spare a bullet even for what looks like a corpse of the enemy. The only losses we had were the full crew and rifle squad in the first armored vehicle and several wounded from the second one. Had all our actions been like that, we would have taken over Chechnya without the much blood that we poured over the years. It was one of several cases when I had a chance to see the result of our job from the point where the entire battle happened in front of my eyes, like on the stage. Most of the other encounters did not give me many opportunities to observe the battle since I was busy transferring coordinates to artillery positions. Only the sounds of explosions were heard, and once we were shot by a high-caliber machine gun, which left a few holes in the armor and some unpleasant but unforgettable mementos in my memory.

Later on, I was transferred to the relative rear where we were mostly involved in the guarding and security service, and besides the few incidents, there was not too much worth recalling.

My service term came to an end, and two years later, I had come back to where I so narrowly escaped. Almost all my buddies have been serving their terms, and I decided not to tempt my fate and move out of my city to a place where nobody knows me. Thus, the ways of my destiny brought me initially to Pskov and later to St. Petersburg.

Random jobs and a lack of connections threw me from construction companies to driving emergency ambulances for the regional hospital. It was tough times: no place to live, rented apartments consumed most of my salary, hardly enough money was left to survive, until eventually I, like a frail dinghy, found myself on the banks of the river Neva in the city of St. Peter in one of many private security enterprises. Initially, it all turned out quite well. Work was not troublesome and was easy. The money paid was not great, but enough to rent a small apartment in Rzhevka. At that time, the criminal case in which I was initially a witness back in Astrakhan and later a suspect, was either dropped or forgotten, and nobody bothered me.

By that time, "the criminal Petersburg" was not as criminal as in the 1990s or early 2000s, and we did not experience many troubles, not with gangs, most of which had already become history, nor with competitors, nor with the police. The latter received their share from our owner, and we occupied a legal niche in that grey and sometimes hardly legal business.

By mid-10th, I was already in charge of the branch in Okkerville and Veseliy Village when I began to see that my efforts were starting to pay off. However, the golden era of private security companies was rolling down. If in the 90th those companies provided local businesses with the same protection as the criminal structures and differed from them only by their legal status, then ten or twenty years later their activities were effectively curbed by police and FSB authorities, which also wanted to be fed by those whom they missed in previous years. So, year after year, we were losing competition with the government security forces and eventually became redundant when the reigning law authorities demanded that we sell our business to the people directly connected to the government. Fighting with the government was an ungrateful business, and our owner, Vitaliy, wisely decided to accept the offered deal; however still unsuccessfully trying to negotiate the offered and unfair price. His battle did not last long, and the once profitable business has changed hands, with all management employees kicked out by the new owners.

That year brought me enough unpleasant surprises: I lost my job and relatively comfortable position together with my wife after an imminent divorce, in addition to the recently bought apartment in Ohta. Several attempts to get a decent position among the former competitive businesses did not go well, and the pricy life in the city on the Neva River started to take its toll. The only good and sellable asset I still retained was my good physical shape. In the security business, it is not the last element required to persuade an unwelcome contingent and, in several cases, particularly at the beginning of my career, it turned out to be quite useful and necessary. Broken jaws and knocked teeth of lighthearted, but equally careless and imprudent guests, were a very good guarantee that protected enterprises appreciate our help and stick to our service in the future. But now it was over, and my perspective became bleak and dull.

Around that time, I heard from my friends and former contacts about a doubtful group looking for people with a former military background for some missions on the Russian border. Payment, they mentioned, sounded unrealistically high. What kind of missions and where they are supposed to be fulfilled nobody knew, and at the beginning, I did not take this information seriously, considering it a common city rumor or some kind of new scam.

However, my time and money were running out while the job options were hardly trickling in, and one morning, after a big night out in one of our former clients' bars, I decided to call that phone number. My head was aching, aspirin did not help, and pickle brine refused to cure my morning disease. There were no calls from the job hunter for a couple of weeks when I found a piece of newspaper that I had saved a few days ago, where I scribbled the phone number and gave a call without any hope that anybody would pick up the phone. Surprisingly nice and sweet woman's voice on the other side politely and clearly confirmed exactly what I heard from my acquaintances and asked me several basic questions about my age, military experience and experience in security business, availability of the foreign passport not forgetting to ask me questions more appropriate to a man picking up a whore, about my height, weight and so. The questions about my physical parameters positively surprised me, giving me some hope that there might be something more serious and materialistic than I initially suspected. At the same time, she refused to give me any answers to my questions, promising to provide complete information at our meeting, which was scheduled for next Monday.

The next day was Saturday, and their office was closed. To give further thoughts to that conversation in my poor state was absolutely useless and unproductive, and I decided to go to the sauna. A sauna cured me, and a few beers in the company of my friends restored my hopes and optimism.

At that time, the office of that mysterious company had not moved yet to my neighborhood on Zolnaya street, and I had to go to downtown, located blocks away from the Fortress of St. Peter and Paul.

The office was nice, bright, clean, and impressive. At the scheduled time, I was invited inside for the interview. However, upon arrival, two rough-looking and not-so-sweet guys were at the reception desk. By their demeanor and behavior, I could say right away that they had nothing to do with police or National, or how it is called now, Russian Guards. Their questions revolved around my experience in the Chechen war, including names of commanders I crossed with, obviously trying to recognize familiar names. I had no doubts that both were in Chechnya, and judging by their questions, were there in both wars. Then the questions shifted to my responsibilities during my previous job. Interestingly, we did not talk about payment at all. I did not raise the question, knowing that it would be a subject of discussion anyway. Pushing it forward at this stage would be premature. They likely had been of the same opinion and did not mention it, considering it unnecessary at this point. After about twenty minutes, they gave me a prescription for a medical test and, without promising anything, told me that I should expect a call. Before leaving, I asked questions about what they expect from me and the geography of my future service. Their response was "Your knowledge of security aspects might be of some interest for us, in regards to geography, we cannot tell you anything specific until signing the contract, however, you might not be surprised if the geography will exceed your most daring expectations".

It was an interesting beginning, also not very informative. Leaving their office, I decided to proceed searching for another job without relying too much on those military log heads. In my previous job, I learned not to trust either my clients or outsiders with unclear goals. On Thursday, when I came home from my daily stroll, I got a message to call their office again for further discussions. I could not say that I felt too much excitement, and their secrecy and adherence to keeping information closed up to the last point irritated me. I was not accustomed to playing such Bond-style games, but still called them.

"Tomorrow at 10, bring your passport and yourself to where you were interviewed," said a male voice.

"Anything else?" I wanted to save an extra trip across the city in case they want to come again.

"No. Just bring what I said. The rest you will be told here. Any more questions?"

No. I did not have any more questions, considering that they are not going to discuss them over the phone anyway.

Next day at the prescribed time, I was in the already familiar foyer. This time, there was only one interviewer, the younger guy, who talked too fast for my taste. I decided to get to the point and find out about payment, conditions of service, compensation, and area and type of service. Surprisingly, the young recruiter promptly answered all questions.

"200,000 rubles at start, payment upon return or monthly on your account, up to three monthly salaries for successful operation, food and outfitting kit are free, compensation for a wound as well as for death," he looked at me as if trying to estimate on me the effect of his last words after what added, "risk of both is high. Training is for three months after which you will belong, together with your socks and boots, to us. We will arrange a medical test for which you already got a prescription at our premises. Further information will be provided before signing the contract."

"What about the area of my duties?"

"You will start as a rifleman of an assault group. Further specialty will be determined based upon your proficiency and talent."

"Geography of service?" I decided it would be better to be as terse as he is.

"Too early to talk about, however, I can guarantee you strong, healthy sunburn," he wryly smiled, looking straight into my eyes.

I understood that the interview was over. We shook hands, and I was going to leave when he told me to be close to the phone within the next few days.

Another few days passed before I got an invitation for a medical test, which was quite basic. Chronic diseases were their primary concern; the rest was even more basic than the draft board medical commission. Two days later, they called me and set a date for me to come to the office with my personal belongings to sign the contract. After that, they emphasized that I am not going home and will be at their total disposal.

It was enough time to tell my landlord that I am moving out, to sell what I could sell, and give away what I could not sell. The rest of my meager belongings I presented to my friends, who did not even try to hide their joy about those freebies, and started to prepare what I had to take with me on my way to the company.

Was I happy? I do not think so, but rather indifferent. Nothing kept me in St. Petersburg, nothing tied me to my lost family and to my friends. I was quiet and consented to what was laid out for me ahead. Did I think about gloomy perspectives, about associated risk waiting for me, or did I already have no doubts? I perfectly realized that such money would not be paid for nothing, and the Company will squeeze from volunteers everything it could without any hesitation or sympathy. After all, I was born in Russia, fought in Chechnya, and worked in a security company, which is why I perfectly understand the price of life in this country. So, I was neither excited nor depressed and treated it as a normal course of life. At the same time, deep in my soul, I was wondering where and how they were planning to deploy me. Later, I understood that at that time, nobody knew the answer to that question, and nobody could help me with my assumptions until I went through a basic military preparation course.

Last day before leaving to the unknown I had a good sleep, called my mother saying that soon I will be seconded to Far East part of Russia where I will be out of touch for a while, had a good breakfast and in the evening went to the restaurant with two of my friends from the company from which all of us recently have been fired. The evening was joyful, and I was bombarded with questions about why I decided to sell my head instead of continuing to look for a job, which would eventually find me if I did not find it myself. I only smiled, swayed my head, and explained that I do not really care about anything anymore, which was partially true. I needed changes, and I recklessly invited them to my stupid head. "Hey guys, there is not too much left for me here, no job, no family. Maybe it is time to change the environment. I do not believe that it will be too bad at my new place. At least that is what I hope for".

One of them tilted his head and looked at me as if I were fatally sick, another one… Another one just drank his beer, deeply submerged in his thoughts. Frankly, I did not believe what I said, but I needed to say something, and what else could I say, anyway?

The next day, I was at the assigned address, which turned out to be some auxiliary military unit on the Vyborgskaya side, where there were about thirty or forty of the same lost souls as myself, some of whom really looked like scum from the Gilyarovsky's Petersburg society. Their age was also a matter of surprise – some were around fifty, although the imprint of excessive alcohol consumption made them look older.

We were lined up on the small drill ground with our knapsacks lying in front of us, with all their contents dumped on the asphalt.

"All alcohol is prohibited; usage of alcohol and drugs will be punished, both disciplinary and financially. Insubordination is a cause for disciplinary action and expulsion without pay. Disciplinary punishment has nothing to do with army regulations, and I would not recommend you get familiar with them. From now on, you are on pay, and all of you from your cap down to your slippers belong to the company. Questions?" A military guy in his thirties, obviously with a military background, was quite straightforward.

It did not look like the Army I knew, and some cold shivers ran along my spine. By no means was I scared, but a strange feeling of dealing with something new, menacing, and ominous had cast an unpleasant shade over me.

"Well, why can't I have a last sip for a good trip. We are not at service yet," a short and skinny guy was trying to start debates.

Our leader looked at him with surprise. "Okay. It looks like I was not clear enough. Hey, 'Bird,' please explain to the newcomer the rules of behavior." He addressed the rough-looking guy staying behind him. 'Bird', was it his nickname, slowly approached the talkative recruit who stayed with a dumb smile, looking with a challenge at the approaching sergeant.

"Pick up your stuff," the sergeant told him.

The recruit sat on his haunches and started to pick up his stuff into his knapsack. He stood up, holding a knapsack in one hand and a bottle of vodka in another, when the sergeant's fist knocked him right under his jaw. Unexpecting such a strike, the perplexed guy with both hands widely sprawled out and still holding a knapsack, hit the ground with his head. Bottle smashed and knapsack flew aside while the unfortunate volunteer shaking his head turned over, staying on his four and trying to stand up.

"Is it clear now? Or you have more questions?" asked our leader.

Well, it could not be clearer than that. I suspected that, at this particular moment, we began to understand where we had gotten ourselves into, and I am sure that some started to doubt whether it was the right choice to join such a merry company.

The rest of the day, and the whole next day, we spent in the barracks of the disbanded military unit. Surprisingly, those days were quiet, and nobody bothered us. We were instructed not to leave the barracks except to go to the unit's canteen. "Bird," the sergeant, escorted us there and back. There were no more excesses with him, although we did not hear a word from him except for basic commands and directions on where to go and how much time was allotted for lunch and supper. When one of our guys asked him a question about our near future, "Bird" threw such a murky glance at him from under his eyebrows, without saying a word in response, that the rest of us lost any desire to ask him more questions.

The next day, we spent time gathering our uniforms and clothing. In the dim, old warehouse, another man in a camouflage uniform without straps handed us two sets of summer uniforms, Panama hats, a standard army rucksack, underwear, a flashlight, a compass, an army kitchen set, and some other small items. Remembering my years in the Army, I was surprised that the man, who was just as unfriendly and even less talkative than 'Bird,' offered us the chance to try on army boots and uniforms that fit our sizes. In my Army experience, this was something new and unbelievable. After the red-haired, red-bearded guy in our group was satisfied with the fit without any trouble, the rest of the volunteers quickly formed a line, trying to find gear more suited to their actual sizes.

An hour later, we began to look like, if not genuine soldiers, then something closely resembling a paramilitary group.

"Hey, bud, can I grab another pair of boots?" my neighbor, a stocky guy with a round, kindhearted face, jokingly asked the storekeeper.

"Soon you might find yourself happy if one of your boots would not become excessive," the yeoman grinned in response.

If it was a joke, then it wasn't well-received. The round-faced guy foolishly smiled and awkwardly turned his head toward us as if seeking our support. Nobody spoke, but some unpleasant creeps ran down my back. "Damn, what a collection of bloody morons in such a cramped space," I thought, which was probably on the minds of the two guys standing nearby.

The day was almost over, but still with another surprise in stock – we had to return all IDs, including passports and driving licenses. Since that very moment, each of us acquired a nickname. Surprisingly, it was a challenge to pick up a proper nickname for some guys. Some of us from the peasant stock picked names more appropriate for yard dogs, some tried to apply heroic callsigns which were obviously in short supply. It was fun to watch them trying to resolve that puzzle and struggling with such a simple task. But it was not a challenge for me to fix the puzzle. Suddenly, from nowhere, the old memories from the Chechen war struck my mind, and I could not figure out anything better than 'Kurush', the name of a Dagestani village where we stayed for some time during the Chechen campaign.

Supper in the canteen was very basic and consisted of oatmeal with one can of meat for two, tea of undetermined color, and two small cubes of sugar with a piece of bread and a standard army cylinder of butter. That part was familiar to most of us and hardly differed from the time of the Chechen war.

After supper, 'Bird' set us up in the middle aisle of the barrack.

"Atten-tion!" 'Bird' knew his business very well.

"At ease," someone we couldn't see yet said condescendingly, give the command. He was a short, quite mature man, clearly an officer, although lacking visible straps. He walked toward our line, slowing his steps and moving from one side of the rank to the other, fixing his gaze on us. His uniform was similar to ours but neatly maintained and not new. The man conveyed the impression of being a seasoned professional officer.

"Guys, tomorrow you will go to the training center in southern Russia. Don't ask questions, do what you are told. It will be tough, but necessary and beneficial, mainly for yourself. You'll realize how useful it is very soon. Stay alert and don't waste time. It will pay off if you want to stay alive. You will be divided into groups based on your military specialties. Any breach of discipline, any," he paused, slowly glancing from one side of the file to the other, "will be severely penalized. Cowardice, insubordination, and stealing from your comrades will be punished with death. With death, my boys!" The last words he shouted to emphasize the point. He paused again. "I hope you heard that clearly. Is it clear? Once more, remember what I just said as 'My Lord' prayer, because there will be no more warnings. And good luck to you. You'll need it very soon."

It was encouraging, brief, and clear. An eerie silence followed. After his speech and before we were dismissed, 'Bird' instructed us about tomorrow's departure: wake-up time, breakfast, gathered belongings, barrack order, and transportation arrangement.

The next day, we left. All of us, except for the guy who wanted one last sip of vodka on the training ground – he was left behind without his monthly pay and two missing teeth as a tribute to his untimely curiosity. I never saw him again; I don't know if he was discharged or stayed with another group.

We had some time to digest the information we heard. Did it make me doubt anything? No, it did not. I was more scared in my past than I am now about my future. I can't say the same for the rest of us. Some were probably influenced by the officer's wishes and warnings, but most of the guys, with nothing behind their penniless and worthless souls, weren't. Still, his speech left a noticeable impression on all of us.

Around seven in the morning, a dull, grey AN-12 turboprop picked up our whole team of about forty people along with some crated cargo at Levashovo Airport. That's how my Odyssey began...

After we boarded and sat tightly along the walls, our leader, since his rank was not marked on his strap but whose authority was unquestionable from his behavior, instructed us not to smoke, not to walk, to sit tight, and to consider this flight as a sky gate into the new life. I do not recall that we were pleased about jumping into an unknown promised life, but it was evident that most of us were trying to put on a brave face, accompanied by stupid jokes in front of the others. Now I can see how stupid it looked, but then it was okay. So, we, as if the seasoned veteran troopers, played poorly performed roles to encourage ourselves.

Several minutes later, engine after engine roared to life. The noise blocked all attempts to talk, so everyone turned inward and sat quietly, eyes closed as if trying to nap, which was impossible in such a state. The section of the cargo bay where we sat tightly along both sides was not airtight. The plane shook for a minute before it started to roll along the taxiway, knocking wheels over the concrete joints. Finally, we reached the end of the runway. We couldn't see it, but we felt the plane slowly turning ninety degrees, stopping for a moment, howling as if flexing its muscles, then pulling all power. The engines squealed wildly, the fuselage shook and rattled after that massive plane, initially slowly, then faster and faster as it sped forward, pounding on the runway. Increasing speed pushed us aside as the front wheels tore off the concrete, the plane tilted back, and took off. The rattling subsided, and old Peter's city was left behind beneath us. It would be a good moment to make a sentimental comment to heighten the drama and say that not all of us would make it back alive. I would avoid such cheap theatrics; we signed up for fair compensation, at least that's what we believed then, so it was a game we willingly chose to play.

Within a few minutes, I began feeling cold. I hoped we wouldn't fly too high, or else by the end of the flight, we'd look like hulks of frozen meat. I wasn't alone in my feelings; my neighbor started stomping his feet, and the guy across, who looked like a bum in a military uniform with small red eyes and a stupid expression, began rubbing his hands on his camouflaged pants. The others followed his lead; someone started shouting at the pilots, who couldn't hear us anyway because of the separating firewall.

I didn't hear his yelling and crying over the noise of the engines, but I could see him and his intentions. A desperate guy tried to stand up while the sergeant, who was sitting not too far from me and across from that guy, jumped out and knocked him right in the chest, clearly explaining to him the proper way to behave on a military airplane. Bloody start, devil take them!

Several hours dragged by slowly, and I can't recall a more miserable flight in my life. It was extremely cold, although I assume we stayed significantly lower than on a typical flight; otherwise, we would probably have died from exposure and lack of oxygen, but we were a bit higher than we would have liked. Still, we survived to be saved for training and future exploits.

Finally, everything ended as everything ends in this world. In about two hours, our bulky airplane began to descend. Our ears popped, and the plane slowly went down. The sound of the engines changed, becoming a little quieter and softer, and soon the plane's landing gear gently hit the runway and rattled at the joints. The plane taxied a little, turned around, and with a howl, its turbines fell silent. We, half-deafened and half-frozen, lined up under the command of our officer and exited the chilly fuselage through the open door.

The captain who met us on the runway lined us up and led us away from the airport building, which was visible a few hundred meters away. There were already three ZIL trucks waiting for us, and we were quickly loaded into them and, without delay, set off in a small but nimble convoy out of the city.

The journey lasted about forty minutes, and there weren't many conversations along the way. Some people looked curiously at the road fading behind us, but aside from the steppe and a few scattered bushes, simple houses, and buildings, there wasn't much to see. The rest sat quietly, as if resigned to their fate; the exhaustion from the flight was clearly showing. To make our mood even worse, outside stretched a dull steppe with patches of shrubs and low trees covered in thick gray dust.

The trucks, with smoke billowing from exhaust and dust rising, rolled into the camp behind the barbed wire and came to a stop, stalling their engines on a small, well-trodden dirt parade ground, behind which rows of large tents were settled.

To the vehicles!" came the command. We started jumping out one after another. "Faster, faster! Move your 'pistons'!" Two soldiers without epaulettes stood on the parade ground. It was clear that they expected us and had dealt with volunteers before.

The military unit, and it was undoubtedly a military unit, consisted of several rows of olive-green army tents designed to accommodate a couple of dozen people each. There were no painted "mushrooms" sheds for guards or posters calling for learning "military affairs in the proper manner," according to Lenin's precepts and other propaganda typical of any Russian military unit. Just tents and that's it. There were no idle loiterers, as was usually the case in military units. There were no painted curbs and paths to impress visiting inspectors, only posts with the names of either subunits or training classes visible near the dusty tents. We were led along the main passageway and then assigned to several tents located nearby.

The interior of the latter was as simple as all the great things: wooden flooring made of planed boards and rows of metal soldier beds with simple army bedside tables. Further between the tents was a dining room, where we were taken after arrival. The food was different from the soldiers' food in its richness and variety, which was unimaginable during the Chechen campaign. So far, there was nothing to be unpleasantly surprised about.

The tent in which I was assigned with another fifteen people stood in the second row from the main "avenue."

"Looks like we can survive here," said my neighbor with a happy, shiny, round face as we left the dining hall. He turned out to be Sasha, call sign 'Raven', with whom we later got along, and a little later went to the "new place of service," but who did not return from there. 'Raven' turned out to be an excellent soldier who had already seen action in Chechnya and Transnistria. I could understand what made him take up this 'glorious' career as a mercenary in Africa. "I was sick of the routine of civil life", was his explanation, and he was drawn somewhere toward King Solomon's mines, following in the footsteps of Stanley and Livingstone. The exoticism and romance he had gleaned from the books he read in his distant childhood stirred his mind and boiled the blood of the romantic who seemed to have already been tempted by life, who ultimately ended up with a broken cervical vertebra from a grenade fragment in the ambush at Beloko in the Mambere prefecture. If the guy hadn't read those books, everything would have been fine. Oh, those books! They don't lead to anything good.

Our contingent was not particularly diverse — there were individual romantics like Sasha or completely crazy 'adventurers' who later were the first ones to look for the first opportunity to return to Russia, and whose romanticism of the cool mercenaries quickly faded away under the scorching African sun. The bulk of the group was a motley crew of ordinary, mostly urban losers who had not found their place in life, were good for nothing, knew nothing, and had no desire to do or learn anything. They were the majority. There was no place for them in the cities or villages of Russia or anywhere else, they were unable to adapt themselves to modern conditions, and at least a third of them would have ended up in prison for some trivial robbery or burglary if it hadn't been for the opportunity to see the world and serve in a private military company. Strangely enough, that enterprise saved many of them from such dubious life prospects, provided, of course, that they managed to return alive and in one piece. Most of them had once served in the army and had since then managed to successfully forget what they knew or learned during their army years.

The greatest suffering for this group was the lack of vodka and beer, and for some, drugs.

The separate group consisted of dashing young men who had managed to go through the ordeal of the labor camps and prisons of our vast country, so rich with that type of accommodations. There were not many of them, although they could hardly be called rare birds. Military service not only did not appeal to them, but rather repelled them, and they went to serve with a single purpose of either to disappear for a while from the radar of police and prosecutors or, as some of them thought, to get loose, enjoy a wild life without the expected consequences, to feel their power with weapons in their hands, and perhaps to vent the hatred they had accumulated over the years towards the whole world around them. Such people were dangerous to the enemy as well as to the civilian population, and it was because of them that we quickly earned a reputation as cold-blooded and cruel, if one can speak of our reputation at all. In a battle, however, they were no better than the others, of course, with some exceptions. Those losers clung to their last chance to find a place under the sun.

Just as I mentioned, all our documents and phones were confiscated, and our connection to the outside world was cut off. Leaving the camp was strictly forbidden. There was no question of unauthorized absences, and I personally can't recall any, but I heard about one poor fellow who was caught attempting such an escape after he was beaten nearly to death in the headquarters tent. I don't know what happened to him afterward, but he quickly disappeared from the camp without gaining any military experience, most likely compensated with an acquired disability. We were not given time to adapt to a new lifestyle. The instructors there were serious people and did not engage in idle chatter. In the campground, everything, from the rules to the camp layout, from the latrine to the speeches on the parade ground, was simple and straightforward. So simple that no extra efforts were required for explaining anything to anyone, and woe to those who didn't understand it the first time, they were simply taught by beating a shit out of them.

Classes started right away. In the army, everything begins and ends on the parade ground. The formation happened without much pomp or fuss. The commanding officer announced the start of classes, reminded us of the familiar schedule, and explained that training would be divided into individual, group (two to three people), and platoon exercises. The information was delivered briefly and clearly, without any patriotic nonsense or lofty phrases so common to everyone who had served in the Russian Army. There was no marching in front of the commanders, no orchestras, and none of the old army's beautiful but pointless traditions. It was clear that time was valued here, and no one would be allowed to slack off. Several ZIL trucks were brought in, and we quickly climbed inside and drove deep into the campground, which only took a few minutes.

Individual training began. We were introduced to small arms, shooting while lying down, from the knee, from behind a cover, and while evacuating the wounded. There was plenty of ammunition, and neither it nor we were spared. Everything had to be done on the run, in the dust and dirt, without sparing our uniforms, weapons, and ammunition, strength, sweat, or scratched and bleeding hands and knees. The weapons we had to familiarize ourselves with were the good old AK-74, PKM, and the old and equally good grenade launcher RPG-7. For most of us, even for those with the intellect of orangutans, this was completely unnecessary, since everyone in Russia could tell the difference between the first two weapons, however, it was very unlikely that they could distinguish between honorarium and gonorrhea.

The RPG training was quite helpful. I didn't get a chance to use it in the war, so the knowledge I gained was not wasted. Then there were classes on adjusting the sighting optics. This is a vital skill, and its importance cannot be overstated. You can shoot as much as you want with an automatic weapon, but it would be useless and lead nowhere unless you have a well-adjusted and tested sight. It's not that critical in close combat, but it's beneficial for aimed shooting, especially with optics. The SVD rifle is a different case, but for some reason, we didn't have classes on it, and it was only the sniper's prerogative. Night shooting was mixed with daylight shooting, and shooting at dusk was perhaps one of the most practical elements. Then there were classes with the AGS-17 and the RPG-30 "Kryuk," although, as we learned in the Central African Republic, we didn't see them in action due to the lack of active protection on enemy vehicles. Possibly one of the most important and useful classes focused on RMG and RSHG flamethrowers, which were a real help to us in fighting light French armored vehicles and working with enemy fortified positions.

Later, we had to go through "fortification" training, which in reality meant digging trenches and foxholes while lying down, kneeling, and standing. That training didn't require much brainpower, and another purpose of those classes was to get rid of our excessive fat when the instructors began to feel that the excess of theory should be compensated with practical classes. However, the camouflage classes proved to be very functional, though in distant and hot Africa, we had to improvise quite a bit.

This was followed by engineering and liaison courses focused on installing and detecting mines and operating radio stations. However, the former had to be refined through practical experience, considering the local terrain and landscape. The latter required mastering basic on-air encryption skills and learning short commands for reconnaissance, correction, and information transmission.

Talking during classes was prohibited; only communication and questioning instructors were allowed. Physical exercises such as obstacle courses had to be completed several times a day until the end of the training.

Medical training was also new and was given considerable time. Applying tourniquets, administering pain relief to oneself and the wounded, evacuating incapacitated soldiers in combat conditions — all this was explained for minutes and practiced for hours. There was nothing like this in the Russian army.

Later, when I began working with CAR (Central African Republic) government units that had previously undergone military training with French instructors, it became clear to me that there was nothing special about the intensive combat training we underwent in Molkino. All African fighters had already gone through this standard course many years earlier, at a time when we were wearing out the soles of our boots on the parade grounds of military units and when, after two years of service, most of us were discharged without having learned even the basics of military service.

Morning exercises, running, and pull-ups with a set of basic exercises became routine. They began to burn off the fat we had accumulated as civilians gradually, and little by little, we began to take on some military appearance. But training took its toll when weeds were separated from chaff, and some overweight and overaged candidates started to disappear. There was not too much time to contemplate where they had gone and what had happened to them. Very likely, they were expelled without any compensation, which did not cause too much regret on our side.

By the end of the second week, we had more or less adapted to the new lifestyle.

"Man, I could use any woman right now. I'd take her like a bear," moaned my bunkmate Ilya, with whom we later went to the Central African Republic and who had disappeared without a trace there in the very first month, like morning dew under the southern sun.

"Shut up, you ghoul, you're making me sick. Whack off your dick if you like or just shut up," said another bunkmate, for some weird reason nicknamed 'Therapist', who had recently been released from prison. 'Therapist' was right, though — such conversations about women and drinking were irritating and annoying and served no purpose. "Hang on, buddy, you'll get your black tarts anyway you want, just let us get to sunny Africa. Have you been to Africa, 'Kurush'?" he asked me. I have been lying on my bunk and smoking quietly, listening to their chatter and not paying much attention. "In Africa, there are gorillas and vicious crocodiles," continued 'Therapist' with that stupid line from the Chukovsky's children poem, "but Anatoly from the third squad has been there. He says that, apart from AIDS, there are no other problems with the local girls, but by the time AIDS gets you, you'll already be dead anyway."

Many people liked 'Therapist's' cheerful personality. Surprisingly, it was people like him who, for some reason, had the best chance of surviving in the African meat grinder, quickly accepting new rules and adapting to those conditions.

Did you know, for example, that bananas in Ecuador are much cheaper than in Russia? Did you know that? I knew that too, but what I didn't know was that life in Africa is valued like bananas in Ecuador. If I had known, I wouldn't have gone there. That price was not only applied to our lives, but also to the local Aboriginals. We will see all this soon, and first, for many of us, it will be, if not a shock, then at least a surprise, which, however, will very quickly cease to be so. In general, there will be more to be surprised about.

Well, for now, we are still in training. Now they are starting to train us in small groups — in pairs and threes. Probably, of all the tactical courses, this one was the most valuable and practical. You can't achieve much when you are alone.

Covert communication with gestures, setting up a fire shield when your comrades are rushing forward, running, hiding, camouflaging, adjusting aimed fire, overcoming high obstacles using a comrade's back as a "step," and making holes in walls with explosive charges. There were a lot of useful drills on these courses. For example, knowing how to set up a MON-50 directional mine might be useful even in peaceful life, but in the army, it is simply indispensable. During a retreat, to slow down the enemy's advance, those mines, even in a standard European green casing in CAR, were a necessity.

Once, after placing it in front of a small bridge over a shallow, muddy stream near Sibut, we destroyed a rebel's Jeep with all its carefree, joyful passengers.

There weren't many fatalities, but everyone on their happy team was maimed or wounded. The Jeep rolled on for several meters before crashing nose-first into thick bushes, scattering its passengers like bunches of bananas from a broken cart. But they didn't suffer for long, no, they didn't. When the camion following behind the Jeep opened fire with a tripod machine gun sticking out above the cab, we opened so heavy fire from three different positions that their camion, with flat tires, hurried to retreat and hide among the green bushes. Using quick following respite, our hot-headed guys expressed dislike of the rebels by shooting the wounded in the Jeep. It was unlikely that their comrades would have picked them up from the field, so the shooting was nothing more than an act of misericordiae. The Jeep was not in much better shape than its passengers; our well-placed little MON mine located a few meters away smashed the front of the SUV so badly that even the most adroit Bangui mechanic would not risk taking it into his workshop.

Training in the field, training in the ruins of the buildings and sheds, classes in tents... Training, training, training…

Nearby, in a similar tent, we heard the sappers at work, and a little further away, the artillerymen. There, they calculated angles and azimuths, computed sights, and corrected the firing of artillery and mortars. I was a bit familiar with that work, but for some reason, they did not take me there. Everything worked out by itself in Africa later, when I had to correct mortar fire, and after that, I was transferred to our improvised artillery group.

In general, I could not think of a better job than an artillery spotter. It is an interesting and exciting job. You can see the results of your work right before your own eyes, but it is better not to be captured while engaging in such activities. Had you been captured, it would be very unlikely that they would leave you alive, and it is only part of the problem; the next part of it would be to learn how you will die, and the discovery might be very unpleasant. Well, any decent job has its disadvantages.

That is how it was in Chechnya, and nothing has changed since then in Africa. In addition, you must sit quietly and not stick your neck out, because there is no more important target for the enemy than a spotter, and therefore, camouflage for a spotter is no less important than fire control itself.

Yes, I wouldn't get tired of repeating that the first aid classes were a pleasant surprise. These classes saved many lives, although sometimes those lives were altered by losing limbs, and I am a sad example of that. However, the benefits of such classes were undeniable. At the time, I often wondered why no one in our Army, in Chechnya, or even in the Soviet Army in Afghanistan was concerned with such courses, and why not only soldiers but also officers had no idea how to use a tourniquet or provide first aid.

At the training center, they said that much of it was borrowed from special forces training—I do not know whether it is true or not. If this is true, then there was nothing supernatural about it, except for common sense, which, as we know, was always in short supply in the Red Army. Why was it taught in the special forces, but not in regular Army units?

In general, by the end of the month, we managed to get rid of the extra fat we had, and from the professional alcoholics, of whom we had an abundance, and created a society, though not of teetotalers, but of a more or less abstinent public.

"Therapist', which country would you like to visit?" I asked him as we peacefully, albeit quickly, ate a cabbage soup for lunch.

"You know, Yuriy," 'Therapist', unlike the other former convicts, preferred to use first names instead of the more tribal practice of using surnames, "I don't really care who I save among those savages and who I knock down. "In Africa, there are gorillas and evil crocodiles," he repeated for the hundredth time the already tiresome line from the children's poem, "as far as I'm concerned, they're all the same. But I have one cherished dream — if I come back alive, I'll spill the blood of the one who drained me to prison. I need a little time. I'll hang around in Africa, my old sins will be forgotten, and then I'll get back to pay a visit to that bastard. I'll get back at him, damn it."

In the end, 'Therapist' returned alive, unharmed, drunk, happy, and covered with money from our African tournee. I do not know if he kept his promise or not, but he was a good fellow and a good fighter, and I do not envy the guy he swore to get back at when he meets him in Russia. 'Therapist' was a good friend of mine, and if he said he would repay the debt, then apparently, he meant it. I only know that very soon after returning to Russia, he signed a new contract and went to either Syria or Mali to tempt his fate again. That is where his trails were lost.

Two months went by quickly. None of us ever left the camp, but we had neither the time nor the desire to do so. We were tired and had no free time. Those who drew up the training schedule clearly knew what they were doing.

The training finished. During those months, we learned so much that, at the usual pace of service in the Russian army, it would have taken ten years. That's just a side note about training in the Red Army.

It all ended on the same parade ground where it had begun, albeit with a speech, but without Soviet pomp, patriotic pathos, and political nonsense. The senior officer, again without epaulettes, spoke briefly and straight to the point. What did he say? "Tomorrow, get on the plane and go forward—to new achievements, to see the world and work for the good of the Homeland, somewhere "in the distant approaches." You were taught well, now it is time to put it into practice". That was the whole speech, and I liked it.

Well, if it is "in the distant approaches", then so be it. But where are those "approaches"? I was interested in that as an inquisitive person, and besides, a southerner, constantly freezing under St. Petersburg rain and indifferent to heat, I had my own practical interest. What could I do — I am an old Astrakhan native, albeit covered with a little bit of a St. Petersburg patina.

We had already received our equipment, our torn pants and tunics had been replaced with the new ones, we had been given backpacks and, as a bonus, new Panamá hats instead of our old ones," so I had one less doubt — apparently, like the geese in the autumn, we would be heading to the southern countries. To the south — that is good, but if only I knew which part of the south.

Then everything went in reverse order: the parade ground, the ZIL trucks, the same road through a moderately bleak area with scrubby bushes and trees, shabby Adygeysk, and the airport where a large TU-154 was already waiting for us. After hanging around on the concrete for a while, we began to embark. There wasn't much room; there were already some wooden boxes attached to the fuselage, but there was still enough room for us.

Before our departure, no one had mentioned our destination or the purpose of the flight, but while we waited, rumors started to spread—either from the pilots or the mechanics—that we were flying to Africa. Yes, Africa. Funny. But where exactly? Africa isn't that small, as you know; I'd even say it's quite large. To "gorillas and evil crocodiles" — damn it, that obsessive line keeps popping into my head too…

We sat down, composed and with little excitement. Suddenly, something began to rattle, striking the fuselage from outside, and through the open door, we could hear snippets of conversation from the fuelers and the hum of the airfield equipment. Then everything went quiet, the ladder was taken away, the door slammed shut, and we heard the engines roar. The airplane paused for a moment, then started to move...

No one told us exactly where we were going and for what purpose. If it is Africa, I would have liked to know at least which part. As a child, I had read bits and pieces about Africa, but my fragmentary knowledge and newspaper articles were clearly not enough to understand what it was like. Libya, with its mad Gaddafi and his Jamahiriya, was one thing, but South Africa, pro-Soviet Angola, or Morocco with its king were quite another, and everything in between was shrouded in a black veil of mystery, as black as the continent itself.

The flight was normal, although noisy. The pressurized fuselage of the civilian aircraft kept us warm from the outside cold, and the flight was much more comfortable than the one to Krasnodar. The uncertainty about where we were headed and what awaited us next overwhelmed everyone, and the fatigue from the past days made us sleepy. We spoke little; no one sang military patriotic songs like in the movies, but just sprawled out in odd positions, trying to find any free moment to sleep, which was scarce on Molkino. Our dream team looked more like the blind men in Pieter Bruegel's painting than a combat unit. In fact, we were as blind as his heroes.

In less than four hours, the plane began to descend. As it descended, the exhausted contingent began to wake up. Four hours is not much time to get into Africa, except for its northern countries. Maybe Sudan? The thought flashed through my mind and immediately disappeared. Hell knows, we'll find out soon enough. Why worry? No one can escape his fate. They'll take you where you're supposed to go. Just sit tight, flat on your ass and wait, everything will become clear soon.

Here is Sasha 'Raven,' sitting blankly staring ahead, and I'm sure he does not see anything, and there's no trace of excitement on his face. His slightly open eyes under his eyebrows are more reminiscent of a drunk old man, judging by his round face. Oh, I wish I could be like that! 'Therapist' is asleep, leaning against his backpack, his head next to the head of the "invisible front's" fighter sitting next to him, who is sleeping with his mouth half open and drooling. They are not bothered by thoughts of "the big picture," neither about Africa nor Asia. They do not care where their ungrateful destiny will throw them to, and they couldn't care less whether it will be N'Djamena or Addis Ababa.

The plane began to descend quite sharply. My ears popped. Someone "fell out of line" by sliding off the bench feet first — a bad sign. It isn't a good omen - sliding off feet forward. Better and safer headfirst, since judging by the soldier's face, there was nothing to damage there anyway. We are coming in for a landing. I could hear the wheels hitting the runway, but the landing was still very soft. We rolled to the end of the runway. I could only guess that it was the end — the plane is large, and the runway in Africa is hardly among the longest ones. Everyone woke up, turning their heads, eagerly awaiting disembarkation and the resolution of the uncertainty.

"I wonder if they'll give us something to eat or just throw us straight into fighting," asks the big guy with the baby face and a dissatisfied grimace sitting across from him, either to himself or to everyone at once.

"Yes, it wouldn't hurt," a chorus of several voices murmured in unison. The plane kept moving under the noise of turbojets, which switched to a high, irritating tone.

In a minute, the plane left the runway, and after a few turns, it stopped. The engines roared and then fell silent. Silence settled in, causing ringing in the ears, and the air was filled with the pungent smell of aviation kerosene inside the cabin. Then, the commotion and fidgeting began. The doors stayed closed. Ten minutes later, they opened, and we tumbled out onto the tarmac via the boarding ladder. The heat was intense. Dry, hot air enveloped us as soon as we stepped out of the cabin, like a felt blanket. God, it was hot! The bottomless pale blue sky and the bright, merciless sun heated the concrete runway, from which heat rises.

"Get out! Get out!" One of our instructors is standing outside with a couple of armed guys. "Line up! Quickly!"

Somehow awkwardly after the flight and the wait, we spilled out one by one down the rickety stairs onto the concrete runway. We built a formation as if on a parade ground, pretending to be lined up, but the officer paid no attention to that. Everyone started turning their heads, looking around, although there was not much to see. Behind us, we could see the airport buildings, and in the distance, a thin strip of greenery. The rest of the landscape resembled a desert. A little to the side, a group of Arabs with machine guns were talking about something, nodding their brown heads in our direction and laughing, pointing their arms in our direction. They had machine guns — we didn't. Ours were packed in boxes in the aircraft's cargo compartment. If anything happens, we'll be in big trouble. But it looks like they're our allies or local natives in their traditional apparel, part of what is always an AKM.

As if reading my thoughts, the senior officer had selected the first four people and, after a short briefing, armed them with machine guns from the first box he found and posted guards around the plane.

"Listen to me, team!" the senior officer said quickly, coining short phrases after phrases. "This is just a stop for refueling. Everyone gets ready quickly and stays close to the plane. We're taking off right after refueling! Is it clear?!"

"Where are we, commander?" a voice is heard from the ranks. "Where are we flying to?"

"This is Benghazi, Libya. Any more questions? No? Then disperse!" He ignored the second part of the question, and no one asked again.

I walked over to the edge of the concrete, which was burning hot, and threw my backpack onto the yellow-red sand to lie down on the ground. Someone else did the same. My fellow trainees from camp joined me.

"Hey! Libya? Where's that?"

"Therapist's knowledge of geography definitely was not his forte, and the answer was predetermined in rhyme, and followed from two sides: "Where is? In the ass!""

"Ah, I see..."

Now everything was becoming more or less clear — we were flying to Africa, Central, or maybe Southern. I remember from the school time that the USSR and later Russia supported communist movements in Angola and Mozambique. But there are no more wars there. They defeated all the white usurpers, led by the Rhodesians, dropped the shackles of colonial imperialism and built an amazing and paradise-like dream country - Zimbabwe. Local revolutionaries cut out most of the white population and expelled the rest, including their black sympathizers, and since then started to live happily and without sorrow, making South Africa follow their wonderful example. So, our great mother country has already done everything it could to restore national independence in that part of Africa without our help, which means that we are not needed there anymore. In other words, we fly to the place where the earthly paradise has not been built yet, and universal happiness has not been achieved.

While the plane was being refueled by some suspicious-looking bearded characters and overly loud technicians resembling Ali Baba's forty accomplices, our guys with their meager army supplies collapsed on the sand along the runway. The aircraft crew hung around closer, watching the suspicious technicians like hawks. That's good; that's encouraging.

"Fall in!" a new command rang out, and the people, exhausted from the sun, terrible heat under hot sand, sluggishly gathered in front of the plane. A check followed. After counting everyone by head, we climbed into the aircraft in two columns, one by one, using the same rickety ladder on crooked wheels, and took our seats. The plane's doors closed, everything hummed and roared again, the aircraft began to maneuver along the taxiways, and then took off into the blue sky. Below, on the left, Benghazi was visible, with a port jutting deep into the city and a harbor more reminiscent of a lake. The Mediterranean Sea rushes by, the plane turns right, and the sea disappears, filling the entire space outside with a boundless desert.

Everything is going well, it's just a pity that there are no stewardesses in short skirts servicing lemonade with pretzels. The flight continues for another four hours or so. Below is a huge desert hidden behind a haze, either because of humidity, although where humidity could come up in the desert, or rather due to the long-time unwashed glass of the porthole.

It is a long flight, but even the longest flights end somewhere. We begin our descent. The scenery here is more cheerful — there is a lot of "greenery" below, either jungle or shrubs. This is the African savannah, but we will find out about it a little later, since there are no savannahs near Astrakhan or St. Petersburg to gain that knowledge. On the left, we can already see houses scattered in amazing disorder, with the trees scattered between them. Soon, the houses grow up, increase in size, and turn into huts, scary and miserable, which does not inspire our confidence in this wonderful place. So, here we will fight for the happiness of the people living here and defend the interests of their Motherland. Hey, Our Motherland, couldn't you find people who are not so miserable and destitute, and what interests do you have among these despairing huts?!

We stay in our seats as prescribed by safety rules. Safety first! Indeed. Everything happens just like on the previous flights, only faster. There are only two planes on the tarmac, and there is no air traffic in this God forgotten place. Outside the window, I read the name 'Bangui International Airport'. Hello Bangui! I can't remember what an amazing country has a city with such a lovely name. It's clearly not Rio de Janeiro, as old Ostap from The Twelve Chairs would say, it's something completely different, more exotic, but for some reason considerably less attractive.

We've arrived, gentlemen. Let's get out. It looks like this is our final destination. The plane boldly taxis up to a modest building with a proud international name, and after a while, a staircase, mercilessly battered by time and usage, is dragged to the plane. We spill out in a crowd, and some of us are led behind the plane to unload boxes of weapons from the cargo compartment. People look with interest at the airport building and the Africans bustling nearby. They are no longer bearded like Chechens and do not resemble Ali Baba's thieves — they are real natives from the very heart of Central Africa. Hello Bangui, the capital of the Central African Republic, as our senior officer kindly explained to us. So, what else do you need? We flew to Africa and landed right in its center. They didn't lie to us — the Company never lies!

This time, we were even officially greeted, albeit without an honor guard. Two very dark-skinned guys in Panamá hats were walking towards us from the airport. As they approached, our old friend pulled up from somewhere to the side; it was a familiar Ural truck with a worn-out tarp and painted in safari colors.

"Well, guys, looks like we're on the spot," said a fighter of indeterminate age with a dissatisfied expression, spitting in the direction of the approaching officers when they were still quite far away.

"Stand still!" Our commander kicked some laggard in front of him in his chest, giving the rest of us a convincing impulse. We lined up, and the officer reported our arrival without addressing anyone by rank.

"All right, guys! Welcome to the hospitable land of the Central African Republic! Now transfer all your stuff from the plane to the camions and we'll go to the base. All instructions will be given there. No questions! I'll give you all the information on the spot."

What I liked about the Company was that they didn't talk much but did a lot. This new commander instilled respect with his simple, clear, and concise manner of communication. It seemed that it would be possible to work with people like him. We'll see how it goes.

Boxes with machine guns and grenade launchers were taken out of the cargo compartment, and boxes with ammunition and sights were taken out of the passenger compartment. We took shelter under the awning, hiding from the sun, which, for some reason, was not as hot in the center of Africa as it was in Benghazi. Soon, the second and third Ural trucks pulled up with an even worse tattered tarpaulins with shamelessly gaping holes, where we quickly loaded the boxes, taking with us only an automatic weapon with spare magazines. Four of our guys climbed into the back of the truck with heavy weapons loaded in boxes, while the rest climbed into the other trucks. Without much delay, we set off. We expected to be at the base in an hour, where we were promised lunch and, most importantly, cold water.

I sat somewhere in the middle of the row, where the view was not the best. Those who sat closer to the edge of the truck bed looked back with interest through the swirling dust of the receding road at the amazing Africa, the impression of which was rather dubious. I did not notice any asphalt in the city. Rather, it was compacted soil with potholes that, even after not the best Russian roads, seemed like real potholes. If this is the capital, then what is the province like? In general, later I noticed only two asphalt roads in this glorious state — we drove on the first one when we left the city, and I had the opportunity to drive on the second one later on, which led to Sibut. And that's right, why spoil the population? Today you give them asphalt, and tomorrow they'll demand city water? No, that's not good. So, the local government was leading the country in the right direction, and our Motherland was apparently adopting their African experience.

It was impossible to drive fast on such roads, but it was possible to shake up the passengers sitting in the back like rag dolls. Dust swirled and got under the awning every time our Ural slowed down, which seemed to happen every fifty meters. Marik, who was sitting next to me and whom I had met on the plane, grimaced discontentedly and muttered something under his breath as he looked at the poor one- and two-story buildings with stone fences and crowds of poor natives on the road and sidewalks. However, the natives clearly did not consider themselves poor and, with a knowledge of their business, busily rolled carts loaded with some kind of junk behind them or proudly carried bags of all possible colors, shades and sizes. People knew exactly what they were doing and busily and expertly followed their mysterious baggage business. Bags were carried in the pick-up trucks, on the carts, in hands, and on the heads. Black as ebony trees, local women were particularly adroit with using their heads for such an exotic way of transportation.

Every now and then, we passed piles of garbage created by respectable and proud citizens. The piles were usually bordered by or located under palm trees covered in dust, which made them appear grayish. The bigger palm tree provided an inviting place for the bigger pile of garbage, exuding a complex spectrum of terrible stench, and the smaller ones accommodated smaller piles, however, of the same stench. All piles were ornamented with plastic boxes and bags of all imaginable colors, which added certain gaiety and merriness to the surrounding scenery.

Concrete and brick buildings alternated in their old-fashioned styles and colors. The ground floors housed shops and stores whose purpose was impossible to guess. Somewhere near the city center, on nearby streets, we could see a few white high-rise residential buildings. Overall, Bangui reminded me of a large, chaotic ant hill. The only pleasing sight was the green hills surrounding Bangui.

"Hey, Marik, why are you so unhappy? What did you expect to see here anyway?"

"And we came here to defend these bums? Who's that idiot who's going to attack them?"

"You don't know what they have in their bags — maybe diamonds," his neighbor on the other side tried to cheer up the disgruntled soldier.

"Rather, they have jackass ears in their bags, what else? Oh God, and this is where we have ended up."

That was the first time I heard some regret about our assignment. However, I was also not enthusiastic about the dreary landscape and poor buildings, and even more so about the people inhabiting this godforsaken country. The glamour and exoticism of Africa quickly faded in my eyes in the clouds of dust swirling behind our trucks. Really? What did you expect? To be taken to Cape Town or Cairo?

From where I was sitting, it was difficult to see the surrounding landscape, so all my attention was focused on the sensations of the road. And there were enough of them, though not too varied. After about an hour of speeding along a highway dotted with potholes and bumps, clearly inferior to the road lost somewhere among the Kalmyk cow towns, we veered off the road and rolled into a fairly large camp compound. At the checkpoint stood a black native whose skin glowed purple in the sun. The shiny and proud native waved his machine gun and shouted something to the driver, and after a brief stop, we drove into the camp.

"To the vehicles!" came the familiar command. We jumped out of the vehicle onto the concrete-hard ground and lined up in front of another commander. This time it was a major with the familiar epaulettes of a Russian army officer.

"Welcome to the shreds of the Great Empire!" (Later, we realized that his salutation applied to the relatively recent and quite weird past of the modern CAR.) He greeted us with a broad smile. "You will now be taken to your barracks, and then we will divide you into groups. Just so you know", he continued," we are here at the request of President Touadera's government to train the republic's armed forces, to protect and, if necessary, defend its interests and property. You will serve alongside the units of the republic's forces, and sometimes as part of them. Try to find common ground with them. Don't offend anyone! They are our allies, and we will be working and serving with them. Is that understood?!"

We stayed silent.

"Well, once again, welcome to the former imperial residence of Emperor Bokassa! You should appreciate the royal welcome you are receiving here. You will stay in this camp until you are assigned to the corresponding group and region of service. Further instructions will be given in groups. Dismissed!"

The imperial residence, which was somehow hard to believe, was a very large and equally dreary estate with the remnants of either a luxury villa or a seedy palace and a mass of auxiliary complexes and buildings once belonging to the mad Emperor.

Within the estate, there was also an airfield and a decent shooting range. Bokassa's two-story palace saw better days with all the glory tied to his imperial African court. However, it is now poorly maintained, slowly falling into disrepair with crumbling mortar and overgrown yards. What added a certain interest to that place was that it had once housed a harem of his multiple wives. But life can be cruel, and it played a trick on his royal descendants - it turned out that half of the service staff, dressed in rags, dirty and tattered, were either his children or grandchildren, and they were indeed the closest relatives of the infamous cannibal emperor.

"How many wives did he have?" Ilya asked with a deep sigh and immediately answered himself, "Many." Then he thought a bit and added, "Our commanders should have pity on us and give one field wife to each, and if they are in short supply, at least one for two." he suffered, dreaming of women since the Molkino camps.

"You, woodpecker, calm down before they feed you to the crocodiles, as was once customary here," someone replied.

A little later, before I was transferred to guard a mine, I had the opportunity to examine the palace and listen to stories that I wanted to believe, but which sounded rather like legends from local folklore.

Remnants of the former luxury could still be discerned among the bullet-riddled and unkempt rooms. The magnificent tiles and stucco molding on the walls and ceiling did indeed claim imperial luxury, but all this, combined with the rest of the glaring wrecking and devastation, reminded me of a homeless person with a top hat and starched jabot. In the basement, I was shown the kitchen where, allegedly, "on special occasions," dishes were prepared for Bokassa from his political opponents. I'm not sure how true all those stories were, but they fit perfectly into the overall picture of luxury and poverty mixed together and paired with the habits of a deranged dictator. This palace was stormed by French paratroopers, who were unimpressed by the luxury of the deranged African dictator against the backdrop of the beauty of Versailles and Fontainebleau.

Once three hundred French paratroopers captured the airport, and then the entire country, including the residence of the crazy emperor. A multitude of buildings and houses were burned down and destroyed, most likely sometime after those events. No one bothered to restore that kitsch. But we still were situated on the premises of Bokassa's palace ensemble, settling in something like construction workers' temporary houses, which wasn't so bad considering that they were furnished with air conditioning. However, it was necessary to keep an eye on the civilian service personnel, who, consisting mostly of the illustrious aristocratic descendants of the hapless emperor, were always ready to thieve anything unattended.

After being divided into sections, 'Therapist',' Raven', Ilya, and I ended up in the same group. Of course, we weren't the only ones in that group. There were twelve of us in total — just like the apostles — half of whom were guys who never held a gun in their lives and for some reason had decided to break bad in the darkest depths of Central Africa.

We were supposed to guard the exploration of minerals, which was predominantly gold, which was very helpful to some Government people, but not very profitable for others. Of course, we had already heard that the minerals we were going to guard might be of some use, and therefore there would be plenty of people willing to put their hands on them, along with the means of extraction, and very likely without asking for permission. Apparently, as a consolation prize, we were given four RPG-7 grenade launchers and one 82 mm mortar with ten boxes of ammunition and mines. They didn't skimp on the underbarrel grenade launchers either, giving one to each of us.

It was good that before leaving Russia, we were given a series of vaccinations against all kinds of nasty African diseases and were instructed to strictly follow the example of Pontius Pilate and wash our hands before eating and whenever possible. Drinking water other than bottled water was strongly discouraged, although that warning didn't prevent two members of our team—one of whom was humorously nicknamed "Barmaley," were struck by severe diarrhea. Of course, it would have been better if paralysis had struck those idiots, but unfortunately, at that time, only diarrhea was available, so we had to leave both sufferers behind at the imperial court and travel as a group of ten, like the Ten Little Indians from Agatha Christie's story. But it was a valuable lesson for everyone that this warning wasn't just empty talk, and following it could help us avoid all kinds of nasty intestinal diseases and their terrible consequences.

So, as an escort for a convoy carrying food, ammunition, and other supplies, we set off westward into the depths of the inhospitable African continent in a convoy of seven Ural and two Renault camions. Of course, so that we wouldn't be bored and lonely on this journey, right before departure, we were assigned a platoon of fierce-looking local natives from the government troops — a colorful crowd, constantly shouting and gesticulating wildly, capable of scaring away any member of Coalition of Patriots, not to mention other bandits of all stripes, just by their appearance alone.

Our sergeant was the taciturn 'Gremlin', who had already been to Syria and managed to get concussed there. He wasn't a bad commander and hadn't bothered anyone about trifles, though he always seemed either sleepy or languid.

The road was long, and the speed was good at first, but only as long as there was asphalt, which didn't last for long. We were told the region was under the control of government troops, so although there was a jeep with a machine gun in front of us, there was no other combat protection. We were our own guards, because, as we all know, "The rescue of drowning people is the work of drowning people themselves."

By that time, the asphalt had ended, the speed of the convoy dropped, and the road turned into a classic dirt road, the kind you might find in Africa as well as in Russia. The savannah, with separate groups of trees, was completely open and easily passable, with space between plants sufficient for SUV pass. Gradually, it began to turn into a tropical bush, and in some places, the road ran through a real jungle. There was less dust, and the road became wetter. Later, we found out that we had passed a local national park with a cartoonish name reminiscent of the old Soviet cartoon "Chunga-Changa," which was accordingly called Janga-Sanga. Our final destination was quite far away and could not be reached that day, so at night we had to camp in the park on hilly ground surrounded by groups of trees.

"Gremlin" consulted with the commander of the indigenous platoon, after which, despite all assurances that these places were under control of their beloved president, we still set up a guard, dividing it into sectors shared with our "allies."

"Guys, there's not much trouble here and supposedly a minimum of guerrilla activity, but keep your eyes and ears open," said 'Gremlin'. "If anyone's up to no good here, it's the local thieves and bandits. They are not really dangerous, though, always ready to dispatch one or two guys if they have put an eye on their stuff. The maximum they do is steal armament for sale; that is how they make a living here, so be on your guard and shoot without warning if necessary. And one more thing — there's one of us will stand on guard over there", he pointed to a group of bushes separating us from the allies, 'those guys', he meant our allies, "don't give a damn about us, just like we don't give a damn about them, so you can't rely on them if something goes astray. So, you, 'Kurush", he said to me," you'll stay there half the night until Iliya relieves you, but be careful not to shoot our native by mistake, or it'll be a war.' They'll probably get drunk or high on drugs, and then the 'call of their ancestors' will draw them into the jungle, and then it'll be a fun and lively party, with shooting and dancing right in front of you. Their sergeant instructed them not to approach us, but I am sure he forgot to tell them not to shoot. So, keep your eyes open if they come at you."

The advice wasn't bad and, as it turned out, quite suitable. Dividing into two camps and having supper near the Ural trucks, we spread out to our assigned posts as dusk fell, which here comes instantly, turning day into night in no time. In the west, the sunset was quietly fading away, and the cloudless sky turned from dark blue to purple. Suddenly, stars started to glow, one brighter than the next, and a faint breeze from the trees carried the smell of some unknown herbs or trees. The cries of birds had already died down, and rustling sounds could be heard, as if something was lurking in the surrounding bushes.

"Quiet Ukrainian night. The sky is clear, the stars are shining," I recalled a line from a long-forgotten school program. But the night was not as quiet as it seemed at first. A fire lit up nearby, and allies, like gypsies from the Free Village, gathered noisily around it. Loud voices and shouts could be heard—our neighbors had clearly gathered to have some fun. "Those bastards, I wouldn't be surprised if they even didn't post guards." Evil thoughts crept into my head. Loud singing rang out. The 'allies' were clearly having a good time. Shadows twinkled around the campfire.

I lay there and quietly watched the native orgy. I had to watch a ninety-degree sector, where a good fire was blazing in the middle, blinding me with sparkles and flames. Someone started beating either a drum or the trunk of a fallen tree. The rhythm was taken up in unison, and the shadows flickered more frequently around the fire. The black sky with a purple tinge seemed to descend to the ground. Even the silhouettes of groups of trees and bushes disappeared, and only the flames of the fire, the monotonous and shimmering hum of singing, and the annoying, repetitive beat of the drum cut through the darkness. "Oh God, what the hell are we doing here, among these devils who are stuck in the last century? They seem to lose the sense of reality. What's the difference between Bokassa and Touadera?" I thought to myself as I lay in the bushes a little away from a frail tree. I was starting to feel sleepy. Strange, sweet smells from exotic trees, the dark purple night, the dancing fire, and the rhythm of the drum did their job. I leaned my cheek against the butt of my rifle. How nice, how quiet... A chain of abstract thoughts flew through my head; they also swirled like the sparks and shadows of the natives around the fire — I was falling asleep.

I was woken up by the noise of crackling branches. Grabbing my AK with the bolt already cocked, I saw something black in the starlight, moving toward me and muttering guttural sounds. In the darkness, I couldn't understand what it was or where this nighttime horror had come from. The enemy wouldn't have attacked like this. There was no time to think, and I fired a short burst at the tops of the trees standing ten meters away from me. There was a screech, but then the footsteps stopped. Someone in the bushes screamed in agony, and I could only make out something that sounded like in the movies about WW2, "Rus, Rus." "Rus, surrender!" No, that didn't seem right, and these people didn't look like Germans. Not at all. From both sides, automatic weapons started firing in my direction. I crawled to the side. Suddenly, a dark figure appeared, waving a long stick with a shirt or jacket tied to it. It stood up, half hunched over, and began waving it over its head, shouting something in its own language, which sounded like the wise monkey from The Lion King.

'Gremlin' was already creeping up behind me.

"How many of them?" was his first question.

"I don't know. There seems to be a negotiator," I nodded in his direction.

Meanwhile, the negotiator had disappeared, but his stick with the rag remained sticking out.

"Are they 'allies'?" I whispered.

"Michel !!" yelled our commander. "Michel!! C'est toy ?!!?"

Somewhere to the side, there was loud rustling in the bushes, and a stick with a cap on it appeared again. "Vova! Vova! Ne tirez pas! C'est moi, Michel!"

"If they start shooting, take him down," whispered 'Gremlin', cautiously getting up. A huge figure rose from the bushes opposite him, impossible to recognize in the darkness. The figure stumbled slightly, waving its arms and shouting something joyfully, moving toward 'Gremlin'.

While the conversation, marked by extensive gesticulation that resembled two deaf people talking, was underway, Ilya crept up from behind. "What's going on? Is the ally causing trouble?"

"Looks like it. Good thing I didn't shoot anyone in the dark. Fucking idiots!"

A few minutes later, 'Gremlin' returned. "The 'allies' got high on 'kush' and wanted to treat us, but you," he said, pointing at me, "didn't appreciate their generosity. And you were right. These morons mix local cannabis with formaldehyde, and then it blows their brains out, which aren't much to begin with. Anyway, I explained to them as best I could that we were very grateful, but everyone was already asleep, and that tomorrow, so as not to offend them, we would come straight to them and smoke their "kush." In the morning, of course, they wouldn't remember a damn thing, since even now they are on the verge of passing out. Ilya, it's your turn now — they're unlikely to come back here, but keep your eyes open, you never know with these idiots".

The rest of the night passed quietly, and no one bothered us. In the morning, after breakfasting on the dry rations we had been given, we decided to check on our allies. Everything was as if nothing had happened. The black faces of the local guards were as expressionless as they had been before. Their sergeant, Michel, remembered the previous night only vaguely, but he wasn't particularly worried; for them, it was a normal night. The guys had been resting; they'd fired a couple of shots, what a big deal, that's what their weapons were for, so everything was fine.

A little later than planned, the convoy set off. Half an hour later, we stopped again — the Allied Renault camion had driven into a ditch after the Allied driver had fallen asleep at the wheel. The journey continued...

The road led through a real jungle. Although we didn't venture there even when we stopped for short breaks, it was clear that it was impossible to get through without a machete. A solid wall of twisted and entangled plants growing on the damp soil and occasional pools of standing water made it impassable. Spiders, the size of fists, snakes, and mainly swarms of insects were ready to devour any ambush, if there was one. This was probably why the road through the jungle, where it was impossible to see anything a meter deep, was quite safe, and any ambushes that took place usually happened in the savannah, which was more suitable for life and how it turned out here, for death. Humidity and stench from swarms of gnats and insects hung in the air. Rare villages, as if taken from old colonial engravings and consisting of round and square wicker huts, did not fit into the twenty-first century at all — the wildness was absolute and complete.

The road led to Nola, the capital of the local prefecture, but we did not reach it, turning south a few kilometers before reaching it and continuing further along the Kadei River.

In the Central African Republic, a country of dreams and unworkable hopes, almost all the gold and, more importantly, diamonds are concentrated in the west, at the junction of the borders with Cameroon and Congo.

Union for Peace, Popular Front, and Anti-Balaka groups and other fronts, groups and gangs covered the entire northwestern, northern, and eastern parts of the country and also controlled the gold and diamond-mining regions of the country, although original and well-established mining was carried out in the southwest along the Mambere River, a fairly full-flowing river, murky and full of all kinds of unpleasant surprises, such as crocodiles. Those creatures felt at home in the gloomy, dull waters of the African river, and if they have not eaten any of our people, it is only thanks to our innate aversion to them, which cannot be said about the local aborigines working on dredges extracting diamonds from the bottom of the gray waters. One such lover of the local fauna had his foot bitten off by a crocodile swimming by while he was washing his legs, sitting on a fallen tree trunk, and another dredger boasted to us of a deep scar on his leg left by the vile reptile.

There were no anti-government gangs in this region, but there were the omnipresent criminal gangs always ready to relieve the local diamond miners of their excess baggage. Recently, during the civil war, there had been an abundance of such "knife and axe" workers, as well as weapons accumulated over the years since French colonization and even since World War II. The people were fierce and raised in the African spirit of freedom, unburdened by questions of humanism and civilization, and ready to shoot at anything that moves in the hope of picking up a few shiny stones that would be worth thousands of euros in Europe.

Another, albeit less dangerous, plague was the monkeys swarming in the local jungle, screaming and brazen and even more thieving than the aristocratic descendants of the former Emperor. I was not sure whether monkeys adopted this practice from the local aristocrats or vice versa. These creatures prowled nearby, ready to snatch anything from a backpack to food left unattended. Several times, these vicious monkeys even tried to snatch a piece of bread from the hands of another animal lover in our team, who was teasing one of them, until 'Gremlin' hit the last one with his helmet, which landed right on the stupid head of the frivolous monkey. After that, it let out a bloodcurdling scream, which attracted several more of these creatures with clearly aggressive intentions, and only after a couple of shots, they, hissing and screaming, disappeared into the jungle.

South of Nola, the road became even worse, with more potholes and even more dilapidated villages. The huts, which could hardly be called houses, were something like huts woven from branches, sticks, and leaves. Some of the huts were somewhat square in shape and were scattered haphazardly. There were no people to be seen among them, only somewhere behind the huts could smoke be seen rising from a fire where the local natives were cooking their unpretentious meals. Apparently, this was how they had lived a hundred years ago, maybe even two hundred, and judging by the course of history, they will be happy and ready to live in a century after. All these evoked bright hopes in our hearts.

So, after another forty kilometers, we rolled into Salo, situated on the river Kadei, one of the godforsaken settlements on the riverbank. It seemed that the road ended there. In the settlement, which consisted of huts, there were even wooden houses. These houses could hardly be called houses per se and looked more like crooked barns, and that is where 'Gremlin' led us to.

"We'll be staying here. Let's unload the food and store it here. We'll keep watch around the clock — if they don't kill us, they'll definitely steal something. I repeat, don't let anyone from the village into the house. In a couple of days, reinforcements will arrive. We'll guard the drugs on the river as well as the mining site and patrol the approaches. I'll be assigning tasks for each of you on a daily basis. For now, settle in and drag everything into the hut."

There was no electricity or water in the hut, so we organized lighting ourselves using our generator, also to power the batteries for the radio station. We dug a latrine about fifty meters behind us, not far from a group of trees. For the first few nights, a sentry was posted outside so that he could watch the approaches to our hut and the other barns. Everyone slept on wooden bunks with their weapons beside them.

Closer to the river, the barracks were located with workers engaged in mining. There was also the employees' kitchen and warehouses with equipment and other technical means, as well as the hut of the local doctor, who turned out to be an excellent specialist. How good he was could be judged by one episode.

In addition to patrolling the approaches to the mine, guarding the dredge and the diamond storehouse, we inspected, as far as possible, the approaches from the western bank, which was in the off zone to everyone except us, of course. The western bank was deeply overgrown with jungles and vines hanging down into the water, and seemed impassable. But it only seemed that way. Sometimes we heard the sound of motorboats downstream, but we never saw any people or boats. However, when patrolling the opposite bank with Edgar, a local guide, we discovered that the bank had been visited and someone was curiously watching us from there. This could not end well, and measures had to be taken. Edgar also discovered the observation posts of the unknown people by the trampled grass, broken vines, and tracks that none of us could make out. There were several paths and observation sites, but it was pointless for us to set up an ambush; no one doubted that it would be discovered. We had no anti-personnel or signal mines with us, but something had to be done.

There were many good ideas, but none of them were practical. The idea came to me, an old river Volga's man.

"Listen, 'Gremlin', in the Volga delta, a while ago, they used to set fishing lines with triple hooks against uninvited guests. You can't see them even in the daylight, let alone at night, but they bite for sure, and they bite hard. Let's set a few of these surprises for the night and see who takes the bait."

"You've gone crazy from nostalgia for your homeland, 'Kurush".

"Do you have a better idea? "asked 'Therapist', who was lying next to me on the bunk. Let's try it, we've got nothing to lose."

That's what we decided. Two approaches, where, judging by the trampled grass, someone had posted a lookout, were covered with thin Japanese fishing lines, with small, sharp hooks, which the local fishermen had in abundance, hung along and around the supposed trail. The hooks were hung at face and shoulder levels, not across the path, but at an angle to the supposed approach in several rows. The hooks were hung a meter apart, and after they were hung up, we could not see them at all.

Everything was quiet for a couple of days, but on the third day, the three fighters on duty at the drag were awakened by a sudden howl right in front of the drag. Jumping into the boat, they quickly reached the shore, firing several rounds in the direction of where they heard a cry. The howling stopped but turned into a rapid, incoherent sound, somewhere between speech and a howl. In the bright beams of their flashlights, they spotted the clumsy figure of a black native struggling among the vines, with one hook stuck in his neck under his cheekbone and another, while he was still struggling, caught his arm, digging deep into his skin. While the poor man howled and floundered like a perch on the line, and under a couple of bursts of automatic fire, his companions did not hesitate to retreat quickly, abandoning their comrade.

Our guys had to approach the poor man slowly and cautiously so as not to get caught on our own hooks. They cut the line, tied the intruder, dragged him to the boat, crossed the river, and delivered him to the doctor's hut, where he had to be interrogated.

The local doctor was not at all pleased to be awakened in the middle of the night, especially after a turbulent evening with a dubious teenage girl, black as night and very scantily clad, who had disappeared momentarily right after our approach. Nevertheless, the awakened doctor quickly got down to business. After examining the poor fellow and baring his snow-white teeth, he unwaveringly wrapped the end of the fishing line hanging from the hook around his finger and yanked it out, tearing it out from the flesh of the poor guy, causing him certain inconvenience. The doctor laughed condescendingly and threatened the man with his finger. Blood gushed from his jaw in a dark red stream, and the kind doctor, in a gesture of mercy, threw him a dirty rag so that he could stop the blood from flowing. The second hook was removed less dramatically, but almost as quickly and effectively, with a cut in the tissue, naturally without anesthesia.

Without wasting any time, with the help of a translator, we were already interrogating the intruder, although he was not particularly hasty with his answers, periodically wincing in pain. Then the doctor whispered something in his ear, after which the answers poured out of him like goods from a cornucopia.

"What did you tell him?" asked 'Gremlin', who had joined us by that time.

The follower of Hippocrates, without hesitation, replied: "I told him that if he will persist with resistance, I would hook him by the scrotum with the very same hook."

No one answered, but I am sure that a brief but evident thought flashed through everyone's mind: "This doctor has a great future in his profession."

The poor fellow turned out to be one of the local bandits who preyed on the gold miners and the roads leading to them, so his fate was sealed right there and then. Handing him over to an allied sergeant, the latter mercilessly kicked him with his heavy army boots and, giving him an impulse with the butt of his rifle, herded the poor creature toward the river. A blow to the back or spine with the butt of a rifle is, as we all know, a sufficient means of persuasion under what even a legless invalid would move briskly. His destiny was sealed right there, on the riverbank, where an allied fighter finished him off with a short burst from the automatic rifle.

He was a scoundrel and a villain with a dark past, so we spared our tears to more noble character. His body was thrown into the river so as not to bother digging a grave. It seemed to me that this was done for practical reasons, that is, out of sheer laziness, but later we learned that it was done for a reason. According to local belief, the corpse of an enemy must be given to crocodiles, to please them and soothe their bloodthirstiness. I'm not sure whether the crocodiles were satisfied with that sacrifice and became more pleasant after that incident, but the natives knew better...

After that, things calmed down, and no one bothered us. Our work was not particularly tiring — we guarded our dredge and warehouses with property and washed diamonds at our mine and two smaller dredges upstream. The entire riverbank was dug up, sometimes on whole terraces. Partial security was provided by local soldiers stationed at the mines. Their duties were more like those of police officers and were limited to maintaining order among the workers and periodically encouraging the slackers. All operations were run by a local party member from Nola. His task was purely administrative and consisted of organizing work shifts, meals, material supplies, and the delivery of the washed diamonds, what was protected jointly by the teams of 'Gremlin' and Louis, the senior member of the local formation. There was enough equipment, and in addition to the dredgers on the river, excavators and heavy dump trucks were soon deployed on the shore. At the same time, in some places we could see simple wheelbarrows loaded with rocks, and if it weren't for the skin color of the local workers, the scene could have resembled the construction of the Belomor Canal in the Soviet Union.

A service in these parts of the country was not particularly stressful; the commanders from Bangui visited us only once, assuring us that our money had already been transferred to our bank accounts in Russia. At that point, it was impossible to verify this, but as it turned out, the office was not lying. This was pleasant and satisfying news, and if the service had continued as it was, it would have been possible to serve here for a long time without any worries. Only once our camion was shot by someone from the jungle. There were no casualties, not even any injuries, and after jumping out of the back and the cab, we scattered along the road and opened fire, albeit rather haphazardly, in the direction of the supposed enemy. There was no response, and it was all over before it began, but the Ural's shot-up tire had to be replaced. Apparently, they did not expect such resistance, and no one bothered us anymore.

'Gremlin' later shared with us an interesting observation: the locals, whether they were bandits, anti-Balaka, or government troops, could not withstand heavy and concentrated fire, and the more noise there was, the more depressed they became. The explosion of rocket-propelled grenades and mortar shells, combined with machine-gun fire, almost certainly guaranteed success and the flight from the battlefield of even the most organized local guerrillas. It was important to create such a concentration of fire, but this was not always possible.

Once all fun has to come to an end, and we were no exception to that ancient rule. A couple of months later, our entire group and a similar one from the Nola area were pulled out and transported in camions with all our weapons to a camp near Berberati. In the north, in the region that was still supposedly under Touadera's control, unrest began, and pressure from the Coalition of Patriots and anti-Balaka forces began to be felt. To counter them and hold the "front line" of the Beloko-Bassangoa region, or more precisely, the main centers along this line, Russian and Ugandan volunteers began to arrive from the south. That was the end of our security duties at the mining region.

A large camp was set up near Berberati, and intensive training of government troops loyal to Touadéra began. The training was organized along the same principles as in Molkino, a lieutenant colonel from Russia, was in charge, but we only saw him from a distance, as we did the other senior Russian military officers.

We were divided into groups and assigned as instructors. I was assigned to the same company as 'Raven' and 'Therapist', with whom I traveled through the CAR until my sad end, and 'Raven' until his.

Berberati made a better impression than Bangui. It is one of the largest cities in the CAR. There were enough stone buildings in the city to impress the imagination of the most demanding CAR citizens, although there was not enough asphalt, which, anyway, was lacking throughout that wonderful republic. The roads were fairly smooth, but driving on them raised clouds of red dust. Some of the houses resembled European ones, although it is quite possible that after our "life on the Mississippi," that is, on the River Mambere, any distant glimmer of civilization gave us the impression of the Champs-Élysées. The city was quite green and, importantly, peaceful. This was probably due to its rear location and relative remoteness from the rebels and various carbonari of all shades that swarmed the CAR. The approaches to both the city and the camp were much easier to guard than the jungles of Nola. Separate thickets of bushes and plants gave way to isolated palm trees and exotic plants, and the open spaces between them provided a decent observation. The African savannah had a certain charm and gave us some confidence that the approaches to our location were under constant monitoring and control.

We didn't have much contact with the city, our entire life was confined to the camp and intensive training, which we had already begun to get used to. Without any hints or explanations, it was clear that soon all these separate units, including ours, would have to be on the move, but when and to where was unknown.

Berberati Airport was a couple of kilometers from the city and close to our camp. One of our immediate tasks was to get weapons, including promised armored personnel carriers and armored reconnaissance vehicles. Some of the weapons were handed over to the Ugandans, who, to our surprise, showed quite a decent preparation and training, contrasting favorably with the 'invincible' Central African troops.

September and October brought heavy rains, turning the unpaved roads, which were the only roads available, into huge red-brown impassable puddles and limiting our activities to theory and working with weapons, which could easily be done in tents.   However, even in such conditions, the intensity of the training did not decrease.

After several months in CAR, we had become good friends with our compatriots from Russia, since the time of Molkino training camp and even from St. Petersburg, what in those inhospitable African places gave us a hope that in the event of impending trouble, we could count on the help of our comrades-in-arms.

A month later, the unit was filled with the camions of all kinds, and engineering equipment was brought in. Two transport helicopters were also permanently based at the airport.

The senior instructor, Captain Mikhailov, who was in charge of organizing the training and preparation of ours and the African units, came to our tent in the evening. "There will be no training tomorrow morning. We are leaving for good and heading north to Carnot. All the details will be provided along the way. Today is the day for checking and loading weapons and equipment. You will receive your rations and water tomorrow. I will not be checking with you individually—you all know what to do, and your sergeants will take care of the rest, but I will check the heavy weapons and ammunition. We will be the advance guard. In the second BRDM, the senior will be 'Raven', and the technical rear guard will be provided by Ugandan volunteers. Reconnaissance and air covers will be provided by helicopters. Communication will be arranged via the old channels. The senior officer will be in the middle of the column; the call-signs you know. The distance between vehicles will be 60 meters. All details will be provided before departure. We are leaving the day after tomorrow at 10:00 a.m. And one last thing: there may be ambushes on the way, so use everything you have learned and known. Any questions?"

Of course, there were questions. It appears that we are required to participate in an operation, but either the captain was unaware of the details or chose not to share them with us.

Captain Mikhailov, whose surname was his call sign, was not known to us, so all the information he provided was critically assessed. By that time, we learned to be very cautious about the information provided and even less to trust unknown commanders.

In general, everything was clear and understandable. According to rumors, the anti-Balaka was already active in the north, occupying separate points and mines. It was also known that while it was still possible to negotiate with the Patriots coalition, the anti-Balaka, consisting of gangs that did not recognize any laws and authorities, left no chance of survival if captured. But that was only half the trouble. Some gangs practiced ritual killings, which I will not describe to save your feelings. In contrast, others limited themselves to the more popular method of execution, in which a regular car tire was pulled over a person's body, pressing the arms tight against the torso so that they could not be freed. Then gasoline was poured into the tire. Then gasoline was set on fire, and a poor guy was left free. The person could do whatever he likes; he could run or roll around on the ground, surrounded by a flame. The burning gasoline could not spill even when he was rolling having been embraced by the burning tire. It is impossible to pour out any liquid from the tire because of its shape. Death from pain shock could take tens of minutes, while the monsters howled with joy as they watched the slow and painful death of their victim. We later found the corpse of one of our government soldiers killed that way who had gone missing while on guard duty. They didn't even try to bury him, leaving him for us...

No one gave the order not to take those bastards prisoner, but no one openly prohibited it either. We did not interfere in this matter, in most cases leaving it to the government troops to deal with their prisoners in their own way. When we needed to interrogate one of the prisoners captured by the local army of their glorious president, we usually got vague results of the interrogation, combined with the corpse of the interrogated object, which was sad and completely unproductive. But what am I talking about? O tempora, o mores…

I remember once, back in the distant and forgotten Chechen war, I was sent to bring two captured Chechen guerrillas to the regiment headquarters. Our artillerists kept them in the artillery battery where they were captured, and taking one soldier with me in a staff UAZ SUV, I set off for the battery. It wasn't far away from our position. The artillerymen were cheerful fellows, but greeted me with confusion: "What prisoners? There is only one here, and even he is not very presentable, so he won't be able to talk sensibly until tomorrow. "Well, where's the other one?" I asked. In response to my question, the sergeant nodded awkwardly toward a D-30 howitzer dug deeply in the rough log-walled position. It stood there with its barrel raised high, and contrary to all regulations and requirements, the tow bar intended for towing the howitzer was protruding beyond its muzzle brake. In combat position, the bar is always attached to the barrel, like a folding bayonet on an SKS rifle, but in this case, everything was against the rules, which explained the situation with the second Chechen. A trigger cord was tied up to the ring of the bar, ending in a loop exactly like the one depicted in photographs of John Woods, who loved to pose with his ancient but reliable instrument, and on which the Chechen was hanging. His body swayed slightly in the mild spring breeze while his feet were almost touching the earthen berm, his tongue slightly protruding, and his face with bulging eyes resembled an artistic caricature. The lazy artillerymen didn't even bother to tie his hands, and the corpse, with its shoulders slumped dejectedly, seemed to be apologizing for the negligence of those sloppy gunners.

"He was not very cooperative," the sergeant remarked apologetically, nodding again toward the hanged man, "and his luck ran out."

"I noticed. You were too quick, guys", ruefully I scolded the sergeant, and we went to pick up the second one, who, as it turned out, needed medical attention rather than an escort.

"Hey, 'Kurush', are you afraid of death?" asked 'Raven' that evening in the tent amid other conversations about the upcoming departure.

"Of course I am, although if I was really that afraid, I probably wouldn't have come here. Why is that all of a sudden?"

The conversation was pointless, and no one expected honest answers. The camp had quieted down; there was no sound of footsteps, shouting, or commands typical of any field camp.

Outside, one could hear the night sounds of the African savannah, the cries of birds and some exotic animals, and the noise of vehicles moving around the camp. Inside the tent, a dim light bulb burned, powered by a generator humming steadily outside.

"We're all scared. Who wants to die? If it was just a wound, I'd go to the hospital or even home; if maimed, it would be a different story, God forbid." A middle-aged soldier sitting deeper in the tent joined the conversation.

"Yeah, I'm scared too," continued 'Raven', "but you know, I look at it differently."

"No matter how you look at it, it's all the same, no one wants to die," continued the neighbor.

"That's right. But look, all my life, for as long as I can remember, I've loved to travel, although, to tell you the truth, I never got very far. On the 'Rocket', hydrofoil boats, that traveled along the river Kama, on the train, well, on the bus to the city. Once I traveled with my father from St. Petersburg to Sarapul, he was seconded to pick up a bus for his company. It was just him, the driver, and I. It was an ancient PAZ bus, a square wonder of the domestic auto industry. It broke down all the way down, and the poor driver repaired it without respite, so the whole trip took almost a week. Since then, I've always felt drawn to somewhere else. And I read all kinds of books, including those by Mayne Reid and Cooper. Indians, America, then watched Eastern Germany's spaghetti western movies..." 'Raven' suddenly fell silent, staring at the ceiling. Then, as if coming to his senses, he quickly blurted out with some malice, "What can I do in my life?! Where can I go?! I have no job, no money, no fucking education! Nothing! Everyone in the village was either drunk from the early morning, or in jail, or dead by his forties! So, I went to Chechnya on a contract, and then to Transnistria. Everything I saw was a war, damn it all... 'Raven' cursed and paused. Then more quietly, he continued, "Basically, my thinking is like that: if they kill me, then I have to accept death as a journey to a place I've never been before. They'll give me a free ticket for a long trip. I will get the ticket and go. I will look around, relax, and enjoy the trip. No worries, no hassle. It's a little scary, of course.   Everyone goes through it, but no one has ever told anyone what it's like there. So, I'll have to discover everything for myself. Like Columbus discovering America... If only I knew where I would be going... And no one knows what's there. So, it's even interesting, maybe even exciting. Just as long as death is quick and painless. A free ride to the unknown"

Did 'Raven' know about his fate then? Did he feel it? We often recalled this conversation later, and it made us feel uneasy. Goosebumps ran down my back, and it wasn't death itself that frightened us, there was enough of that around, but his clear premonition. Grim Reaper was there with us, the swing of its wings made us feel its presence, but at that time we didn't know for whom it paid a visit. It was as if the guy was telling us what had been awaiting him in three days.

God is great in his unmeasurable wisdom and sometimes sends us signals that are understandable only to the initiated, and at that time, the one who was initiated was 'Raven', who was preparing for his last journey. Where is he now? Did he reach his destination or still continuing his flight to the unknown? But what he had planned came true, and I will never forget that evening in the tent when the guy told us about his future, and not only his future, because one day each of us will start his own glorious tour, or as he called it, a "journey." And when the bell will knoll the measured time, it would be better to be prepared like 'Raven' was.

In the morning, we set off for Carnot. There were about fifty vehicles, with one BRDMs at the front and one in the middle of the column. At first, the mood was high. It was time to fight. Jokes and swearing could be heard everywhere, a usual unhealthy excitement before the imminent. We loaded the camions as if we were going for a fun ride. A helicopter hovered overhead, providing aerial reconnaissance and cover in case of attack. The front vehicles were already loaded with ammunition and equipment, and soon we finished what had been allocated for our part of the column. The heavy weapons and ammunition had been stowed the night before, so it didn't take long to complete preparation.

Everyone is sitting in the camion's cabs and in the back on the benches under a tarp. The first one sitting by the side of the trunk is a machine gunner with his assistant in case of attack. If an attack happens, they will be the first ones to jump out of the trunk and cover the rest with fire right from under the camion. The engines are already running, showering us with exhaust fumes. We're about to move. But as always, something goes wrong. We wait; the driver has stalled the engine. We can hear the guttural speech and swearing of the black guards. Someone is running along the vehicles, shouting something as he goes. The Ural's starter rattled, the vehicle started again, jerked forward, shaking us like rag dolls. We're moving. Slowly at first, then faster, kicking up red dust from under the wheels.

Individual huts, palm trees, and bush came into view. The vehicle shook and bounced over bumps. The conversations stopped. People lit cigarettes. Those sitting closer to the edge of the truck bed all look back through the thick dust rising in calm air, at the faded houses of the Africans. Under the tarp exhaust fumes mixed up with fine dust. Someone in front of the truck bed opened the tarp window above the cab to ventilate the truck bed. The exhaust fumes lessened, but the dust from the truck in front of ours drifted under the awning. Coughing and swearing. Now it is not the time for smoking. Everyone withdrew into their own thoughts. It is good that no one had put on their body armor. Sweat streams down our dust-covered faces. Our hair had turned gray from the dust. I am getting thirsty...

It was about eighty kilometers to Carnot by a dirt road. After Berberati, the savanna gave way to jungle in places, and from Banzum to Gaza, with rare clusters of poor huts, the road passed through dense "green" areas — dangerous, wild, and unwelcoming places — ideal for ambushes. In the jungle area, a helicopter circled the convoy, scanning the approaches and possible areas suitable for an attack, and providing flank protection. The sound of the rotors, which sometimes reaches us, sitting in the trunk, gave us some hope that, if necessary, we can count on air reconnaissance and support. The convoy moved slowly, but so far there was only one stop, the road was blocked by a stalled camion. Otherwise, the journey continued without incident.

I wonder how things are in St. Petersburg now. No one there even knows about some godforsaken republic in the heart of black Africa. If you ask any of my friends, hardly anyone knows where it is, and no one can name its capital. And why would they? It is not a tourist destination. No, they certainly don't need to know that, but then why do I? What am I doing here, and who would help me if something happened? I try to push the bad thoughts away. Why are they creeping into my head? So far, everything is going well, money is trickling into our accounts, or at least that's what they tell us. There haven't been any combat clashes yet, but will there be always like that? There will be, for sure, there is something in stock for us, otherwise who will be paying us such money? Special attention has been paid to this march and raid, then rest assured, something is definitely going to happen. But what and when? Everything is fine for now. But only for now. Look at those fighters sitting there, what are they thinking about?

The Ural camion shook, throwing us to the side, but we didn't stop. We drove around an old roadblock that had been set up by the rebels and never completely cleared, then we crossed the dry riverbed at the edge of the road, which had turned into a decent-sized hole, we were thrown around as we made our way through the improvised crossing. The last stretch of jungle, or forest, closer to Gaza, becomes very dense. This is the perfect place to mine the area, shoot at the convoy, and quickly get away. But everything is going well, and soon the open savannah begins, providing decent visibility to both sides. Not much further down the road we made a halt, placing the native soldiers as guards hundreds of meters from each side of the road. Meanwhile, the helicopter disappeared somewhere.

This is not encouraging, although the terrain is becoming more favorable for moving. There is more visibility, and there are hardly any defiles where we can expect mines or a sudden attack. Surprisingly, there are no people around. All the huts are deserted, with no smoke visible and no laundry hanging around the shabby shacks. The people have either hidden or left although that's unlikely. Where would they go? Most likely, they are hiding or trying to stay away from the military convoys. It's better for civilians to stay out of them, and it doesn't matter whether they are pro-Balaka or anti-Balaka, a Patriotic coalition or government troops, nothing good can be expected from either of them.

Three hours later, we reached Carnot without incidents or issues. The city was the same as the others, only bigger, dirtier, and full of angry, emaciated people. Motorcycles and pickup trucks with and without passengers, but always full of bags and sacks of all imaginable calibers and colors, scurried around the city. Rows of one-story buildings resembling sheds with omnipresent awnings in front of them, lined the streets. Dirty and wild people with carts filled with worthless junk were all over. On the main street, which is as wide as Nevsky Prospekt, there were even stretches of asphalt. Then white painted peacekeeping vehicles appear. There were plenty of UN peacekeepers here, and they were all as black as our fighters with the only difference that they acted with pomp and significance. Significance? What were they good for? They were not taking part in skirmishes not to mention any battles and not risking their lives. What a job! They were full of arrogance and saw us as real and dangerous competitors. Until recently, the peacekeepers ruled here, including the local administration, but now they have to make a way when we arrive with part of the government troops. They clearly don't like it, and the convoy stops, apparently for negotiations.

We jump out of the vehicles to stretch our stiff legs and backs.

"What's going on, guys?" Our volunteer from the neighboring truck approaches us. "They say the peacekeepers aren't letting us through. The commander is negotiating with them."

In front of us, two local boys are herding a flock of goats and sheep. Both the goats and the boys are extremely thin. Their bleating and cries drown out our conversation. Traffic stopped so as goats. Pickup trucks full of dirty people sitting in the back and even on the roof of the cabin yell at the boys, while the boys yell at their goats, and only the goats have nobody to bleat to; an idyllic and rustic picture is the epitome of African romanticism.

'Raven', 'Therapist', and the interpreter come to our group to take part in the discussion and to kill time.

"How long are we going to stand here?"

"Are you in a hurry?" replies 'Therapist', covered in dust. "Ah, I cannot do without a beer now. How much longer are we going to hang around here?"

I look at the 'Therapist's' shaved head, which resembles a poorly molded ball. Somehow, I hadn't noticed this before. The bulges above and behind his ears clearly indicate the aggressiveness and thievery of his happy owner. Once, in the distant and forgotten past, I was fascinated by reading about the long-forgotten and now discredited pseudoscience of phrenology. Scientists, doctors, psychiatrists, and medical luminaries of all stripes long ago condemned this once-glorious trend, and they were probably right. But just look at his head! It's not a head; it's a dream of a phrenologist and a perfect specimen for the St. Petersburg Kunstkammer! His head clearly refuted the conclusions of all medical dignitaries and scientists. You could easily read the character and criminal predispositions of its owner, judging by its shape. What a beautiful head he had! It's not a head, but a treasure trove of evidence, ready to blow all theories of phrenology opponents to smithereens. I smiled while staring at his bald head in the rays of the hot Central African sun. He fans it with his crumpled Panamá hat and notices my lingering gaze.

"What is wrong, 'Kurush'? What are you staring at?!" He looks at me with indignation and surprise. "What's wrong?"

"Haven't you heard of Gall? Once there was such doctor and scientist."

"What!? What are you talking about?!" 'Therapist' clearly suspects something wrong and doesn't want to be the butt of jokes, but I don't try to go into details or engage myself in enlightening activities in the African country. It's better for him not to know about old Franz, otherwise poor Gall will be in trouble.

The senior officer of the column passes along the line of our group and the Republican soldiers and stops a few dozen steps away from us. Platoon leaders from both ends of the column move up to him. He explains something to them, after which the commanders disperse to their units. Our lieutenant is the first one to approach us.

"Okay, guys, we're moving in half an hour. There's been a hitch with the peacekeepers. They don't know that we're coming, so we'll move on while they are sorting things out with headquarters in Bangui. Take a smoke break. There'll be another short stop on the way out of town, past the airfield, where the column will split up. All the details I will give you there. Once again, we're moving in half an hour".

We're in Carnot downtown, so it would take about ten minutes to get to the outskirts of the town, to get a better understanding of our further actions.

"Hey guys, where are we going to?" A small guy with the face of a professional drunkard whom I haven't seen before approaches our group. His question goes unanswered. We smoke. Cigarettes taste different here. I wonder whether it is because of nervousness or just scorching and dry air? Empty chatter begins about nothing and everything: about the

UN and peacekeepers, about what we see around us, and about the local women walking past us with the bodies as if carved from black marble and with faces that might scare Death itself.

"Damn it, they couldn't even tell us how much further we have to go, bastards!" says 'Therapist', who is in a bad mood. He takes his automatic rifle off his shoulder and leans on it like a cane.

"Don't rush. I think we'll stop again for lunch in an hour, and then they'll tell us where we are going to."

Our fighters are still crowding in groups, but gradually begin to disperse among the vehicles. The uncertainty is certainly depressing. So is the heat.

But now there's a commotion ahead. The command "To your vehicles!" is heard. It is repeated and echoes back and forth, and in a few seconds it covers the column as a tide wave. Without rushing, we climb under the tarpaulin of the truck bed, our temporal home in this African safari. One by one, the vehicles start up, spewing clouds of smoke into the still air. The hot air is thick with the smell of burning fuel and unburned diesel. We move, jerking and jolting. Everyone is falling on top of each other. One of the volunteers sitting in the middle of the truck hits his face on his neighbor's rifle barrel, breaking his lip and knocking out a front tooth.

"What an asshole is driving this thing?! I'll fucking kill him!" Someone in the front of the camion bangs his fist on the roof of the cab through the open front window in the tarp, but the driver pays no attention. The convoy moves forward. We can't stop; we keep going. The guy wipes the blood from his torn lip and curses. I can understand him...

Another ten or fifteen minutes, and we pass the white trucks and peacekeeping reconnaissance vehicles, leaving the city barracks behind and entering the open countryside outside of the city. Black peacekeepers standing in groups look at us, if not with malice, then without any sympathy. Another few minutes pass before we reach a big flat plateau. Outside, we hear commands given in French and our vehicles lining up in surprisingly organized order, like at a parade on Red Square.

A halt is called. We jump out and form a line. The guy with the broken lip and now missing front tooth grabs our black driver by the collar and yells at him. The driver can't understand anything — this style of driving is natural to him; he doesn't know any other way how to drive a camion with people or without. Situation is getting hot and we might get a fight between blacks and whites, which cannot be beneficial in the current situation. They are pulled apart — the black fighter pulls the white man, the white soldier pulls the black... Push and shove, damn it. What a fun...

After the stop and lunch, we refueled the vehicles with the help of the peacekeepers. We see their reasons, but there's no need to thank them. The reason for their zeal and willingness to help us is simple and understandable, even to our driver — the peacekeepers are staying at the rear, in Carnot, while we are moving into areas controlled by the anti-Balaka. "Have a nice trip, you, log heads", 'Raven' summed up the situation, meaning that the peacekeepers are ready to help us in any way they can, as long as we get out of their base and pull chestnuts out of the fire for them. If we do it right, the UN will get all the credit; if we mess up, well, it's our own fault, the peacekeepers had nothing to do with it. This philosophy is as simple as all great things.

From Carnot, our convoy split into two directions. We were all in one team consisting of 21 trucks and a BRDM at the head of the convoy. Our goal was Beloko, from where we had to drive out the anti-Balaka in case of resistance, and then secure the defense of the area. The rest are moving to Bouar with a similar task.

Beloko is a village in the far west of the country, located right on the border with Cameroon. We were told that there is an enforced company of rebels positioned there who must be driven out.

The first vehicle in the column was a jeep with a local sergeant who knows the area, followed a few dozen meters behind by a BRDM for cover and a truck with a mix of our and government soldiers, and two hundred meters behind was the rest of the column, with our Ural camion closer to the end of it.

The road to Beloko was quite long, and the day was drawing to a close. Our convoy had to cross the Carnot again from west to east and then move northwest across the bridge over the Mamberé. The night march through the area leading towards the rebels did not bode well, and the task was to cover about twenty kilometers to the same Mamberé River, which separated the provinces of Mamberé and Nana-Mamberé.

"They're not very imaginative, these guys. Everywhere you look, it's Mambere. Mambere rivers, Mambere provinces, just with different prefixes: nano, micro, macro. Good for them, they are not bothering themselves too much by making complicated names. They'd better do by assigning them numbers ", said 'Therapist', smoking and sharing his impressions of Africa with a bottle of beer he had managed to get hold of somewhere." Hey, 'Kurush', have you heard that in the States, all the streets except Washington and a couple of big cities are marked only by numbers?"

"Really? Have you heard about Brighton Beach?"

"Yes, of course I did. But that's different because Russian Jews live there."

"Is that why they named their neighborhood Brighton? Use your head, if you have one."

"Get lost." He expressed himself somewhat differently and continued, "There was a shoe repair shop on our street. An old Jew named Fima worked there. He got his son into the business, and then, lo and behold, his shop was closed. It stood closed for a week or two, but Fima was already in America, his brother lived there, the Jew as him and also rich".

"It happens sometimes", said I, "He's a Jew and his brother is a Jew, and I thought he was Chinese". I was amused by the American stories of "Therapist."

"Fuck off. I'm telling you, I don't know about Fima, but his son is already running a shoe factory there. They pooled their capital and got the business going. He's a millionaire!"

"Really? Well, of course, had it not been Fima's capital from the shoe booth, what would his brother be doing?"

"Get lost," repeated the 'Therapist'. His faith in American capitalism seemed to have cracked, and his American enthusiasm began to wane.

Before reaching the bend in the Mambere River, the convoy stopped. We did not cross the river in case there would not be a route to retreat had we been under attack. Trapping ourselves in the bend of the river would have been the height of stupidity. On the other side of the river, we still set up a post with a machine gun that provided some protection and blocked the approaches to the bridge from the north. On the side where the convoy was, a cordon of pairs of soldiers was set up, and closer to the river, but under the cover of camions, we placed a mortar with a couple of dozen mines at hand.

Night fell. There was no traffic in the same direction as ours. All transport, which consisted of a couple of motorcycles and cars traveling in the same direction, was stopped until we crossed the bridge the next day. The discontent of one of the drivers was quelled by a government sergeant who explained the situation to his slow-witted black comrade with a blow to the stomach with the butt of his rifle, followed by a blow to the back. Enlightening without bloodshed is ideal, but sometimes lessons need to be persuasive. The cars and motorcycles of all those detained at our camp were temporarily confiscated, and their owners were sent to spend the night under the nearest palm trees.

Aerial reconnaissance did not report any enemy movements. Another night in the savannah passed quietly. The sky was studded with stars, and the night was filled with the scents of the savannah plants, inviting peace and tranquility, although this feeling was very deceptive. There was no peace from the ubiquitous monkeys, who were as thieving as the local population. Shooting at them was forbidden so as not to cause false alarm and panic—fire was to be opened only against the enemy. If the allied soldiers weren't drunk or high, they were certainly tipsy from only to them known stuff, so their sergeants were busy ensuring discipline among them, while we stayed aside, not intervening in their business. The first part of the night on guard duty fell to me and a group of two other men. As a senior stormtrooper, I was assigned to watch the northeast sector, which was some distance from the river, but my attention was constantly distracted by the government soldiers loitering around the camp. Their commanders were in no better shape, but somehow the night passed without incident.

In the morning, one of the allied fighters who was on guard was missing. He had been on the other side of the river, guarding the approaches to the camp from the north. The last people to see him said that he had walked toward the river and then disappeared. He did not cross the bridge. A search along the riverbank yielded nothing. The soldier, who was not from the area, disappeared without a trace. Whether he deserted or swam away in the company of the travelling crocodile rushing for his business, remained unclear. No one blamed the reptile — people hunt crocodiles, crocodiles hunt people — it was a fair game.

In the morning, we crossed the bridge, and the column slowly moved northwest. The speed dropped significantly due to the poor condition of the road. The road led through dense bushes alternating with sparse trees. Sometimes the trees thickened, turning into a jungle. Visibility was limited to a dozen meters, and an ambush could be expected almost anywhere. There was no longer any air protection, but reconnaissance was still present in the form of a helicopter that occasionally appeared from nowhere. Occasionally, we came across settlements that could hardly be called villages. The huts, made of whatever materials were available, were overwhelming in their poverty. In some places, there were cultivated plots of corn and millet. How the locals survived on these items remains a mystery. On the other hand, the natives had no problems with garbage disposal, they just piled it up or dumped it literally behind their sheds where they lived.

A survey of the locals yielded nothing. It seemed that there were no anti-Balaka in the area. Some trucks passed by, but it was hard to say what political movement their drivers belonged to or sympathized with. Questioning didn't provide much information. The locals would tell you what you want to hear, but definitely not the truth; they did not want any trouble either with the government troopers or with the rebels. Their behavior was understandable, as the locals were not particularly eager to cooperate with the military of any side, knowing from experience that such encounters did not bode well.

Afternoon, we reached Abba – halfway to our goal in the village, which was as poor as all the others and differed only in its size and even more disgusting smell. There was a garrison of local paramilitary guards. The task of those vagabonds was to guard the cistern with diesel fuel, which we used to refuel our voracious camions.

Everything was going well, but the heat, dust, monotonous and already tiresome landscape, combined with hours of jolting, dulled our vigilance and senses. Stilted conversations, flaring up and slowly dying down, did not derail our trip. Dozing people succumbed to their destiny, looked tired and indifferent to the scenery, and slowly dragged time. They smoked incessantly after that, falling into a stupor, which was interrupted by a good kick from the truck bouncing over the potholes.

"What sins did we commit to end up in the asshole of black Africa? Others went to Syria, where, though a desert, there is also a civilization." My neighbor was clearly not thrilled with our odyssey.

"In Bangui, I heard it's okay," added 'Raven', sitting opposite, "not Transnistria, of course, but not bad. The wine was good there", he added thoughtfully, smacking his lips and almost singing his last phrase.

The gloomy looks directed at 'Raven' made it clear to him that he should change the subject. The topic of alcohol, given its almost complete absence, was a painful one and had become a taboo in order to reduce temptation. The conversation that had begun again died down as quickly as the previous ones.

After a rest at the edge of Abba and lunch, the journey continued. There was one more night to go, and we needed to find a place that was suitable for defense. Soon after Abba, the terrain became more mountainous, and the road more cheerful though strewn with stones and small rocks. The heat subsided, and the forest became a little less dense. Hills began to appear in the distance, sometimes with granite cliffs also covered with forest and picturesque bare slopes, which were a welcome change from the evergreen background.

One of the Ural camions broke down due to overheating. For the locals, repairing an engine or simply troubleshooting was a superhuman task. They were incapable of doing anything more than replacing spark plugs on a motorcycle, and they operated the equipment until it breathed its last breath. Repairs were unnecessary — the allies, whether the French or Russian, would provide them with replacements anyway. So, all the repairs fell to our guys. The pump broke down. Surprisingly, there was a spare one in stock. The repair did not take too much time. Somehow, we made it to Baidoke, another collection of ugly huts surrounded by jungle. We didn't stop there but drove another kilometer north and settled on the slope of a fairly steep mountain. The top of the rock was well-suited for observing the approaches and part of the road. At night, of course, you can't see much from the mountain, but you can see movement on the roads and the lights from far away. And, of course, the sound - trees and jungles absorb noise and generate a whole spectrum of uproar from living fauna. From the rock, however, it was possible to hear the sound of moving vehicles. After questioning the locals, it became clear that armed men had visited the village, but it was not possible to find out who they were or what their purpose was. Information from frightened and ignorant residents should be treated with great caution; their sympathies were unknown. In any case, it was a sign that we were entering dangerous territory and that the area was no longer controlled by Touadera's men.

The posts were reinforced. The road was blocked by a machine gun post. Paired guards were placed away from the road, and BRDMs were positioned under the rock on the terrace so that the firing sectors covered both ends of the road and the front of the jungle, while the equipment was divided into two groups and pushed closer to the foot of the hill. The rear was covered by a rock with an observation post on top and a machine gun nest in one of the crevices.

"Hey, 'Kurush,' are we going to fight?" asked 'Grey' as he took off his bulletproof vest.

"We're going to fight, brother. Just get out of the way and let me take this place. I am not going to lose a minute of my sleep." I picked up a spot under the shrub on the softer soil to use my bag as a primitive bed.

Our commander, Lieutenant, as we called him, although I never learned his real rank, led the column. He is also positioned on the mountain. It was a good spot on the top of the rock to control the situation in case of emergency —breezy and beautiful scenery around, plus all our troops were under full supervision, positioned like on a plate. There was no radio communication, only in case of an alarm. Complete radio silence was a must.

"Truly, I tell you, some who are standing here will not taste death before they see the Kingdom of God." That's what the Evangelist Mark said about Mount Tabor", suddenly said 'Raven'. "This mountain, Tabor, is the gateway to a new life."

"Wow, 'Raven', I didn't know you were so well-versed in theology. Where did you learn all that?" I was perplexed to hear something like that from anybody, and in the middle of nowhere.

"My grandfather had strong faith. He was a true believer. He took me to church when I was a kid, even before it became a popular trend. He was friends with the priest, and when they drank together, he often debated the New Testament with him. I listened, even though I didn't understand enough, but something stuck in my mind. When my grandfather died, I read all four Gospels myself, although I never managed to get through the rest of the books of the New Testament. I even wanted to go on a pilgrimage to the holy sites. Unfortunately, it didn't work out. And this mountain reminded me of Mount Tabor, even though I've never seen it.

"The Kingdom of God, you are saying. I don't think we'll find the Kingdom of God here... Are you a believer yourself?"

'Raven' looked at me before answering, then grinned and asked, "Weren't you a believer when you were in Chechnya?"

Now it was my turn to pause before answering. "I have become one, or maybe I had been before, I do not know. I also sometimes went to church when I was in school, hiding to make sure that nobody would recognize me; otherwise, there might be a problem. But you surprised me with your knowledge. Nowadays, as you know, there are believers everywhere, but do they really believe? Do you remember, "Many are called, but few are chosen" ...

"I see you've read a lot, 'Kurush'. Maybe when we get back..." Here he faltered.

"What do you want to say, 'when we get back'?" I asked.

"Oh, never mind. I just wanted to invite you to church when we get back, but it is nonsense, church is not a restaurant, one can't just invite someone there."

There was a long, awkward pause that needed to be broken somehow. Then 'Raven' asked a question that I had been looking for an answer to for a long time, but couldn't find. "And why did you come here yourself?"

I sat, staring at the ground, and said nothing. "Why? What else was there to do? Once upon a time, back in Russia, there was a choice. There were specialties, professions... then everything suddenly disappeared. Those who had money remained, and those who didn't disappeared from active life. The latter were not counted at all. Choices in life had become too simple. It turned out that it was easier to make money in war than anywhere else, and for that, not much was required—no knowledge, no education, and hardly any experience. No one can build a career without money or connections, and they won't let you anywhere near power. If you want to get ahead, go to war or die. The country doesn't need you, and you don't need a country like this. If I had a specialty, I would have left this business long ago. That's why I'm fighting for that asshole Touadera, even though he's not much better than his predecessor, Bokassa. So, I do not have many alternatives, unless you have something in stock for me".

The night was quiet, although rare gunshots could be heard somewhere on the side of the mountain behind the settlement. No one knew who was shooting or at whom; most likely, it was local gangs. Otherwise, everything was calm.

In the morning, we checked our equipment and weapons before setting off. On that day, we were supposed to take Beloko. There was no confirmation of enemy forces other than the information we had received earlier. We expected to oppose about a hundred or so anti-Balaka fighters in that settlement, and since the town was not fortified, we thought it would be relatively easy to drive out the insurgents. All of our information turned out to be incorrect: instead of the anti-Balaka, we stumbled upon the "Coalition for Patriots," and not in Beloko, but a bit earlier. In general, during my time in the CAR, I came to the conclusion that our commanders, at least at our level, did not have a clear understanding of "who's who." Their clever talks about anti-balaka, "Patriots," 3R groups, Lord's Resistance, and Arabs in the north of the country were worth nothing, and hardly any of them could distinguish one party's program from another. Neither could we.

Descending from the mountain like Moses with his commandments, our commander gathered the senior members of the group around his truck to convey the plan for the attack. A convoy with increased intervals between vehicles was to proceed to Bakobo, from where a reconnaissance group supported by a platoon of fighters would be sent to attack Beloko from the south along the border with Cameroon. Meanwhile, the main group would follow along the road, with the flank covered by BRDM. We did not rely particularly on aerial reconnaissance. When encountering a checkpoint, the usual and standard measure was to suppress it with a mortar section and then destroy defenders with hand-held grenade launchers. Ideally, the frontal attack should have come from the road, as the flank approaches to the checkpoint were likely to be mined. The plan was excellent, and like all excellent plans, it had its flaw, namely, inadequate reconnaissance of the area.

At about eight in the morning, the convoy set off. The camions' gearboxes were grinding and motors spewing blue smoke from yet cold engines. The speed was reduced. Everyone puts on body armor and helmets, ammunition, hand grenades, and smoke grenades on their belts. There was a feeling of tension and readiness for the upcoming assault.

It took about an hour to reach Abau, a small settlement like all the others, stretched out along the road. There were no people to be seen, no sound of barking dogs. The convoy moved cautiously forward through the hilly savannah, green and dotted with groups of trees on rocky ground. It became easier to observe and breathe as the road slowly but surely climbed upward, alternating between gradual ascents and descents. Small canyons and ravines began to appear on either side, some bare, some covered with dense shrubs. The landscape was changing, and definitely for the better. My mood also changed. After the briefing, the morning tension began to evaporate, and a boyish confidence emerged that soon we would "put things in order." It was funny to see that the most excited in this regard were guys who had never smelled gunpowder in Chechnya, Transnistria, or any other troubled regions before.

In just over half an hour, we reached Yerima, a settlement similar to Abau. Without a map, it would have been almost impossible to tell one settlement from another. Global civilization had swept through these places at full speed, without lingering or bothering either itself or them with unnecessary attention, and if anything reminded one of its existence, it was only the old tires scattered all over the place and, for some reason, the Coca-Cola signs that were so popular here and sometimes used instead of walls for the shacks. The road took us south, then turned west again, bypassing reddish granite mountains, then south again, gradually turning north 180 degrees. The camions shook. The rocky soil prevented dust from forming, but it was generously compensated with shaking and aggressive vibration. The helicopter had not been seen since the morning, or maybe we just couldn't hear it from under the camion's awning. The road was plainly going uphill. The air was still, or maybe it just seemed like that to us. The leaves weren't moving, the radio was silent, as it should be, someone was smoking, and those sitting closer to the side were looking at the pretty scenery.

An explosion! Somewhere ahead… Immediately followed by the continuous trills of the machine guns, somewhere ahead, probably where Jean and the BRDM are. The Ural jerked sharply and stopped. Short bursts of automatic gunfire followed us from the right side.

We jumped out of the truck on both sides and threw ourselves across the road onto the ground. The rest jumped after us. The Ural behind us continued moving without braking, rolling straight toward us and gradually veering off the road, its left wheel falling into a ditch where it came to a halt, half overturned. The windows of the Ural camion were smashed, its the driver was wounded or killed. The fighter sitting next to him jumped out through the door under fire and rushed toward the source of the shooting, immediately throwing himself to the ground next to the nearest bush. Shooting began from all sides. It was unclear where the shots came from and where the enemy was. It seemed that our guys were already firing in the direction from which the shots were coming. Further behind, another explosion was heard, most likely a rocket-propelled grenade, and a camion caught fire. In addition to the shooting, screams were heard from all over, with easily distinguished cries of the wounded. The airwaves were filled with commands. "Enemy on the right! A group in the bushes on the slope! 'Bayan', respond! 'Bayan', shooting from the mountain! 'Fourth', cover us with fire! Where are the mortars?! 'Mikhas'!, 'Yakut'!, To the foot of the mountain! Cover us! Crush the machine gun!"

I couldn't see who my neighbors were. Everyone was pressed against the ground. Bullets ploughed the ground in a punctured line. Ricocheting bullets screeching nastily in my ears. I had to figure out where they're shooting from. I quickly ran across and threw myself under the wheel of a truck. From there, I could observe what is going on, but lying under the vehicle is the worst of evil: you are visible, and the vehicle is on the road, which can hardly protect you. This is one of the biggest mistakes learned since the Afghan and Chechen wars. This hiding behind the wheels of a vehicle feels relatively safe, but this is just an illusion. The camion is visible from a mile away, there is nothing around it, and it takes seconds to spot you behind the wheel. You will either be shot or burned along with your shelter—the camion. The right thing to do, but also the most dangerous, particularly in the first seconds of the skirmish turmoil, is to jump away from where you are in the direction the shooting is coming from and use cover, bushes, pits, ditches, and boulders to get closer to the enemy. That way, you are at least even the odds by getting closer to the enemy, unless, of course, you get killed before you reach a cover. This option has been proven, although, I repeat, it is very dangerous. The problem is that everything has to be done smoothly and in sync, and how is that possible to do in a surprise attack? If you're in the right spot and there's a gap in the ambush line, which is usually quite long and sparse, because they have to cover the entire column with fire, you can break through, and if you are lucky, get to the flank of the militants, if not behind them, and that's the key to success. Lying under a camion, hoping that no one sees you and that you are protected by a flat tire and wheel's rim is self-deception and a road to nowhere; you will be dispatched in no time.

I'd been lying there longer than I should have, trying to determine where the shooting was coming from. To my left, one of our black allies who had been sleeping the whole way threw himself under the front wheel and fired his automatic weapon. I hoped he could see where he's shooting at. As if reading my mind, he turned his head in my direction and shouted something. He had lost his helmet. His face was glowing, either from fear or excitement. I waved him with my left hand and pointed to the opposite side of the road, inviting him to come with me. I had to do something. Another minute behind the wheel and I am done. I gathered my strength and will and dashed across the road towards a small boulder. The boulder turned out to be quite small, as a matter of fact, too small for my taste. Now I heard the nasty sound of a bullet hitting the flat surface of the rock on the opposite side of the boulder. My helmet had slipped to one side. I still couldn't see where the shots came from. I realized that I couldn't lie here. About fifty meters ahead of me, right on the bare rock, I could see the explosion of our grenade. While there's still noise and confusion, I had a respite, just a few seconds, and holding the automatic rifle in my right hand, I literally flew several meters forward from the boulder and landed under a bush. There was a small hollow here; it wouldn't cover me, but it almost leveled my outstretched body with the ground level. My face was pressed against the ground. I expected a burst of fire at any moment, but so far, it's quiet. Although quietness was only relative, and only around me. Either they didn't notice me, or they're not interested in me right now. Good. If they're not shooting at me, maybe they didn't notice me. I slowly raised my face off the ground and looked at the gentle slope in front of me. Now I could hear where the shooting was coming from, but I couldn't see the fighter. Cracks in the granite rocks and sparse bushes hid the shooters. I spotted what looked like dust or gunpowder smoke not far above me. They hadn't noticed me. I took aim and waited. A head appeared, turned, and seemed to be shouting something. I fired a short burst. The head disappeared. Did I hit it? Hell, if I know. I tried to concentrate and observe the sector in front of me. No one appeared. There seemed to be movement behind a bush, but I couldn't make out any shapes. I fired a few short bursts. My magazine was empty. I changed it hastily, losing the second one from the vest. I grabbed it with my left hand and somehow shoved it back in. I needed to change my position. I couldn't stay in the same place for a long time. A little to my left, I saw the same guy whom I saw under the camion, a government soldier. He's firing desperately from his automatic rifle. How did he have so much ammunition? Ahead and slightly higher up, there's something like a stone cornice about half a meter high, with a small thicket of stunted bushes above it. The bushes were rather puny and frail, but they're better than nothing. I rushed over there. There's the sound of gunfire all around, but return fire could already be heard from our side of the road. It's our guys. So, they've learned something! To my right, I heard grenades exploding. Hand grenades. But who threw them, our guys or the guerrillas? The explosions were slightly above me, which means it is likely our guys threw them. Someone is getting up ahead, trying to run up the slope, clearly not our guys. I shot.   Another burst. He fell. Excellent! I saw one of our guys breaking away to the right, behind a small, gnarled tree. Another one followed him. But then I saw that they were being covered by a long burst from a machine gun. Another one. Bullets hit ground in front of me and whizz over my head with a nasty sound. An explosion ahead. Only now did I notice that the radio was constantly blaring, but I couldn't hear it or simply didn't understand what it said.

Closer to the top of the hill, a mine exploded. It's very far from the enemy. Half a minute later, another one. Our mortar gunners had joined the battle with their 'Trays', 82-millimeter mortars.

An 82 mm mortar mine for the 'Tray' mortar is a pleasant lady in all intents and purposes. Its explosive charge weighs just under three and a half kilograms, but produces up to six hundred fragments, so it's quite a darling for whoever is nearby. It flies far and lands accurately. A good spotter with equally good gunners can put it within the radius of three meters from the target with the third shot. And that's usually enough. I got to know 'Tray's' work back in Chechnya, and I can't say anything bad about it, except for good. I've also had the opportunity to correct them.

I couldn't see where they're firing from, but they're firing with the main charge; at such a short range, it could only fire using this charge. As a matter of fact, it is even better, fire rate is higher with a main charge since no additional powder charges need to be tied up to the slim waist of the mine beauty.

I couldn't hear their spotter's commands; he must be somewhere around here, unless he's been wounded or killed. I remembered where the enemy's machine gun was fired just seconds ago. I grabbed my radio and shouted: "Tray'! This is 'Kurush'! Target: machine gun!" "I have no way of knowing what they were aiming at, so I shouted, "Lower your sight by two notches! Five-zero-zero to the right!"

The shooting continued around us. Somewhere to the left, at the head of the column, I could hear grenade launcher shots, but the mortars were silent. Either they didn't hear me or they're adjusting their sight, although I still couldn't hear their spotter. I waited, keeping out of sight, hoping that the mortar gunners would return fire. Suddenly, amid the cacophony of commands and noise on the radio, I heard: "Roger, 'Kurush'! Observe the explosion!"

I stopped shooting and tried to spot the explosion. Somewhere behind me, either behind the camion or further down the road, a mortar roared. An explosion… I didn't have binoculars and couldn't stick my head out, but I watched it out of the corner of my eye. It was too far to the right, too far away from the spot where I detected the machine gun. The distance seemed right, though it's hard to judge without optics or a chance to take a closer look. "Same target. Sight - zero-forty!" "Got it! Observe!" I heard in response. A few seconds passed, but it felt like minutes. Again, the mortar roared, and there was an explosion. It seemed to hit the target area. "Target hit! Three shots!" I observed three more explosions. I couldn't hear the machine gunning anymore, but I'm still not sure if we hit the machine gunners. Maybe they've already left, although it is very unlikely that they had enough time to do it.

Our guys have recovered from the initial shock. Behind us and somewhere to the side, I could hear grenade launcher explosions, but I couldn't see where the fire was coming from. However, the moment of surprise passed, and it looked like the insurgents were slowly withdrawing from the battle. It made sense. There's not much point in firing into thin air, and there's no reason for them to prolong the battle. Those retreating were still being covered by another machine gun fire, and I gave our column artillery new target, aiming at the machine gunner. Gradually, the shooting subsided, and I noticed that our men were advancing up the hill. It did not appear that the enemy had maintained a defense on the crest of the hill anymore. However, I couldn't provide coordinates without seeing the target, so I climbed up with our guys, running from bush to bush, stumbling and falling, as we tried to reach the hill so that I could give the mortar crew a new target coordinate.

The granite hill curved smoothly, and we were now at the top. No one was shooting at us, and there were no enemies in sight—they had all disappeared into the thick bushes behind the hill. I did not see potential targets anymore.

I provided approximate coordinates, but I was unsure if anyone was in the area of the explosions. The battle has its own momentum, and the mortar shooting, ineffective now, was directed toward the retreat route where the enemy was supposed to be. Mortar firing was now useful only for raising the spirits of our own troops and harassing the retreating enemy.

Gradually, the shooting died down along the entire column, or rather what was left of it. Behind us, there were fires and clouds of smoke from the burned camions. A few meters behind me, a wounded coalition fighter was being dragged out of the bushes. His leg was, and his pants were soaked with blood mixed with dirt; he was rolling his eyes wildly and did not respond to the questions shouted directly at him by our interpreter. One of our volunteers jumped up from the side. "What are you doing?! Don't you know how to deal with him?! You bitch! You will be singing for me now!" He pushed the interpreter aside and put the barrel of his AK to the insurgent's lips, continuing to curse him. The insurgent didn't understand what was going on and looked at the fighter in fear with wide-open eyes. Then the fighter pushed the end of the barrel with muzzle rifle sight into his mouth right through his closed lips and clenched teeth, crushing his teeth and tearing his lips to shreds, and started rotate the muzzle with the steel sight of his AK-74 left and right in his mouth, tearing his gums and palate, crushing the remaining teeth and bones of his mouth. The Patriot's mouth turned into a bloody mess that flooded half of his face. He could no longer speak or even yell and was only moaning while blood mixed with brownish bubbles was rushing out of his mouth. He grabbed his torn mouth with both hands, but it did not help.

"What are you doing?!" shouted the enraged interpreter. "Stop it! How will he talk?!"

"He doesn't need to."

The fighter stared blankly at the writhing insurgent and fired a short burst into his head. The body jerked and stilled with both hands partially covering his messy face. Face was a bit more than messy because three bullets teared off the back side of the guerrilla's skull, leaving a formless, gory mass hardly resembling a human head.

"Sorry, I got carried away," the volunteer turned his head to the interpreter and, without waiting for a response, started to wipe the blood-stained barrel of his rifle on the sleeve of the dead insurgent. Guerilla's hand slipped away from his face, so the fighter pinned it down with his boot and continued to rub the sight against his camouflage. The others watched silently, unable to forget the burned corpse wrapped in a car tire.

'A la guerre, comme a la guerre.' What else is there to say? The battle ended as suddenly as it had begun. How long did it last? The retreat routes of the "Coalition Patriots" had been mapped out and well prepared, and they withdrew in an orderly fashion, leaving us several dead and wounded. That is where they had an obvious strength — not to bother themselves with their wounded. Everyone survives or dies on his own. It's not easy to fight an enemy like that…

Our convoy was pretty battered. Three camions were burned to the ground; another one was smoking at the front of the convoy. Several more camions were standing with broken windows and flat tires with cabs punctured with bullets. The BRDM was a little luckier. A grenade hit the axle hub, knocking out a wheel, but the crew was alive and uninjured. Surprisingly, we did not have many casualties. Six dead and about eighteen wounded, five of them seriously. Three of the dead were Touadera's soldiers, and three were our volunteers.

After examining the dead and wounded coalition troops and posting guards on the crest of the hill, the lieutenant organized securing the area along the ridge and replacement of wheels, inspection of equipment, and the loading of the wounded into two vehicles. Three of our volunteer medics were already working with them, as the government soldiers were of little use in this field.

"Where's 'Raven'? Have you seen him?" when I heard the voice of 'Therapist' behind me. I haven't seen him since the start of the battle. I didn't see any of our guys when I was surrounded by black fighters, and I didn't notice anyone during the skirmish. I turned around. 'Therapist' was running towards me. "They got 'Raven'! You know that?!"

"What?! Where is he?! Is he wounded?!"

"No..." 'Therapist' was without his helmet, disheveled, somehow slumped over and looking off to the side.

"What?! Speak! What happened to him?!" 'Therapist' turned his head toward me and waved his hand listlessly.

"'Raven' is done, they dispatched 'Raven'..."

The old convict "Therapist" looked different. Gone was his former prisoner swagger. Standing before me was an ordinary guy, unlike I've seen him before.

"What!? Where is he?"

"Down there, behind the Ural with mortar crew."

A couple of our guys and I ran down with 'Therapist', jumping over crevices and dodging the sparse bushes. Where is he? There were no dead or wounded by the truck. The mortar gunners were working there with their equipment. One of them, Gena, came up to me.

"Hey, 'Kurush', well done, I didn't know you knew how to adjust fire, where..."

I interrupted him. "Have you seen 'Raven'?"

"Who?"

I waved him away to leave us alone. Together with 'Therapist', we walked toward the Ural, where several volunteers were loading stretchers into the back of the camion. There were stretchers with ours and guerrillas wounded.

"Hey, guys, is 'Raven' here?"

They're not paying much attention to us; they're busy with the wounded.

"Hey, you!" I grab the sleeve of a soldier bent over a wounded ally." Where, I'm asking you, is 'Raven'?

"If you mean our guy, he's over there with the 'two hundreds,'" he said, pointing into the back of the camion. 'Therapist,' someone else, and I scrambled aboard. The truck was already full of stretchers with wounded fighters.

Some were moaning, some were screaming in pain. All this cacophony, mixed in Russian and French, grew into a vague hum. It was impossible to get through. We had to save those who still were alive; the dead would wait; they're in no hurry. Somebody from outside was calling us back, and we jumped out from the trunk, where there was no use for us.

"Okay, we'll find him later."

"Are you sure he's not wounded?" I shook 'Therapist' by the shoulder. "Did you see him by yourself?"

'Therapist' nodded. Always so talkative, now you couldn't get a word out of him. "How did it happen?"

How? No one really saw when or how it happened. There was shooting and chaos at the start of the battle, just like always at the beginning of a skirmish. Nothing was clear, and confusion was everywhere. Gunfire was coming from all directions. Everyone was on their own. We were hit with grenade launchers and small arms along the length of the column. One of the grenades went off near 'Raven'. That's how simple and banal it was. Behind him were Chechnya and Transnistria. Experience, whether you had it or not, was irrelevant — life was decided by a fragment of a single rocket grenade... And there was no need for philosophy. Whatever might happen has already happened. In this battle, someone else pulled the ace from the deck, and 'Raven' pulled out the six of clubs...

We gathered together to remove the burning trucks off the road, two of the three of which were blocking the passage for the rest of the convoy, and started to wait for a helicopter to evacuate the wounded. Our only reconnaissance drone burned out along with the camion where it was kept, so we had no information about the enemy.

Soon, a dot appeared high in the sky and began to circle around us, gradually lowering its altitude. We couldn't hear the radio negotiations with the helicopter; our lieutenant was in contact with it from his improvised headquarters, but it was clear that the helicopter was not in rush surveying the area from a safe altitude, looking for a safe place to land. The sound of the rotor blades grew louder, and then, slowly, hovering for a few seconds above the ground, kicking up dust, the chopper landed right on the road behind the convoy. The landing zone was already cordoned off to protect the helicopter from a sudden attack.

As I suspected, the main spotter was wounded and was being sent with the others to the rear in Berberati. After that attack, I was assigned as an artillery spotter.

The camion with wounded soldiers pulled up while the commander was talking to the pilot. The conversation took place inside the helicopter via the internal communication system, as the noise of the rotating blades made it impossible to hear voices. The medics were preparing to load the wounded, but suddenly they were ordered to stop. Only two wounded insurgents were loaded on board, along with "Bayan," a burly thug and assistant to the lieutenant who had already spent enough time in the CAR, and one of our fighters with an interpreter.

The helicopter began to spin its rotors faster and faster, and everyone instinctively stepped back, crouching and shielding their faces from the prickly dust stinging their skin and eyes. After hovering for a moment, the helicopter began to take off, and everyone looked at each other in embarrassment, wondering why it had left the wounded behind.

"What's going on, commander?" asked the sergeant standing next to the lieutenant.

"No worries. They'll be back in five minutes."

The helicopter rose into the air, picking up speed and tilting forward like a huge bird of prey, and flew in the direction of the enemy's retreat. From the ground, it seemed as if it was hanging in the air until turning into a hardly visible dot in the azure sky. Ten minutes passed, then another five, and then the chopper reappeared in the sky, gradually obtaining real shape, approached and landed smoothly, raising clouds of dust, in the same place from where it had taken off minutes ago. Our guys jumped out of the helicopter and immediately began loading the dead and wounded.

Then it dawned on me. Two wounded insurgents and the commander's aide were on board. The wounded will now tell them everything and show them from above, like on a map, the coalition group's route of retreat and possible ambushes along our way. I saw something similar in Chechnya.

There are two insurgents on board. No matter how good they are, there is always a strong one and a weak one among them, or simply a smart one and a fool. In a moment of danger, these qualities manifest themselves instantly, because a moment of real danger is like the litmus test we used many times in secondary school, and one doesn't need to be a psychologist to determine who is who. Interrogating two people at the same time is not a rewarding task. The second one will automatically adjust his answers to match those of the first, so they need to be interrogated one at a time, separately, but not in this case; there was simply no time for that. Therefore, the helicopter will return with only one villain on board, while the stronger one, in full view of the weaker one, who is more ready to talk, will be thrown out of the helicopter. Of course, both of them will be scared or, as they say now, "uncomfortable." However, the first one will be a little more "uncomfortable" when he will be slowly dragged to the open door and pushed overboard amid his wild screams. His fear will pour out through every pore of his body, and his cry will suppress the noise of the engine. He will promise to tell you everything he knows, presumes or doesn't know at all, if you wish, but no one will be listening to him. He will scream wildly, fighting back as best as he can, but it will be useless. Nothing will help him, and nothing will save him. After a few terrifying seconds, his body will begin its free fall to our sinful earth. Maybe he will die before he hits the ground, maybe after, that we will never learn, and it is not important anyway. What is important is that his comrade will be given a chance, and he will undoubtedly take it and tell everything he knows and more above. This is, of course, inhumane and contrary to the laws of war, but in the end, it will save many other lives, so now it is time for someone to make his final step from the flying machine into eternity…

But it turned out that I was wrong. Neither the first nor the second insurgent came out of the helicopter. It is true that the first one was kindly asked to leave the chopper to make the second talk, and the second one followed his comrade after telling our guys everything, apparently because he was no longer needed. He told us everything we needed to know. You doubt it? Besides, there wasn't enough room in the helicopter for our dead and wounded, and there was no need for useless ballast…

I took one last look at "Raven". His jacket was soaked with blood, but his face was calm, his eyes closed. He tasted death, contrary to what Saint Mark said, and entered the Kingdom of God or was on his way there. He had been ready for this since his first war in Chechnya, even more so in Transnistria, and apparently now already knew that he was one step away from it, remembering the Transfiguration of the Lord and Mount Tabor just a day ago, and today he found his own Mount.

'Grey' and 'Therapist' approached me. Farewell, 'Raven'! Today, as you said, you received your free ticket for your last journey. Farewell, restless soul!

No traces of the retreating enemy were found in the dense jungle, hiding them well, but the road seemed clear, according to the captives. Of course, they might not have known everything, and most likely they didn't, but nothing was detected from the air, and soon we set off again, much slower than before, towing the damaged equipment behind us.

Still feeling the tension of the battle, everyone was on edge, ready for another ambush, if it was possible to be ready for such a thing. It took almost two hours to reach the main road to Beloko, and from there it was just as long as to our final destination.

The convoy stopped five kilometers from Beloko. According to the plan, part of the group surrounded the village from the south, reaching the border with Cameroon, while we entered in two groups along the road from the east. There was a delay due to the clearing of a small forest just in front of Beloko, but no enemy was detected. We entered the village simultaneously from two directions. The enemy had apparently retreated in advance, leaving us this important border post.

To organize a defense was easier than storming a fortified position. To the north, the mountains and hills rose a little higher, and to the south, we were covered by the state border. The only road running from west to east was blocked by us directly from the border post a little west of the village, and from the east on the road we used to get there.

Our stand was not interrupted by any events. Fuel, food, and ammunition were delivered within a couple of days. Another BRDM arrived, which we dug in at a slight elevation, securing the firing sector from the east. A pair of 12.7 mm machine guns delivered with the BRDM covered the approaches from the mountains to the north, where, according to our information, the insurgents had dug in.

Then there was Sibut. There were isolated but minor skirmishes with anti-Balaka in the central part of the country, which are also worth mentioning, although for some reason, most vividly, I remember our trip to Beloko and the ambush we got caught in. Everything was going fine until the inevitable happened. That's how it always happens: everything seems to be going fine, and then, boom, and you suddenly find yourself either in a hospital bed or in a coffin, and no matter how comfortable the latter is, it's still not the best outcome of the situation. And yet, up until that very moment, everything had been going fine. That's pretty much how it happened to me.

Time passed slowly in the CAR, but it was quite varied, so I didn't really have anything to complain about. Gradually, I got used to this mindless African country, its terrible poverty and hopeless squalor, its heat and beautiful nature. What can I say—people are such animals that they get used to anything, given enough time. Money also came in regularly, and although we hardly ever saw it, the feeling that it was being deposited into our account warmed our cold, lost souls. There were significantly more of us now than when our group arrived. Some units consisted entirely of our people.

I had already become a recognized mortar spotter, and that suited me just fine. Those with whom I had started serving here were scattered to different places, and I don't remember ever running into anyone, except once in Bangui with 'Therapist'. By that time, he had changed, acquiring a certain "mercenary" gloss and losing his more characteristic jailbird swagger. However, showing off had always been his trademark. We met at our headquarters and didn't have much time to talk. We enjoyed a recollection of past events in the west of the country and talked about Russia. At that time, he was returning either to Bouar or Bossangoa and was already commanding a detachment of "former ZKs" (former prisoners), modestly forgetting that he himself had come from the same tribe. Then, as I already mentioned, I lost track of him. He returned from the Central African Republic safe and sound, drunk and happy, all covered with money, spent some time in Russia, signed a new contract, and left for either Syria or Mali. Since then, I never heard from him…

With me, everything happened simply, trivially, and sadly. After we repelled the anti-Balaka attack near Sibur, the three of us were sent on a reconnaissance mission towards Grimar, on the border of the Ouaka prefecture.

According to our information, a guerrilla group had been spotted near Bo, a little south of that settlement. The possibility of an attack, an ambush, or simply road mining could not be ruled out, so we had to dismount and survey the area, not engaging in combat, with the sole purpose of reporting the location of the camp if one is found. Bo was no more than ten kilometers from our temporary location along a passable road. 'Location' was just a name, since groups like ours usually stayed in or near populated areas, while we cruised along the roads, patrolling it rather than guarding it.

Bo is a fairly orderly settlement, consisting of ordinary huts standing in the middle of the African savannah. A kilometer before reaching the settlement, we turned off the road to the south into a small forest, where we left our UAZ SUV, and camouflaged it with a net and branches. Then we started moving southeast along the edge of the forest. The left flank was more or less open, and the terrain was under observation, but we had to move in a line, one after another, through the forest at a distance where we could see each other. The forest was empty. We saw no signs of enemy presence until we reached the local road leading south from Bo.

It was clear that the local road had been used recently; there were tire tracks and flattened grass. We moved along the edge of the road, with 'Feeble', the guy from our squad, a few dozen meters behind us, covering our rear. The road wound between groups of trees, disappearing into the bush, hidden by a natural strip of trees.

Suddenly, just beyond a small grove, we stepped into a small clearing where, very recently, a camp had been set up. The fire was no longer smoking, but it was still warm, and there were several empty water bottles and some trash lying nearby. It was quiet around. But there was something unpleasant about that silence. It's hard to describe. It was a feeling similar to trepidation or real fear in anticipation of something inevitable, unknown, and looming over you from nowhere as if someone was watching you. I don't know if my companions felt it, but I could clearly sense it. 'Feeble' checked the coals and waved us toward the edge of the forest beyond the clearing. I followed on the right, and 'Buryat' covered us from behind. Suddenly, about fifty meters to my right, I heard automatic gunfire. Right at the same moment, I felt a sharp pain in my right leg and fell down, firing in the direction of the shots. I heard the crackle of automatic fire behind me. 'Buryat' was shooting. The pain in my leg became so excruciating that I dropped my automatic rifle and reached for the ransack to bandage my leg. I knew I was seriously wounded without even looking at my wound. My pants were torn and soaked with blood. When I pulled a ripped piece, the fabric tore along the seam, and I saw that blood was gushing under my knee, but that wasn't what worried me. The intense pain in the bone above my foot made it impossible for me to even move it. The bone was clearly shattered by a bullet. I was lying in deep grass, covered by low tree branches. The grass was so tall that it hid me completely, and I couldn't see anything a couple of meters away from me. I tried as best as I could to bandage my leg and inject painkillers. Writhing in the tall grass with my leg completely out of action, I presented a pitiful sight as I tried to stop the bleeding.

Things were bad. If our guys were beaten back, I would be left here and, in the best-case scenario, I would not be noticed, although that was unlikely. And then there was the prospect of being captured by the anti-Balaka, which did not bode well. It was a scary prospect. I felt a cold sweat of uncontrolled fear on my forehead. I reached for my automatic rifle and pulled it closer. I would shoot back until I ran out of ammunition, and then... I didn't want to think about it. Of course, I still had grenades, but I had no desire to blow myself up like a hero in a cheap soviet movie. Fear crept quietly under my skin...

Somewhere ahead, I heard 'Feeble's' AK-74 firing, then the explosions of hand grenades, but I couldn't tell who threw them. Strangely, the shooting soon stopped. I was lying there waiting for the pain to subside, listening to the sounds of the battle dying down. Suddenly, it became quiet, and then there was a rustling sound behind me. Someone was moving through the bushes. I put my machine gun on my chest and aimed it in the direction of the approaching noise.

'Buryat' came out from the tall grass. He stopped in front of me, slowly turning his head from side to side as if waiting for something. "What's wrong, brother? Lie still. I'll be right back." Without pausing, Buryat crouched down and quietly made his way away. I continued to lie without making any noise. Ten minutes passed, or maybe it just seemed like that. In a state of prostration, I heard someone else making their way towards me, quietly saying my call sign. They were 'Feeble' and 'Buryat.' They examined my wound. 'Feeble' shook his head.

"Not good, brother, not good. 'Kurush', we can't carry you to the UAZ, it is too far. Let's do this: help us as best you can, and we'll drag you to the edge of the forest near the road. I'll stay with you, and 'Buryat' will go back to bring UAZ. Got it?"

A deep indifference overwhelmed me, and my strength left me. Apparently, my injury, the dull pain in my leg, and the effects of the Tramadol were taking their toll.

I hugged 'Feeble' and 'Buryat' with my shoulders, hopping on one leg until I was completely exhausted. Then they tried to drag me, but the result was not much better. Somehow we made it to the edge of the forest. How far was it? Two hundred meters from that place or a little further, it's hard to say. I was in a state of deep prostration. 'Buryat' was gone, and we were left alone. It was quiet. In a semi-conscious state, I listened to the sounds of the tropical forest, the sounds of birds, the flapping of their wings, and some kind of whistling or singing. Was it delirium or did I really hear it? I was terribly thirsty...

I didn't hear when our UAZ drove to pick me up. They dragged me into the back seat, and we set off back. The road to our base was not long, but the car shook and tossed us from side to side. The pain returned. Then I passed out completely.

The chopper was already waiting for us at the camp. The only other wounded person besides me was another fighter I had never seen before. He had been shot in the stomach and was moaning constantly. I don't know if he survived, but I never saw him again. Then there was Bangui, where my African journey began. A makeshift hospital in tents and amputation of my lower leg below the knee.

In short, it turned out that a part of me, albeit a significant one, and quite a useful in daily routine, was already buried in Africa, in the terribly hot and poor Central African Republic, in Bangui. It is already buried, but I am not yet. I wish I knew where its grave is. Although what for? It is very unlikely that I will visit my leg's grave. But in my main grave, which one day will open its gloomy womb to embrace me, I will have a little more space than the others, which most of you cannot boast.

In Rostov, I was sent to the district hospital. Rehabilitation, prosthetics, compensation... The war was over for me. On the one hand, that was good— the others didn't come back at all or came back in a worse condition than mine, on the other hand, I ended up where I had started my African Odyssey, minus my right leg, though with material compensation for the lost weight plus headaches and bunch of related problems for the rest of my life."

There were already three empty wine bottles from Alexander's cellar on the table, and the fourth one was almost empty. It was already dark outside, and it was time to leave. We went out to the front yard to smoke. Lush, low trees lined the front entrance, and several steps with a winding path led down to the street. A light breeze gently rustled the leaves. It seemed like we had lost all desire to continue that conversation. The sharp shadows cast by the branches, as the bright full moon emerged from the clouds, drew fanciful shapes on the freshly mowed grass. Long-forgotten days came to mind from the country that had also been forgotten long ago, the country that neither Alexander nor I had been to since we left.

"When are you leaving?" Alexander broke the silence.

"Next Friday. I have to go to a meeting in Kansas City, and then I'll go home."

"You mentioned something about Victor?"

"Oh, yes. You probably haven't heard about him?"

"Of course not! Maybe, then, you enlighten me and unveil the mystery," he said sarcastically.

"I'm not so sure about your ignorance. You know everything about Yuriy, but I lost touch with him long ago. The last time I saw him was before I left Russia".

" Alright, but what do you know about Victor?"

I silently watched the moonlight filtering through the linden leaves swaying in the light breeze. I could smell lilac and some flowers I couldn't recognize. The scent came in waves, covering us with a southern aroma. There were no cars or people on the street. The city has fallen asleep, preparing for a new day. What time was it? What the hell is the difference? It's so quiet and peaceful around there.

Alexander snapped me out of my meditation. Why did he do that? I was so happy... "So what?"

"Things are much easier with Victor — there's no more Victor. And his grave is so far away that nobody could find it."

"What?! Come on, tell me!" Alexander clearly wasn't expecting that answer.

"Not now. My head is already hurting. Let's do it the day after tomorrow."

"The day after tomorrow?" Alexander threw his hand up to look at his watch, as if he could see his weekly schedule on it. "It's a deal. Come over to my place around six."

"Okay. But now it's my turn and my port."

"Hmm, port... Port has always been your favorite drink since school time. I don't mind."

Cab had already pulled up to the house and was waiting for me a few steps below the edge of his front yard. We shook hands, and I walked down to the car. My legs were slightly wobbly, and the blue frolic moon had already begun its sky play, dancing from side to side, hiding behind the branches and reappearing again. My head was spinning.

"All right, buddy! See you the day after tomorrow." I waved my hand. My head was aching. What a stupid head. It'll be OK tomorrow.

Stumbling over the curb, I almost fell, leaning on the trunk of the cab. Waving my hand again, I fell heavily into the back seat. We drove to the hotel…

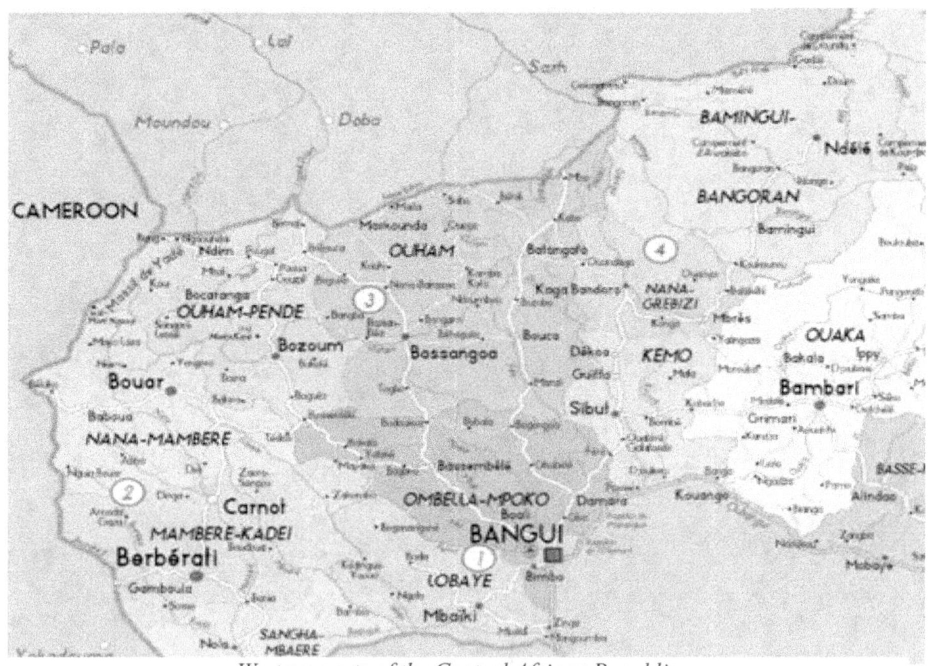

Western parts of the Central African Republic

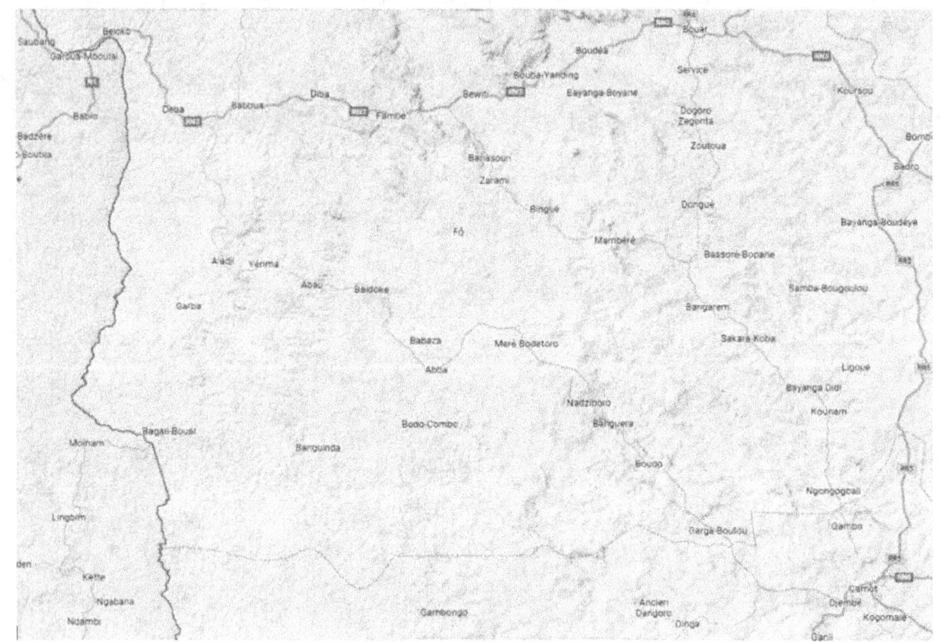

The Road of Beloko

Chapter 2

In The High Seas

The meeting with the company's contractors ended later than expected, but all issues had been resolved, and the contract was signed. Saturday was ahead, so although our plans with Alexander were disrupted, we could postpone our party for a few hours. I took an Uber from the hotel, and ten minutes later, with two bottles of ten-year-old Graham's port wine, I was standing in front of Alexander's house with its trimmed bushes and well-kept yard, resembling a picture of the Grimm Brothers' fairy tales. He was already waiting for me, and as agreed, we decided to have a dinner of fried potatoes with pickled cucumbers to recreate the atmosphere of the old days in Astrakhan but now on the soil of St. Joe, Missouri. However, we did not succeed in doing so, apparently because of the port wine, which could not compare to the disgusting but so dear and familiar port wine from the long-gone Soviet days, and because Alexander's house did not resemble our Astrakhan apartments in any way.

Fried potatoes, without any frills, seasoned with a glass of good port wine, went down well. A conversation began, at first lazily, from a distance, about the banalities and routine of the past few days, which were of no interest to any of us until finally our tongues loosened up and the huge gap of time that separated us and our friends narrowed down.

"Last time you said you knew something about Victor?" Alexander was clearly eager to ask this question, but it would have been inappropriate to start asking questions before the ritual supper with potatoes, pickles, and wine. It was necessary to wait so that the uncertainty would disappear, our heads would clear up, and out of the fog of the day's hustle and bustle and the treacherous sobriety of the past days, from which, as we all know, nothing good can be expected, a mature conversation would flow.

"According to the logic, today we should be drinking rum" , I began, "since the conversation will be about the South Seas, exotic lands, captains, sea dogs, and pirates, but not like those described in the novels of Sabatini and Cooper, but the most harmful and repulsive villains who would do better by adorning with their own bodies the yards of the modern clippers.

About five years ago, I tried to get in touch with Victor through "Odnoklassniki" site or some other social network. I don't remember. I never managed to find him; however, one stranger approached thorough the same site and claimed that he had sailed with him under a foreign flag on an old tub and got into trouble in Africa, which we had discussed a couple of days ago. There, right before his eyes, as he wrote to me, Victor died.

He wrote to me that he will be sailing from St. John's, Newfoundland, on such and such day, where he will stay for several days waiting for his boat. It happened that at the same time I was on my vacation in Nova Scotia, and it wasn't difficult to adjust my schedule so that I could fly from Sydney to glorious St. John's. So, we agreed to meet there. My wife and I drove from Halifax to Sydney, from where she flew back to Toronto, while I flew straight to St. John's, as it was not far — I really wanted to find out about Victor. I didn't have high expectations for this guy, didn't know who he was, and he could have been a complete fraud and failure. There was some risk, but in the worst case, I will visit Newfoundland, that was so close to my heart. Who knows who that guy is? But I decided to take a chance anyway, since it was only an hour-long flight.

I was already familiar with St. John's. It's a wonderful city in all aspects, built according to all the principles of progressive urban planning –right in the harbor, two blocks from the piers, in the heart of the city, there is a place dear to every sailor - famous George Street. The whole street is a focal point of life—pure delight and bliss—bars, restaurants, and strip clubs. What else do you need for complete happiness? Any sea dog, vagabond or vagrant traveler as well as all other respectful visitors to the city, do not to waste their precious time visiting Signal Hill, Cabot Tower, and Jellybean Houses—everything they need is right here, and there's no need to climb the hills, no need to scramble up the slippery Duckworth Street to the strip bars looming at the top with a beautiful women in a short red skirts and black stockings tempting good travelers for dubious and so easily achieving pleasures — everything they need is available in abundance on the wonderful George Street. Baron Haussmann wasted years of his life and mountains of precious francs rebuilding Paris but never came up with such an amazing and simple architectural and urban planning solution as the one found in St. John's, where good citizens do not waste time on trifles and keep everything necessary for life together and close at hand.

My counterpart, like me, had also been here before and appreciated its merits, and of course, he knew enough about that wonderful street. We met there in one of the bars, the name of which had long since slipped from my memory like water from St. John's Harbor at low tide, but which was easily found on the cheerful and drunken street.

The bar was dimly lit, with noise compensating for the lack of light. Lights twinkled merrily, television screens glowed, voices were loud, and laughter rang out. The bar was a focus of fun, but it was impossible to have a conversation in such an atmosphere. "Yes, my comrade was too hasty with his choice," I thought to myself, and quietly, looking around, started moving towards the bar. People were crowded around the pool tables, so there was no point in looking for the "mysterious stranger" there. Maybe behind the bar? But there, too, no one was craning his neck to look at the walking-in stranger. Everyone was absorbed in their own equally important business, silently watching the game on huge bright monitors or simply having lively conversations with their equally drunk neighbors. In the back of the room stood several tables, and there was almost no light, provided by a lone monitor that cheerfully broadcast the latest news and events.

So as not to embarrass my counterpart with the wrong choice of alcohol, I decided not to order anything, but to slowly make my way to the back of the room where he might be sitting. My intuition did not deceive me. As I approached the second table, I caught the eye of a man of indeterminate age in a denim jacket, whose face clearly revealed him to be either a professional sailor or a staunch devotee of strong alcohol.

"Oleg?" He looked at me questioningly, without smiling, as is customary in Canada, and even more so in hospitable Newfoundland, clearly betraying his Russian origins.

"Igor?" I replied questioningly, approaching his table.

He stood up and extended a stiff, sinewy hand. "Thanks for taking the time to come."

"Nice to meet you," I replied. "May I sit down?"

"Of course, of course. What would you like to drink?"

"Well, since we're in Newfoundland, God himself would say screech."

"Great. I'll have one too. I haven't had one for a long time. Not since my last voyage here."

We struck up a conversation. Where he is from, where he is going, whether he goes on a merchant or fishing vessel, what flag it is flying, and so on, of course, I'm not a sailor, but as a former and long-time resident of Astrakhan, having grown up a hundred meters from the famous RybVTUZ, the Astrakhnan Technical University, I had some idea of the seafarers trained there and could support maritime conversation.

Igor, as my conversation partner was called, had been a chief engineer on a freighter ship flying the flag of Benin, spending his entire conscious life, or at least most of it, at high seas. He was originally from Kharabali, a small town lost in Astrakhan sands, and after graduating from the mentioned university, he ended up first in the Far East and then moved to Murmansk, where he settled permanently. Since then, he had been sailing, first on trawlers in the Grand Banks in the North Atlantic, and then, when everything in his historic homeland went downhill, on merchant ships with mixed international crews under different flags. In St. John's, they picked up some construction equipment that was supposed to be taken first to Colombia and then to Angola, with a cargo of coffee or some other stuff.

We drank, then drank more, reminiscing about Astrakhan and RybVTUZ, trying to find mutual acquaintances, which proved futile. Finally, the conversation shifted to Victor, for whom the meeting had been arranged.

"I didn't know Victor for long, but we hit it off quickly, and it seemed like it would last," Igor began his story. "At that time, our old tub, which had seen better days, although it still rattled and leaked like a sieve, sailed between Europe, North, and South America until the leaks became a threat to the cargo. When we left Halifax for Brazil, we encountered a storm and had to call into the nearest port to avoid damaging our cargo.

It must be said that our boat was already an old-timer by any standard, having sailed the seas for years, and it was time for her to retire, but she was still running and puffing away. She was built in East Germany in the early eighties, and German quality, combined with proper maintenance, prolonged the life of the old steamer. It was owned by a Murmansk company, which had no intention of scraping her, and the company was trying to squeeze everything it could out of her old body. This was understandable: state subsidies had long since ended, and credits had become much scarcer, so no one was in a hurry to sign new long-term contracts with our company. So, they continued with what was still working, even though she was leaking, but thanks be to God, not sinking yet. Repairs were carried out either at our shipyards, which were affordable but of subpar quality, or in Norway, where the quality was impeccable, but the price was unaffordable.

I was hired to that steamer as chief engineer when Victor had already been there for several months as an assistant captain, and we quickly became friends. "Dony," as he was called on board, was also in charge of ballast, cargo distribution and securing, loading works, safety, and who knows what else.

Our steamer, the Arijon, was one of those vessels that can now only be found in some God forsaken backwaters. Although she was old, she looked handsome, with classic shapes and lines, unlike the ugly modern container ships. She was small but still full of steam and power. Despite the incomparably lower level of automation of that old tub, our crew was surprisingly small, numbering eight people, of whom only three were the Russians, including Viktor, the captain, and me. The rest of the crew was mostly from the Philippines and Indonesia. In general, the crew was typical for this type of vessel, consisting mostly of idlers and vagabonds from all over the world who were unable or unwilling to live the life of ordinary people and, for the most part, did not stay on the ship for more than couple voyages. There was no ship's cook or doctor, which was not really necessary, as everyone cooked for themselves, performing miracles of culinary art based on their ability to choose the right cooking time on old Korean microwave ovens.

When the loading was finished, we were ready to cross the equator once again. We quietly left Halifax Bay, which made me indescribably happy because I had spent all my remaining money on my new girlfriend, who lived conveniently near the port, which saved me my time but not my money. When the money ran out, suddenly and without warning, as is often the case, my love affair came to its logical end, and my Annette disappeared from my horizon as quickly as the sun over Grand Banks, so I had to spend the rest of my time living on Victor's expense, drinking away his hard-earned money in the bars of the hospitable city. But that didn't last long either. The loading was finished before the dockers' strike, that scourge of maritime transport and all fair sailors, threatened to begin, because without money, even the most cheerful port in the world can inspire nothing but despair, gloom, and melancholy, since neither beer, whiskey, or love on credit would be available there even if you are a three-time union member, and no port girl will offer you any discounts for your noble membership.

The weather was calm and peaceful, and we left Dartmouth with its buildings and structures, which did not impress us in comparison to Halifax, located on our starboard side. Passenger docks floated past us, and on the port side we enjoyed the awesome view of the McNabs Island with its once formidable fortifications and the Maugher lighthouse jutting out deep into the strait. Opposite the lighthouse, in a strip of fog behind the trees, the fortifications could be seen, long since transformed into a city historic landmark and delighting the eyes of sailors passing by. Once, during the war, from here, naval Arctic convoys left for England and the Soviet Union, which had long since been gone. Here, the strait became much wider, and after a few miles, we were out in the open ocean, heading south toward the southern seas from cold and foggy Canada. The ocean was calm while we were under the cover of the coast, but after rounding Parliament Rock, the ship started to sway on the cold waves in the fresh southwesterly wind. My diesel engine was quietly humming its familiar song, mercilessly spewing exhaust into the engine room, and I left it in the care of my Filipino mechanic and climbed up to the bridge to chat with the captain and gaze at the receding shore, which I always enjoyed.

"Hi, cap," we spoke to him in Russian, although the helmsman was as Chinese as my Filipino assistant and knew practically no Russian except for Russian swear words, although in the latter he could give even a Murmansk sailor a run for his money. This did not prevent us from communicating in Russian, and anyone who didn't like it could go to hell at any time convenient for him. Political correctness was not an issue, and we spoke all imaginable and exotic languages on board of our old tub without any risk of offending one another. "Everything's fine. Pressure and consumption are normal, temperature too. What's the weather forecast?"

"East of Bermuda, a low-pressure front is moving north. They're promising a storm. Winds up to a hundred twenty miles per hour. It'll be a good blast. Are you ready?"

"I am. But I'm a little worried about the leak. It's in the engine room. The water is coming in from outside, and there's no more bilge water than usual. With a leak like this, we'll last a few more years if nothing changes, but if we get hit hard, God only knows what will happen. The old girl has already lived her happy years."

"All right, we'll see. Keep an eye on leakage but now let's go for lunch."

He gave his last orders to the helmsman, and we went down to the dining room, our self-served galley.

There was a common supply of food stored in cupboards and large commercial freezers, plus everyone took food to his liking and kept it among the household refrigerators. Neither I nor the captain, whose name was also Victor, by the way, had any particular preferences, and the only thing we sometimes allowed ourselves was a hundred grams of whiskey or rum in his cabin, usually the three of us, our entire Russian crew, who were sometimes joined by Marcos, a Filipino who, among other things, served as the ship's boatswain and was the terror of all his subordinates.

The dining room was spacious and bright, although a little rusty, which did not add to its appeal. In general, everything on our ship was a little rusty or rusty enough, so we didn't pay much attention to it and weren't upset in the least. The crew of this ship used to be larger, but after several upgrades, it was reduced by a third, so there was plenty of room for everyone. The only thing that was depressing was the lack of hands to fight corrosion, and although there was nothing particularly scary, I had seen worse, brown rust was showing here and there, which, however, was forgivable for a ship of such respectable age.

Steamships of this size rock on the waves like a swing, almost like trawlers on Flemish Cap in the fall. The further south we went, the stronger the rocking became. Strong winds drove low clouds that seemed to rush right over the top of the mast, salty spray stood in the air like a solid wall, and the deck was flooded by oncoming waves. It was a beautiful sight. The bow of the ship rose smoothly on the wave, then suddenly dropped down, digging its nose deep into the next steep wave. Spray enveloped the bridge, water streamed down the windows, reducing visibility, and suddenly a squall tore through the clouds, and a lonesome ray of sunlight broke through. Then everything around flashed with some kind of unnatural fire, the white foam on the crests of the waves began to glow, the dark waves suddenly pierced you with their cold blue, and in a moment when the sun appeared everything was glowing white blinding everyone momentarily switching from semi-darkness. All you could hear on the bridge was the howling of the wind and the waves crashing against the ship's side. At times like this, it's good to be in the dry cabin with a cup of hot tea in your hand. Stand still, keep your balance, and don't spill the precious liquid! But then someone rushes into the cabin and a cold wind whistles onto the bridge. Thousands of salty sprays fly in, and water streams down from the sailor, while the bow dips down and the stern rises into the air before beginning its next smooth and deep descent into the dark abyss. And you sip your hot tea, burning your lips, trying to make out the horizon through the white mist. It's great!

But it's time to change mechanics, time to go down to the hold, to the heart of the old ship, to the banging and roaring diesel engines reeking of diesel fuel and poisonous exhaust fumes. A job is a job…

We were tossed about all day and all the following night. The wind gusts exceeded one hundred twenty miles per hour, and although it was far from the strongest storm we experienced before, it rocked us thoroughly. Waves washed over the deck when the bow dug into the high waves. Salty spray covered the bridge every now and then. The windshield wipers could barely keep up with the water flooding the glass. Shreds of clouds, like smoke, rushed toward us, rubbing the tops of the mast. The clouds took on bizarre shapes, resembling the angry faces of animals or distorted faces from Goya's paintings. It was impossible to stay on deck in such a storm. The raging ocean could be heard howling wildly outside the wheelhouse. The howl rose to a high pitch, turning into a whistle and then into a low, steady roar. The ship rose on a high, long wave, then began a gradual, accelerating descent that seemed as if it would never end and would swallow us up into the abyss. But the old ship stubbornly continued her struggle with furious elements, pulling her bow out of the overwhelming waves, to raise it proudly again on the next wave before dropping it down. The picture of the unending struggle was both terrifying and beautiful.

At night, the wind changed, and the waves began to run from the starboard side, causing the ship to sway. The pitching intensified, becoming transverse instead of longitudinal, rocking the ship from side to side.

There was no serious damage done; only the radar stand broke down; it could not sustain the consequences of its furious nature. However, the leak in the engine room intensified. I couldn't understand where the water was coming from.

The bilge pump was working incessantly, but water kept coming in. We checked the holds, and there was water too. There was no threat to the cargo in the hold, not yet. The storm and the pitching clearly weren't helping to prevent water ingress.

Victor was busy, too, trying to find out where the water was coming from. The entire crew was involved, but no one could succeed. It seemed that the water was coming from under the keel, closer to the stern where the power units were located.

We passed Bermuda when the weather calmed down a bit. The islands stayed far off to starboard, so we could not see them. The trip was definitely not the best one. Everyone was tired. The periodic checks of the hold were getting on everyone's nerves. Water kept coming in, even faster than before.

The storm was over. The sun was setting quietly in the west. It was no longer as round as it had been in the sky. Distant, narrow white clouds cut across the sun's disc as it touched the water. The sun dimmed and lost its shape, no longer dazzling the eyes as it gradually disappeared from view behind the horizon. The captain, Victor, and I gathered together in the dining room for dinner for the first time during the voyage. The storm had passed, the rocking had stopped, and our steamer was steadily and busily cutting through the sea, heading for São Luís, Brazil.

The captain was having a heart-to-heart chat with Victor. This happens when all the topics have been exhausted, the old jokes have been told several times, and everyone has already learned everything about the port fights in Monrovia and Abidjan, as well as the women in Havana and Luanda. Apparently, the captain was interested in how Victor ended up on the high seas and why he decided to leave hot Astrakhan for the high seas. I sat down and listened silently to Victor's story, finishing another huge mug of not the best coffee.

"My uncle, Anatoly, was a true sailor of the roughest kind. The sea was his real home, and on land he only felt comfortable when he was pretty drunk. The main excuse for his bad behavior was that alcohol was not allowed on board of trawlers while at sea, which he often reminded his sister and my mother, who was pretty upset by his behavior. He was married several times, but his family life could not withstand the stress and trials of more than a few short years, after which he divorced, only to marry and divorce again. Earning very well by Soviet standards, he acquired nothing but a car and a one-room apartment in Murmansk, where he died absolutely alone in his small abode, where his body was found a few days later.

He spoke little about his travels and expeditions to Antarctica and the African countries on the west coast, and it seems that the ethnography of those places did not interest him very much. Of all his stories, I remember only his description of St. Helena, where they made an unexpected visit due to the illness of one of the crew members. Somehow, he managed to get beyond Jamestown limits with its bars, into an inland area that he did not usually frequent, to Longwood House, where Napoleon was held and died, as well as to the city fort with its famous 700-step "Jacob's Ladder." I remember that when talking about the advantages of knowing foreign languages, he cited an example from the Longwood House, when a young female guide offered a group of Russian tourists the opportunity for couple pounds to lie down on the ottoman where Napoleon once rested, to which one of the sailors who could handle English replied: "Only if you join me, miss."

Such a response would hardly have gone unnoticed today, but this was back in the distant 1970s or 1980s, when emancipation and political correctness had not yet reached such appalling levels as they have now.

Little of his stories about the sea stuck in my memory, such as his descriptions of storms and fogs on the Grand Banks east of Newfoundland and of the Portuguese fishermen "tangling our nets".

The last story I remember him telling me about foreign countries and southern seas was his tale of his last voyage to the Philippines, when half the crew, and it was during the hungry though cheerful, 1990s, gathered their modest seafaring belongings and, after saying goodbye to the captain and the rest of the crew, set off for shore in search of a better pastures, never to return. Since cases of escape from the trawlers and other Soviet boats were not uncommon in the past, they were carried out secretively, very secretively, and with a certain grade of artistry and skill, as sailors were allowed ashore only in groups of at least three, accompanied by an official or, more often, an unofficial informer.

The would-be fugitive would usually drink with his comrades in the local bar after that suddenly disappears on the way to the washroom or ordering another round of whiskey. After that, the ship was moored in the port, although all the sailors were firmly anchored on board and forbidden to leave the boat to the shore. Then the Soviet consulate was notified, and further diplomatic negotiations were initiated until the fugitive declared himself a political refugee. Upon returning to the Soviet Union, the crew was deprived of their bonuses, and the ship's political officer or captain was denied a visa for further visits to the coveted "foreign countries." However, mass desertions from boats were a unknown practice at that time, and if people did flee to the West, they did that quietly and without fuss, observing all the appropriate decorum, but to do so openly, brazenly ignoring the captain and the political officer?! No, of course not! But what could they do when a half of crew suddenly decided to abandon their 'Bounty'? The ship was left in Manila harbor for a long time, waiting for a replacement crew to arrive, as it could not leave the port with only half its amicable team.

I think it was after this incident that my uncle was transferred to coastal shipping, and shortly after that, he retired. Only after that event, when voyages abroad were a thing of the past, did Uncle Anatoly become a little more candid in his stories about life at sea. Then he told me how the crew was tightly penetrated with a network of informers, some of whom did it purely from ideological beliefs. As usual, that glorious team was led by a political officer, whose job was nothing more than watching personnel and ensuring political indoctrination. Typical political officer was good for nothing except warming his belly on the deck in fine weather and putting up posters similar to "More fish for the country!", depicting a bushy-browed fisherman who, for some reason, resembled Communist Party Leader Leonid Brezhnev. Once, being so burdened with his duties, in my uncle's words, their political officer failed to cope with the party-educational aspect of his important work when, preparing for a long voyage, he loaded, either by mistake or due to a shortage of the required posters, instead of the bushy-browed fisherman who looked like Brezhnev, completely different posters that bore resemblance neither to Brezhnev, nor to the actor Petr Velminov, who often played collective farm chairmen. Then the cabin and corridors turned out to be covered with outdated slogans "Sow corn with wide-cut mechanisms!", apparently stored since the days of Khrushchev.

Upon returning to base, a third of the crew would seclude themselves from prying eyes and sat down to scribble denunciations and reports about the unworthy or simply provocative or suspicious behavior of their colleagues. Most of them did this because they had once 'slept up' somewhere and were therefore obliged to write 'reports' to the Special

Department in order to be allowed to go abroad again. I suspect that most of the reports contained worthless nonsense and rubbish information; otherwise, the entire Soviet fishing fleet would have been transferred to coastal waters, adding a shortage of herring and pollock to the general food shortage in the USSR. However, there were also the volunteers among the informers, of whom there were many. Such well-wishers were concerned about the moral character of the builders of communism, the corrupting influence of the West on Soviet sailors, and, of course, the prevention of any attempts at their recruitment by the despicable Western secret services. After all, every true patriot knows from barefoot childhood that there is no greater joy for those vile foreign secret services than to recruit a drunken Soviet fisherman into their ranks. In this way, zealous informers and secret agents made their careers by interpreting Christ's command to the Apostle Simon, "From now on you will catch men", in their own way. Since then, all these stories told to me by my uncle, a cheerful man, and a free sailor, had stuck in my head, and for better or worse, I decided to follow in his footsteps. To this day, I don't know whether I did the right thing."

"You won't believe it, but my story is not very different from yours. I'll tell you about it sometime," replied the captain and. "Well, how are our engines doing?" he asked me after a minute of silence.

"I'm not sure I can give you any good news, Captain," I replied with a sour smile. "Water is coming in, and I'm not sure how we'll make it to the port."

"Let's go take a look. Victor, come with us."

We set off on another inspection, which was becoming almost routine.

"Captain, the bilge pumps are running constantly. If the leak gets worse, we could damage the cargo," Victor replied.

"Let's go take a look," the captain repeated.

The water was rising. It was becoming clear that at this rate it would reach the cargo in the hold before we got to São Luís. Water was already visible in the third hold. At that time, we were about six hundred miles northeast of Puerto Rico.

The next morning, the captain summoned all the crew members who were off watch. "Water is coming into the holds; you all know the situation. We are currently pumping water with the main pump. If the leak continues, we will have no choice but to pump with the engine cooling pumps, but I hope it won't come to that. We are now changing course and heading for Puerto Cabello, Venezuela. There, the cargo will be transferred to another boat, and we will undergo repairs. So, gentlemen, our voyage is taking an unpredictable course and will be extended."

Silence fell. In principle, it didn't make much difference to the crew. Going to Brazil or Venezuela didn't really matter. Brazil is, of course, a country that would promise more fun, and there you get a better time than in Venezuela. In the latter, you could say it's not fun at all, not to mention the unstable situation in the country, but what can you do? On the other hand, repairs are not such a bad thing; while the repair crew will be taking care of the leak, you will likely have plenty of free time. Some people might even get vacation time, depending on how long the repairs take.

The ship has changed course to the southwest, and we are headed in the direction of St. Maarten.

It's a quiet, peaceful day. The sea was as smooth as a pond, and traffic was gradually picking up the deeper we moved into the Caribbean Sea. A huge tanker was passing by, and "merchants" of all kinds and flags were heading towards the Panama Canal. In the distance, a cruise ship appeared, beckoning with its tall white decks. Closer to the Lesser Antilles, yachts of all sizes and displacements emerged as if from nowhere, some sailing, others not bothering to set their sails and motoring along. One yacht, or perhaps it was a cruise ship, launched a helicopter that rushed past our stern, paying no attention to an old workhorse like our steamer. The sea was calm. The bow cut through the quiet surface like a knife. The wake behind the stern disappeared far beyond the horizon, dissolving into a whitish haze. Everyone off the watch was standing on the superstructure, some smoking, some chatting in their foreign languages and dialects.

Silence and peace. Even the swell seemed to have subsided. We were sailing at medium speed, scaring away small yachts with our proud but rusty appearance. One more night, and tomorrow we will be in Puerto Cabello.

There, in Venezuela, they are building Latin American communism en route fighting American imperialism. Communism will end as it always does, wherever it is built, in poverty and ruin, blood and hunger, but our Venezuelan friends don't know that yet, they are only beginning to guess, and we won't rush them — let them build it with accompaniment of the cheerful Latin American songs, with the enthusiasm of the Caracas communist youth organizations, let them drink full cup of happiness before inevitable sobering will clear their heads.

Perhaps they will understand later, because one can never appreciate the joys of sobering up without a good hangover. They say that history teaches us only that it teaches us nothing. And this is true – the experience of Cuba and its cheerful fools have taught them nothing, and the specter of communism – the brainchild of the bearded Marx – easily crossed the Atlantic and continues its victorious march to disturb the still unstable minds of joyful and musical Latinos.

The quiet night passed peacefully, and in the morning a light breeze arose. The ballast pump broke down, and the lights went out at hold number one. Those off watch, led by Victor, went down into the hold to repair the damage, but there were only a few hours left before we should have reached our destination. The electricity was restored quickly, but the pump repair took some time and effort. Since there were no spare parts, the coupling had to be welded. Oh well, we'll fix it properly when we reach the port.

Puerto Cabello is a magnificent port, sheltered from all the storms and other unpleasant surprises that the Caribbean region can offer. Puerto Cabello is certainly no Caracas, but the main thing is that it is the country's main cargo port, and we hoped that they would be able to patch us up there, which was what our steamer badly needed. A local pilot, who looked more like a traveling salesman barely making ends meet, led our crippling boat into the harbor, where the brotherly revolutionary comrades promised us repair assistance. We entered the port through a narrow strait, leaving an imposing Spanish fortress on our port side, along with the Venezuelan naval base, which surprised us with the number of its aging and dreary naval ships peacefully rusting under the hot South American sun.

Our steamer, leaking through every crack, slowly made its way to the pier under the watchful eye of the pilot, Don Pedro, after which hours of waiting gradually turned into days, which was quite unusual. All cargo ports are similar to each other, at least in that they never sleep. Ships are constantly unloaded and, once unloaded, immediately begin loading new cargo. Demurrage charges are high, so everything usually goes quickly. According to Murphy's Law, light cargo arrives first, followed by tungsten, copper, pig iron, or bulky containers. Therefore, you have to wait for the arrival of heavy cargo while losing valuable time, and only after that can you start loading. And here you need to keep a close eye on things. Now, of course, everything looks simpler—load the containers and don't worry about the sequence. However, even then, everything is done to make life more difficult. The containers are not standard, coming in all possible sizes and standards, so stacking them is far from easy. But in our case, everything went as usual, that is, not according to the plan.

We didn't go ashore, waiting for the unloading to begin at any moment. Finally, on the second day, "any moment" came, and a giant crane, as rusty as the Venezuelan navy, began to pull the cages and containers out of our holds. The work proceeded slowly, with frequent breaks for lunch, technical problems, or the sudden disappearance of the crane operator. However, eventually, the holds were emptied, and we began cleaning and pumping out the excess bilge water from all the cargo compartments. The water was pumped out in preparation for the arrival of the promised repair crew.

The glorious city was surrounded by a chain of mountains, completely overgrown and constantly covered with low gray clouds. The damp air, combined with the unwelcoming clouds, threatened to turn into a tropical downpour, but for some reason did not live up to its threats. The weather was clearly not conducive to hard work, and after finishing all the work on board before the arrival of the repair crew, our crew went ashore. As we entered the port, our pilot, weather-beaten by the all winds and hard life, kindly warned us that the local revolutionary youth were quite keen to replenish their revolutionary coffers at the expense of foreign sailors and anyone else who was careless or distracted, so going into town alone or even in small groups could end badly, as there were plenty of weapons on hand, but not enough police. To avoid unnecessary conflicts, we were advised to stay in San Milan, where there were more military but fewer prostitutes and bars, which did not match our expectations.

So, the advice given by the old sea dog was good, but impractical, and that is why in the first two days, two of our Filipinos returned to the ship with traces of unfriendly treatment left on their Eastern faces and completely unloaded from the currency they had had before going into town. The exchange was quick and fair, with almost no bloodshed, but it did not bring much joy to our comrades. Another day passed, and another one of our comrades disappeared. At first, we thought he had disappeared for good, as sometimes happened, especially in African countries that had thrown off the shackles of white imperialism. But after a few days, our unfortunate comrade made himself known. More precisely, we were informed about his whereabouts by the local infirmary. Our amorous hero, by prior arrangement or by a sad coincidence, was found in the bed of a local whore, by her suitors who beat him long and hard, possibly even with their feet, after that the unfortunate man came to his senses on a hospital bed with a swollen face, broken ribs, and a mild concussion, but relieved of all the money he had at the time.

Our town trips with Victor did not make any particular impression on us and left no unpleasant consequences either. The local tacos and bean cuisine were not remarkably varied, and the local Polar Pilsen and Solera beer resembled diluted swill, evoking nothing but southern sorrow. Clouds, gray as the smoke, hung constantly over the mountains and our steamboat, bringing neither freshness nor optimism. The voyage was going to hell, the cargo left in the port had been taken to the warehouse, and there was no new cargo for our boat. At the same time, there was no desire to hang around in this godforsaken hole, poor and torn apart by the followers of the revolutionary Chávez and his opponents.

As we suspected, the leak on board was coming through the propeller shaft seals. However, it turned out that water was also entering through rust-eaten welds in the hull in the area of the third hold, necessitating repairs using underwater welding. The Venezuelan crew worked slowly but steadily, and after three weeks, we could expect the repairs to be completed. This did not give us much joy, however, as our cargo had already been shipped to Brazil on some tramp vessel. No news came from Murmansk, and all we could do was to wait, gazing at the bright South American stars twinkling dimly through the clouds at night and languishing from the idleness, looking into the dirty water overboard, which was full of bags, boxes, planks, and other junk that can always be found in ports like this.

That evening, Marcos, a Filipino watchman, spent the evening standing on the deck, sucking on nasty local beer, thoughtfully spitting into the murky water, and philosophically watching the circles of rainbow colors cheerfully sparkling on the fuel oil film as they spread out from his spittle when an imposing SUV Tahoe pulled up to our steamer and an important gentleman with a rather sour expression got out. The gentleman opened the door with an air of importance and slowly lowered his bulky body onto the dirty pier, calling out to Marcos to ask whether this ship bore the proud name Arijon, even though it was clearly written on the rusty but rather high bow of our boat.

Marcos slowly finished his bottle and, holding it by two fingers, tossed the empty bottle overboard, then deigned to respond briefly and affirmatively, "Yes, sir," to the impertinent but slow-witted gentleman from the SUV. The gentleman, however, was clearly unimpressed by such treatment, cursed under his breath, and moved decisively toward the gangway, where Marcos just as decisively blocked his way.

"What the fuck, Mister?! Have you lost your bearings or what?!"

The gentleman clearly did not expect such a heartfelt greeting, after which he froze in the middle of the gangway with a dissatisfied expression on his face.

"Hey, call your captain!"

"Really? Why not God Almighty?" Marcos was not a timid man and had seen dozens of ports, so a dandy like this gentleman was unlikely to make much of an impression on him. The latter apparently realized this and slowed down a little, still trying to impress the seasoned sailor.

"I am a vice-consul of the Russian Federation, and I need to see your captain."

"I see now. Stay where you are, mister. I will call the vice-captain if he is available."

"If he is available?!" The gentleman was clearly not used to being treated this way.

"Indeed, sir. If he is available, he will see you; if not, you are welcome to come tomorrow, our shift is over".

"Is there a duty officer? Can you call him, please?" The gentleman had apparently figured out how to behave in the company of well-mannered people.

At that time, Victor, who was on duty, and I were sitting in my cabin playing backgammon and finishing off a bottle of good Canadian Crown Royal from our supplies when Marcos came to us with a report: "Hey, Chief, there's a guy out there who wants to see the captain, saying he's a Russian consul."

"A Russian consul? Are you sure the guy isn't lost? Tell him the captain isn't here and will be back tomorrow."

"I told him. He wants to see the duty officer."

"Okay. I'll see him. Don't let him on board. Let him wait," Victor replied. "Let him wait while we finish the game," he continued, turning to me.

"Ah, Victor, you don't like vice-consuls as far as I can see," I said, throwing down the dice.

"You know, I'm not very fond of consuls either."

We laughed and drank another shot of whiskey; the consul could wait for two busy gentlemen. Then we continued our game.

"All right, I'll go to see him." Victor closed the door behind him and went to see the uninvited guest.

I must say that this brotherhood, I mean the Russian consuls, vice-consuls, and other embassy secretaries with all their diplomatic entourage of all colors and shades, have never been particularly loved among us, the Russian sailors. There was no use of that crowd, but plenty of troubles while each of them was no less arrogant than their boorish foreign minister. As for me, I'd rather deal with a cop from a backwater village than with any of these people. Victor was of the same opinion.

"Hi, I am a vice consul of the Russian Federation, and I want to see the captain of this boat," said the gentleman who had imprudently tried to come aboard, proudly introducing himself.

"You can speak Russian, vice consul." Victor switched to the Russian language. "The captain is not here and will not be here today. I advise you to come back tomorrow."

"Do you really understand who you're talking to?!" The vice consul turned into a typical rude diplomat. "Allow me to board the ship to talk."

"I'm afraid, sir, you didn't notice the flag on the mast. I understand that today is dead calm and it's not easy to see it, but I'll help you — this proud ship sails under the equally proud flag of the Republic of Liberia, so even if you are three times a consul and twice an ambassador, you have no business on board of this boat until the captain permits you, and if you continue to be rude, I won't let you on it at all. Hey, Marcos, show our guest the way."

"Who are you?! What is your position?! I will report your behavior to the captain!"

"You know what, Mr. Vice Consul, go to hell."

I watched this scene from the bridge and saw the poor diplomat's reaction to Victor's last words, and I burst out laughing. The imposing gentleman, whose arrogance had slightly faded, raised his head and looked in my direction. Obviously, my laugh did not improve his mood. I couldn't say that his eyes flashed, as it would have been in some book, but I was close enough to see how he ran away like a beaten dog and quickly made his way to the car waiting for him.

The next day, neither Victor nor I was on board our ill-fated vessel when that dandy showed up again. We weren't there, but the captain was, as we learned upon returning from the city, where we had spent our time in a port tavern, as was customary during a long layover".

Igor, like his heroes from his story, got drunk and began to repeat himself.

We had already drunk enough, and lost count of how much Screech was used, while Igor was mixing his screech with beer, which, as every child knows, should only be done if both ingredients are in short supply. I was also in a 'good' shape, but not good enough to continue the conversation. My head was starting to hurt, and we hadn't gotten to the point yet, and it was unclear when we would get there, although it was interesting to listen to this sea vagabond. "Listen, Igor, let's call it a day. I'm a little tired after the flight," was my businesslike suggestion.

"That's because you didn't drink beer. If you had, you'd be like me — like a boatswain at a naval parade."

"Yes, it is very well might be, my friend, but it's time for me to take off."

Igor said something else, trying to convince me to sober up with Jamaican rum, apparently forgetting that Screech is the embodiment of that drink, and that for some reason we had not managed yet to sober up after consuming it.

"Listen, let's meet tomorrow for lunch at some more decent place, because I probably won't be alive until lunchtime."

"Oh, Andrei, I have so much yet to tell you. You seem like a decent guy, just a bit weak. I bet you need more practice. Okay then, let's weigh the anchors and get out of here."

Then there was a little protracted pause during which my fearless companion stared into his beer mug as if looking for his ship lost in the bay of distant Puerto Cabello. He muttered something I could not hear, waved his hand, and said that it was time to go, after what he thought for a moment, and said that he wasn't ready to leave this pier yet. We parted our ways. I took a cab and headed to the Hampton Inn near the airport, anticipating a rough night, a headache, and a guaranteed hangover, which I experienced to the fullest extent.

Early in the morning, after alternating between coffee, shower, and tea, the headache I had envisaged yesterday intensified, so I went for a walk in search of fresh air and a few thoughts I wanted to think over. The morning walk didn't help much, until I did find a jar of pickled cucumbers in a convenience store, which ended my morning misery. Pickled cucumbers and brine! What could be a better cure for the morning hangover?! Nothing, of course! If that brilliant idea had occurred to me earlier, I would have flown to foggy Newfoundland fully equipped with a whole supply of jars of pickled cucumbers. Why do wise thoughts come so late? Why do travel agencies and air carriers not post lists of "good advice" for travelers and display them on large screens in international airports? Why? Such questions plagued me and awakened doubts in my weary soul, and upon my return to Ontario, I vowed to send a letter to my district MP with a proposal about that amazing discovery.

It was noon, and we agreed to meet in a quieter, less crowded place. The effects of the previous day were still lingering, and my memory, as is often the case in such situations. I failed to retain either the name or the exact location of the restaurant where I had to continue listening to the saga unfolding before me, courtesy of my new acquaintance.

We met and Igor carried on: "We climbed the gangway, proudly but with the caution prescribed by the safety instructions after consuming a certain amount of Jamaican rum. On deck, the watchman was waiting for us and told us that the captain was waiting for us in his cabin right upon our return.

Shipboard subordination is a matter of utmost importance! If the captain is waiting, there is no time for delay and excuses, and we must go, though it was not an easy climb, staggering unsteadily up the steep steps to the captain's cabin, cursing and stumbling. But we conquered our Everest and knocked at the door of his cabin, where he was reading something, sprawled in the only chair on the ship, dressed in a fancy dressing robe.

"Captain, we're here as you ordered!" I reported briskly, but with a slight stutter, and added for some reason, "I and him."

"I noticed. And you, old pal, are drunk," he said, pointing at me, "you're setting a bad example and undermining discipline instead of strengthening it!"

"I'm sorry, Captain, but why am I an old and why am I a drunk? I'm still in my prime, good, solid, and at your service as always."

"Shut up and sit down." Our captain could not be more straightforward. "And you could be a little nicer to our fellow countryman, who is a diplomatic representative after all," the captain continued, turning to Victor.

"Ah," Victor drawled, "I see where the wind is blowing from. That nasty little upstart has already been reported on me! Well, he should know, given his rank, that it is extremely discourteous of him to step onto the deck of even an old tub like ours, but confidently plowing the seven seas under the majestic flag of the Republic, whatever it is called. Yes! Liberia! He should have known that, but he hadn't."

"All right, you two, go and get some rest and sober up. Tomorrow at eight sharp, be in my cabin. That's all. Now get out of here!"

We left and started to go downstairs. One of us fell and slid down two steps on the ladder. I don't remember who it was. But we decided not to tempt fate and followed the advice of our just captain. The captain, in fact, was a fine man and knew his way around rum and navigation, so no one would have dared to compete with him.

We parted ways until the next morning, and at night, I had a scary dream that the Foreign Minister of the Russian Federation, Lavrov, climbed aboard our ship, for some reason clattering his hooves and belching loudly. On his back, he was carrying several sacks from which white powder was spilling out, and on the sacks was written "From Argentina with love." Marcos tried to stop Lavrov, while Viktor and I stood at attention in front of him, until suddenly someone behind me shouted, "Why is the horse unattended?! Where is the rider?! The captain wants to see him!" Lavrov smiled maliciously, shook his head, and continued to hiccup loudly, kicking the gangway with his hoofs.

I woke up all covered in sweat. There was no Lavrov, no horse, but someone was banging loudly on the door of my cabin and demanding that I immediately report to the captain. What a dream! What could it mean? If my grandmother were alive, she would have used a dream book to help me solve this mystery. But at that moment, I had neither time nor my grandmother around.

It was ten minutes to nine I had overslept... Jumping up, I quickly washed and tidied myself up, then hurried to the captain's cabin and knocked energetically.

"Dear engineer, you are neglecting your duties, and it's starting to annoy me." The captain was clearly in a bad mood.

I don't remember him ever raising his voice at anyone, but his voice lost its usual pleasant tone and was filled with angry sarcasm when he spoke to someone whom he had been reprimanding. That was usually enough for the culprit to draw the right conclusions.

I apologized and stood silently in front of the captain. He was not alone. Victor was already there, sitting on a chair near the window.

"All right. Sit down. In a few words, the situation is like this: the gentleman you did not let on board returned here after consulting with our ship owner. Murmansk has already confirmed his authorities. We're picking up a new cargo here in Puerto Cabello and heading for Calabar in Nigeria. The bill of lading for the cargo states that the cargo is silica gel, so the containers will be sealed to ensure airproofing. Everything seems fine, but there is a small nuance…"The captain paused, turned around, and walked over to the window.

We sat silently and looked at the captain's silhouette against the window, lit by the bright blue sky outside. He turned and looked at us: "I don't know what this silica gel is, but the entire crew will be issued automatic weapons with three magazines each, plus a box of ammunition. Among other things, we will be given a PK machine gun, which should be kept in the wheelhouse, with two tripods installed, one on each side. The most interesting thing is that no one will be allowed on board on our boat in neutral waters. If anybody attempts to do so, we are to use our weapons. In territorial waters, we are to be met by the Nigerian coast guard. That fop was talking about pirates, but that's nonsense. I've been in those waters before, heard about them, although I've never encountered any. Besides, we've never been issued weapons."

He fell silent. We also remained silent, assessing the situation.

"Well, it might not be so bad, Captain," said Victor.

"Maybe. But it might not be so good either."

"Yes, the situation looks like... Will our eastern brothers agree to participate in this circus?" I asked.

"I don't know. I have no doubts about you, but I'll have to talk to them. I've already contacted Murmansk. They're promising us double pay for the trip. But they don't know what it's all about, or they're just keeping us in the dark. Hell knows... Igor, you'll be the machine gunner."

"Me? Why me?"

"Because you drink the most, so you'll be in charge of the machine gun," the captain concluded logically. "And you'll take Black Steve as your assistant." After a pause, he added, "It's strange that they're so insistent on giving us weapons. I don't remember this happening before. It's as if they know something they do not want to share with us. Anyway, that's how it is. I'll talk to the crew myself when everyone's on board. If anyone wants to jump from the ship, which I doubt, they're free to do so. Although, where would they go? And Victor, next time, be nicer to the vice-consuls. He really had it in for you."

"Screw them all," Victor stuck to his guns.

"All right. We should get the cargo tomorrow. In the meantime, check that everything is ready for the voyage. Report back when you're ready. Silica gel, damn it... Yes, sure…"

In the evening, the captain briefed the crew on the details of the voyage and special conditions. The crew's reaction was normal, as he expected. Some of my mates had military experience in their national armies and were familiar with small arms; it is also known that even a monkey can be taught how to use an AKM.

The next day, containers with silica gel arrived, along with boxes of automatic weapons and ammunition and a machine gun with two mounts. While we were in the port, all the weapons were locked in a storeroom on the bridge. The representative of the Russian consulate whom Victor had so emphatically sent to Hell was present while the containers were being loaded on board. The diplomat frowned and sweated, but he did not bother anyone else with questions or conversations. There were no further incidents, and soon the dapper gentleman disappeared just as quickly as he had appeared.

The leaks had been repaired, small problems were fixed by the crew, and the boat was refueled. A day later, some more cargo was taken on board, but there was still more than enough space in the holds. It seemed that no one, including the ship's owner, was particularly concerned about the lack of main cargo, as our holds were almost empty.

The departure was initially scheduled for eight in the morning. However, due to some delays with the port service, it was postponed to ten o'clock, and then again for another two days.

With a mournful howl, the steamer sounded its siren. The propellers slowly began to turn, churning up the water and stirring up the mud from the bottom. We cast off and slowly began to move away from the pier. With a creak and a groan, the steamer backed away from the pier, turning around in the harbor at a low speed to begin moving to the narrows, indicating the exit from the harbor. The view of the city was gorgeous. On the port side, the city buildings were visible, while to the starboard, the low, dark superstructures of Venezuelan Navy warships hung over the water. Then the bastions of an ancient Spanish fortress appeared, and after rounding it, the steamer set a course strictly north.

The day was clear, but twilight and then darkness fell quickly as soon as the sun sank behind the mountains surrounding the city, when we were already far out at sea. In the distance, a dark strip of mountains was still visible, but the first stars were already lighting up the sky. It seemed that the whole city, barely visible in the darkness, as if covered by a veil of lights, had decided to show itself in all its glory one last time, turning sideways to the steamer. But the sight of the Venezuelan handsome was indifferent to our boat.   During her long life at sea, she had seen many like him on all continents of all seven seas, and with the indifference of an old courtesan who had quickly forgotten her latest passion, she hurried businesslike toward her native element laying in the blue distance, while her old engine was humming old familiar tune, her steel heart was steadily beating known rhythm and propellers were churning up the dark water behind her stern, gradually pushing her away from the unwelcoming but beautiful city.

Leaving any port is always an event and a beautiful sight before the monotony of the boundless sea. We gradually moved away from the shore, and its lights faded behind us. Soon, the ship's course changed, and we headed east to pass between Grenada and the island of Tobago, leaving the warm, calm waters of the Caribbean Sea behind us.

In the morning, the calm and quiet sea was idyllic. We were about sixty miles from the coast of Venezuela, so we couldn't see the land until we passed Isla de Margarita. There were many yachts sailing around the island, and the place was truly heavenly. The tension and anxiety of the last few days melted away under the gentle sun, and a light, warm breeze carried all troubles far away beyond the horizon. The only thing that reminded us of the unpredictability of our mission was that the captain first sounded training fire drill when we took up our positions according to schedule, after which we were briefed on the schedule in case of a possible provocation or attack at sea, where and how we were to obtain weapons, and who was to occupy which post. Then, I already told you, I was assigned to the captain's cabin with a machine gun and with the second member as the machine gun assistant, while the captain took control of the ship and Victor was supposed to be on the forecastle, from where, in case of a boarding, he could keep the deck under fire if someone managed to land on it and tried to approach the bridge. The rest took up positions along the side of the ship and one at the stern. In an emergency, my assistant was to remain in the engine room. Until we approached Africa, the submachine guns remained where we had stored them upon receiving and were handed out as we approached the black continent. After that, everyone was required to keep their weapon with three magazines ready next to their bunk and were forbidden to appear on the deck with a weapon until an alarm sounded. The only one who took his automatic weapon and ammunition was the captain, and a machine gun with machine gun belts had to be kept on the bridge at all times. By the way, we never installed any tripods, so in case of an attack, I was not going to fire from the open part of the bridge in a standing position, exposing full silhouette, which was a bad idea. Instead, I would shoot lying on the floor, providing least target to the potential attackers.

At the same time, we conducted training and a brief "young soldier" course to demonstrate how to use personal weapons with precision shooting, which proved quite useful, as either the submachine gun sights were not adjusted, or we had all lost our long-forgotten skills of aimed shooting. We placed empty bottles on the deck and fired two magazines each, first single shots and then short bursts. Particular emphasis was placed on firing frequent single shots, unless the enemy was in close proximity. I, remembering my army days, during which, admittedly, I had never fired a machine gun, began to master the new technique. However, a PK is not a space shuttle, so I managed it. After firing, we cleaned and put away our weapons, and our "anti-piracy" training was successfully completed.

We began our journey towards Africa, where the closest coast we should be near is Liberia, under whose flag we were crossing the Atlantic.

The warm Caribbean Sea was left behind. The luxurious yachts and huge tourist liners disappeared as if they never existed before. However, the ocean was not empty. We were sailing along one of the main routes connecting the two continents and could see huge freighters in the distance, rushing to both Americas from Africa and Asia, as they circled the Cape of Good Hope. The vast ocean had long since ceased to be a watery desert and turned into quite a busy water highway.

We were sailing across high but smooth waves. The ship rose and fell calmly, as if rocking on a huge swing. The engine beat steadily like the heart of a healthy person, and I, like a good old and experienced doctor, felt and probed it while this huge mechanical heart was beating somewhere deep below the deck, sensing its healthy beat through the barely perceptible vibration of the hull.

It was the usual routine at sea. Everyone took care of their business without haste or fuss, doing the work assigned to them. The initial anxiety caused by our sudden arming and the demand to be ready to repel a boarding party had long since passed and left us nothing more than a chain of jokes. The ship moved slowly forward, farther and farther into the ocean.

"What do you think about all this machine gun nonsense?" My question was apparently expected.

We were sitting in the dining room with Victor, killing time with small talk.

"I don't know. The captain says he hasn't received any more information from Murmansk. Most likely, the pirates recently captured a ship, and that's why all the fuss has started, and this is our reaction to the latest events. That's what I think. It's just strange that they sent the consul to solve this problem when they could have easily dealt with the local authorities and our military instructors."

"It worried me too. Of course, it might be rough in the bay, but it's not like Somalia. However, I'm not against putting those bastards on the pitchforks. Let them come."

"Don't rush. You'll jinx it. We've got some strange cargo. Silica gel. To Nigeria… Sure... It looks like someone really needs this 'silica gel' or whatever this shit is. Well, we'll see."

The ocean remained calm, and the forecast did not promise any major changes. Soon we crossed the middle of the ocean at its narrowest point, between Brazil and Africa, and set east course for the shores of Liberia. There were no more leaks in the hold, and except for a slight oil leak in the oil radiator, we had no serious problems. Everything was going according to plan. As we approached the coast of Africa, the captain sounded another alarm, this time with weapons, to remind us that we were approaching the West Africa High Risk Area, which had recently expanded to almost the middle of the Gulf of Guinea. The most unpleasant thing about this was that the highest density of pirate attacks and hijackings occurred precisely off the coast of Nigeria, which we had to enter at the maritime border of Côte d'Ivoire and Ghana, where the risk of incidents was adjacent to the highest Level 2 area, covering the waters of Togo, Benin, and Nigeria, which we had to pass through, no matter how far we were from territorial waters.

However, there was a silver lining: we considered any approach to our boat hostile, naturally understanding that the size of pirate boats was hardly comparable to that of even a tramp ship. Our position was not entirely consistent with international laws, which Western countries followed to the letter, for which they subsequently paid dearly in the form of ransoms and even the lives of their citizens, which was not entirely in line with our interests. They could treat the situation as much as they like, and we will handle it our way. Therefore, having been given carte blanche for our defense, we decided to play by the same rules as the local rabble, adding only a small but piquant addition: "take no prisoners." And why should we? We didn't have yardarms to hang them up in, like in the good old days, so we should be more practical and businesslike.

By the way, I'll digress a little from the main subject. I began my maritime career after graduating from Astrakhan Technical University, formerly RybVTUZ (I have always preferred the old name). I worked for a short time on Shikotan, near Hokkaido Island, where I trawled for pollock and cod on Russian trawlers. I was then transferred to Murmansk, where I started sailing under the flags of Norway, Panama, and now Liberia. I have never had any desire to stay on Russian soil. Although I am a Russian citizen, I tried and still continue to "love my homeland from afar," staying as far away from it as possible, because its unpredictability has always made me uncomfortable. It made a negative influence on me, which I naturally tried to avoid with all my might. However, there is one thing that I have always respected and admired in Russia: common sense and determination in matters of security when it served its interests. It is a pity, of course, that Russian common sense was only evident in this aspect, though not as often as one would have liked. However, it did sometimes come to the fore.

Well, take our situation for example. In no other foreign company could I have imagined such a carte blanche as we got now, to "use all available means to protect the crew and the boat". In any other foreign company, the shipowner would have been ready to hand over the boat and the crew like a lamb to a slaughter to avoid bloodshed and, God forbid, injure any of the attackers, which, you must agree, is stupidity or insanity of the highest grade.

In our case, everything was different, simple, and clear. Everything depended on us, and if something had gone wrong, we would have had no one to blame but ourselves. Of course, it would have been nice to have that imposing gentleman from the Russian consulate on board to hand him an automatic weapon and give him the opportunity to participate in such a carnival. But unfortunately, we were deprived of that pleasure.

Another thing we didn't have, which would have been useful, was an anti-boarding net stretched several meters above the side of the board, consisting of a simple metal mesh fence. Climbing over such a net would be terribly inconvenient, and if one got such an audacious but equally stupid idea, he would have to expose his body in all its glory, so that shooting such a fool would not be more difficult than shooting a sitting duck. But there was no net, and the sides of our vessel were not as high as we would have liked them to be, as is the case with modern boats.

The twelve-mile territorial zone was no obstacle to pirates, and the High-Risk Area stretched from the western border of Ghana to São Tomé and Príncipe, if we could trust the maps we had received. We tried to stay seaward in international waters, keeping a course exactly along the four-degree north latitude, following the northern border of Equatorial Guinea, with no intention of inviting more escapades than necessary.

As we approached Africa, the captain announced to everyone that there would be no more training alarms and that the next alarm should be treated as a real attack on the ship. This was a good idea, as it allowed everyone to take the situation seriously and acknowledge the associated risks. All weapons and ammunition were already distributed among the crew to be held at hand right at the bank bed.

Our captain's thinking was undoubtedly correct. The likelihood of an attack, if there is one, was highest as we approached Nigerian territorial waters. Since it was our country's destination and the information and order to arm the ship came through diplomatic channels, there was a suspicion that we might be ambushed somewhere in that zone. I am sure that we would never have been given weapons with explicit permission to use them if the embassy had not had specific information. From my own experience, I had long been convinced that these guys did not do anything for no reason, so I tried to keep a distance from them.

We approached the continent near the maritime border between Liberia and Côte d'Ivoire. The calm ocean rolled high, with smooth waves far apart from each other, and at night, the sky was full of stars with the fading moon, still providing enough light.

In case of a night attack, the captain doubled the watch, which was not easy to do with our already small crew. Among other things, after leaving Porto Cabello, additional searchlights with halogen lamps were installed on the bridge and on the sides of the ship to blind the potential enemy. Blinded by such a dazzling light, it would be quite difficult for them to provide accurate fire, let alone to spot targets. Among other things, the glare of the searchlights would reduce the blinding effect of our machine gunner's fire.

So far, everything has been going smoothly. We had not yet reached dangerous waters, and according to the charts, the highest threat was expected when we crossed the Prime Meridian.

There were no more than two days left before reaching Calabar. By the evening, we should be 170 miles from São Tomé, that is, in the middle of the High-Risk Area. We came across a tanker sailing at full speed in a westerly direction, with several more ships visible on the horizon. Everything was peaceful, calm, sunny, and humid. We could only hope that the night would pass just as calmly. In the evening, we checked our weapons, and it was noticeable that tension among the crew was growing.

The guys, free of duties, were spending their free time smoking at the railings of the superstructure, looking out for suspicious boats on the surface of the ocean. However, everything was as usual. Several times, someone thought he saw the low profile of long boats gliding over the crests of the waves glistening in the sunset, but it was just a figment of his imagination. Most attention was focused on the port side, facing the African coast. Night fell, and the ocean was as calm and quiet as before. Stormy weather at that time would not have been out of place, but it was what it was. At supper, all conversations ended in one way or another with a discussion of a possible attack. In general, the anticipation of any kind of threat is usually much more unpleasant and sometimes even more frightening than the actual danger itself. Uncertainty and the unknown are the worst enemies, whether it be a fire, a major leak, or an attack on the boat. When something happens on a boat, the crew acts according to the established regulations, and the tension subsides as soon as one knows what to do. In the rush and bustle, everyone recognizes his role, which is usually clear, simple, and understandable. When you are waiting for something that you don't know for sure, your imagination begins to paint scary pictures, whether you want it to or not. That was the exact case with us.

Night enveloped the ocean. The deck was empty. All attention was focused on the radar, which showed nothing suspicious and seemed to have fallen asleep at the end of the voyage. The watchmen scanned the ocean, whose waters phosphoresced in the starlight. The moon was in the last quarter.

The engine was running at a lower than maximum power, humming steadily, and leaving a small reserve of power in case of an emergency. Victor went to bed earlier than usual, preparing for his watch in the second half of the night. After exchanging a few words with the captain, I also went to my cabin.

It wasn't wise to waste time dedicated to rest, so I tried to use it as effectively as possible. By tomorrow evening, if everything goes as planned so far, we should be in Calabar, and by morning, at the narrowest point between the southern coast of Nigeria and São Tomé.

I woke up several times during the night to check the clock. Time passed, and nothing happened. A strange thought that there would be no fun we expected for so long and that all my worries were in vain crept into my head and drove my sleep away. Finally, I fell asleep again, only to wake up again in the morning when dawn was already breaking. Thirty miles north of Santo Antonio, the ship set a course north-northeast toward the wide mouth of the Cross River, through which we were to enter Port of Calabar. Less than two hundred miles remained to the territorial waters of Nigeria, where we were to be met by the coast guard ship.

According to the High-Risk Area charts, we were right in the middle of the African villains' activity in the Gulf of Guinea. After washing up, I went to the engine room to check the machinery. Everything was fine. Leaving my assistant to check the oil leak that had been fixed earlier, I went up to the bridge.

It was already light. In the east, on the starboard side, a hot African sun was rising above the water. The sea was as calm as when we first entered the Gulf of Guinea. The captain was already on the bridge. I wished him a good morning and asked how things were.

"Normal. Nothing new."

I looked at the radar, which showed a fairly large number of objects. This was because the radar had been switched to long pulse to detect smaller targets, whereas in clear weather at sea, it operated at medium range, which was quite sufficient. As we approached the coast, the traffic became denser. Three miles ahead was a group of boats, most likely fishing vessels, and slightly to the right was a larger vessel moving on a cross-course. It was a small trawler capable of going deep into the sea. Otherwise, everything was as usual. However, after a few minutes, it became clear that the trawler would soon be in the near proximity to our boat unless it changed its bearing.

We continued to follow our original course, targeting at the mouth of the river, and were still fifteen miles from territorial waters when a command to stop at the request of the coast guard came over the loudspeaker of the trawler. The Nigerian flag was raised on the trawler, but it seemed that the Nigerian 'admiral' had slightly overstepped his rights.

"Captain, it looks like it's starting," I said quietly, lowering my binoculars.

"Looks like it. Get your 'howitzer' ready," he said, nodding toward the machine gun, "and when we get within 300 meters, fire a burst in his direction so he sees the splashes. I'm sounding the alarm."

A siren sounded, and within a minute, the entire crew was in their designated positions with their weapons at the ready.

My assistant hadn't yet climbed up to the bridge, so I lost a little time loading the cartridge belt into my PK. Opening the door to the bridge on the starboard side, I kicked back the bipods and placed the machine gun on the deck so that its barrel rose slightly above the railings. Lying down, I cocked the bolt, aimed almost without looking, and fired a burst. It was not easy to see the flashes of bullets, but they had to interpret our actions correctly.

"Here they are, bastards! Attack from the port side! Igor, machine gun to port! Fire at the boats! Don't let them get close!" yelled the captain.

Over the loudspeaker, he ordered everyone to stay on the starboard side and the crew on the bow, where Viktor already was, to repel the attack from the port side.

Only then did I notice two low, long boats with a group of people in them flying straight towards us from the port side. It was hard to say how many people were there, maybe five or six in each longboat. Their low profiles blended with the water, either because of their color or because they had lost some of their paint. They were equipped with powerful engines. The closest of the boats was moving towards the bow, where Victor and Marcos had already taken up positions behind the bow rail. I fired a long burst. I couldn't see splashes of my bullets, but that didn't slow the attackers down at all. The slight swell and ripples on the sea hid the splashes. Now bullets were hitting the bridge. It was very difficult to ensure accurate firing from the longboat jumping on the waves, so they probably expected to scare us by returning fire. The glass on the side of the wheelhouse shattered above me. A few more bullets clanged against the metal and ricocheted away with a nasty screech.

From the starboard side, I could already hear the automatic weapons of our glorious Filipinos firing back. Later, I learned that they were shooting from two positions: from the superstructure below us and from behind the wheelhouse.

"Igor, aim at the nearest boat! Long shots! Shoot long shots! Take out those bastards!" The captain put the engine to full speed, but it did not make too much difference considering the speed of the attacking longboats.

Something flew right past the bridge windows. It was a propelled grenade, but we didn't see it; only the powder trail was visible.

The captain turned the ship sharply to the right. He did this to bring the stern closer to the attackers so that the boat would be closer to the propellers spinning at full speed. Being close to working propellers is an unpleasant thing in itself, but being sucked under them is twice as bad. At that moment, the less agile trawler found itself directly abeam, heading straight for the middle of our ship, but she did not want to collide with us. It slowed down and began to turn parallel, but in the opposite direction to our movement, when she received a full volley of shots from two positions. How many hit the trawler's wheelhouse and whether anyone was hit, no one knows, but the wheelhouse windows were covered with a web of cracks. One window was partially shattered and fell out.

Their shooting was coming from behind the bulwark where the guy with a grenade launcher was standing on the platform above the wheelhouse. My assistant, Steve, handed me the second box of ammunition and, fumbling around, helped me to get the end of the cartridge belt. It slipped from my grasp just as a bullet hit the open door right above my head.

Steve was on his knees trying to attach the belt, but it didn't fit. The boats were already a hundred meters away when I slammed the barrel cover and cocked the bolt. The boat, which had been flying at full speed until then, slowed down to catch up with our boat's speed and board us. And that was their mistake.

I aimed, even though it took no more than a couple of seconds, and fired a burst. This time, it seemed the bullets had hit their target. One of the attackers, wearing a green bandana with a strand of black hair covering half of his face, bent over in half. Another fell over the board of the longboat. Confusion broke out in the boat, and I kept firing again and again into the pile of bodies.

A 7.62-millimeter rifle cartridge is a serious thing, not like an automatic transition cartridge of the same caliber as the AKM. At that distance, it will pierce any weirdo who happens to be in the way, regardless of his size, ambitions, or political views.

Some of them were naked to the waist, others were in white or colorful shirts. Only now did I notice that there were seven of them. I continued to fire directly into the center of the group. Two of them returned fire, but I didn't hear any bullets hitting the boat. "Oh, it's tough for you guys," a sudden and short as thunderstorm lightning thought flickered in my head. Meanwhile, the longboat increased its speed and started moving away from our boat, but was still close enough to our foredeck, where it fell under fire from Victor and John.

It was a rush; it was pure ecstasy! I had never experienced such an orgasm with any woman, and I had plenty to compare it to, from Luanda to St. John's and from Murmansk to Montevideo. I kept firing round after round, hoping to turn the whole human mass into a uniform mass of reddish mincemeat. It's hard to describe the feeling — it was a mixture of hatred and delight. With a feeling like that, people are not taking prisoners. It's a thrill of battle, a real astral of animal feelings. With that feeling, it's easy to kill and easy to die, and if you die, so be it; the main thing is to take with you as many others as possible!

Then the longboat started to move at full speed away from our boat until we lost sight of it. Whoever was inside that longboat didn't expect such a welcoming reception.

The enemy trawler changed its course, starting to trace a sharp arc at full speed in a counterclockwise direction, trying to get out of the firing zone deeper into the sea. But here, too, they were unlucky. As they moved away from our boat in a sharp arc, they came dangerously close to our stern and came under fire from the guy positioned under our wheelhouse, who was shooting at them over the gunwale. The boat began to turn more sharply to the left and, at full speed, headed parallel to our course in the opposite direction into the ocean. It seemed that they had not expected such greeting. However, I lost sight of the second boat. "I got carried away, I got carried away," the thought pierced my head.

"Where's the second boat, Steve!? Can you see it!?"

There was no sign of the boat anywhere. At that moment, there was an explosion below the deck. The second grenade from the trawler hit below the bridge, somewhere near the captain's cabin. With big bang it shook the structure and black smoke started rising slowly right in front of the bridge windows.

But I had to figure out where the second boat was. It seemed that it had entered the dead zone under the superstructure, that is, directly below us, where my machine gun couldn't reach them. I grabbed my automatic rifle sitting in the corner and rushed to the railing outside the wheelhouse, and leaned down to find the boat. At that moment, a burst of fire hit right next to my head, coming from under the side of our ship. I immediately jumped back and was not hit. All I noticed were two black figures climbing onto the deck via the ladders. There may have been more of them. I couldn't tell whether they were climbing one after the other or using two rope ladders. I stretched out my arms with my AKM gun and fired a long burst blindly downward. Steve had already joined me. He also fired down at the boat without aiming. Did we hit them? I don't know, but we couldn't let them climb aboard.

As I reloaded the magazine, I noticed that our guys were already firing from the front of our boat along its length toward the superstructure. That meant the pirates had already managed to climb onto the ship. Steve rushed to the door leading to the ladder leading to the main deck. I heard him open fire. They had already penetrated the superstructure. Damn it! I leaned out over the rail again. There were two men left in the boat, one was standing, holding onto the ladder to follow the others, and the other was also standing closer to the overboard engine, balancing in the rocking boat, holding an automatic rifle to cover the first one. I fired two bursts. The one standing nearby the engine managed to stay on his feet, but a burst of automatic fire hit the one, who was already climbing the rope ladder. He slipped down, falling between the longboat and the ship's side, and disappeared under the water. Whether he was caught in the propellers and fed to the fish was no longer important; at the very least, he was guaranteed to drown.

Victor and Steve were firing in the direction of the superstructure. We could hear automatic weapons firing back from somewhere below. It was useless to stay up in the wheelhouse and wait when the pirates paid us a visit there—I couldn't see what was happening below, let alone to shoot, no matter how much I leaned over the steel rail. I grabbed my submachine gun and ran to the door leading to the ladder through which Marcos had previously passed. Carefully descending, I was prepared to find either his body or one of the attackers.

However, the ladder was empty. Smoking from the fire that had started in the superstructure began to seep in and sting my eyes. Descending directly in front of the door to the deck, I noticed traces of blood. The door was wide open, but I heard no shooting. I cautiously peeked outside. A meter from the door lay an unusually thin bandit with a wild expression on his face, holding his bloody stomach with one hand and tapping the deck with the other in a ridiculous manner, as if trying to send some kind of signal to those below. He no longer posed a threat, and no matter how I wanted to finish that bastard, I didn't do it because

I didn't want to reveal my position. I looked out the door toward the stern. There was no one there either. I decided to go further to make sure the stern was empty, but before that, I looked back at the wounded native. He was trying to reach the machine gun lying next to him with his left hand.

With one leap, and he was only a few meters away from me, I was next to him and pinned his arm to the deck with all my strength using the AKM butt. He screamed so loud that it drowned out the sound of the shooting still ringing in my ears. I could understand him; he must have been in pain. Note that the back of the wooden butt of the AKM is encased in a steel plate that had effectively turned the pirate's palm and fingers into a pancake of flattened bones. I kicked his AKM with my foot and moved to the stern.

I needed to locate the other intruders already on board, which wasn't hard. Quietly, I moved along the superstructure's wall further toward the stern. Around the corner, I spotted Marcos holding his automatic rifle aimed at another native, who resembled the first. The native faced the bulwark with his hands raised; his left arm was bleeding above the elbow.

The machine gun lay around in front of him. He muttered something, clearly trying to explain that he was surrendering. Meanwhile, our sailor Leo appeared from the starboard side where they had repelled the trawler's attack. Pointing his automatic rifle forward, he slowly moved toward our uninvited guest, who looked at him with wide, terrified eyes, mumbling something in his own language. Little Leo approached him closely and, stopping without paying attention to us, fired a short burst directly into the native's stomach. The latter's face twisted in surprise, and without closing his eyes, he began to slide down, still leaning his back against the bulkhead. A large red spot covered half of his white shirt, though he was still alive, sitting against the side and shaking his head from side to side.

"Well done, Leo," I said.

Leo turned his head toward me, smiling broadly showing his pearl-white teeth. Suddenly, bullets fired from the moving-away trawler struck the side of our boat and the superstructure above. Although the trawler was quite distant, making precise hits unlikely, the sharp sounds of bullets ricocheting off the metal and the screeching noise prompted us to duck behind the bulwark.

"Guys let's check deck by deck down to the engine room. We need to make sure there are no bastards here."

"Chief, that was the last one. There were three of them on board, one fell overboard. What should we do with this one?" Marcos nodded in the direction of the wounded pirate.

"What should we do? What do you mean, 'what should we do'?", I repeated quizzically.

Logically, according to all maritime traditions, we should have hung him up, if not on a yardarm, which we didn't have, then at least on the rail. But we didn't have a rope at hand, nor did we have time, but we had plenty of excitement instead. We couldn't go looking for a rope... What a pity… "What should we do?" I repeated again. "Let him feed a fish. Throw him overboard!"

Marcos and Leo lifted the native, who was no longer shaking his head, and who, with his head pressed against the bulwark of the boat, was lying on his back, still staring at the world with wide, astonished eyes, as if he were seeing it for the first time, and threw him overboard.

Falling into the wake of the propellers working at full speed, his body instantly disappeared under the foam-covered water. We followed back to where the last villain remaining on the ship was lying with his broken palm. He looked at us with a look full of malice, and when Leo and Steve started to pull him up, he continued to scream and try to fight them off with his uninjured right hand. He apparently guessed the sad fate that was awaiting him and, like a wild beast, bared his teeth at us.

But who was to blame that he had grown up so bad and ill-mannered, rather than kind and good? Leo grabbed him under the armpits, trying to pull him over the high rail, but because of his short stature, he couldn't do it. The man writhed and screamed, fighting back with his good arm. Then Marcos lifted him by his legs, which were clad in some kind of canvas sneakers, and tried to throw him over the fence while Leo pushed him from behind. The aboriginal struggled, and one of his legs broke free from Marcos's grip and kicked him in the face. The soft sneaker softened the blow, but did not soften Marcos's anger, who dropped the gangster's second leg, when his body fell onto the deck with his legs spread out.

Without thinking twice, Marcos kicked him in the groin with all his might. The scream stopped and turned into a wild howl. The second attempt to throw his legs over the rail was more successful when his body swung over the wired fence. "These guys know their business very well," flashed through my mind, "as if they've done this before."

The wounded man continued to howl wildly, but it was too late. Even the most notorious pirate cannot defy the laws of physics, and he certainly hadn't studied physics, skipped classes at school and didn't listen to his teachers. But he should have. Then he would have known that there was no way he could get back on the deck.

His body lost its balance and started to fall to meet his sad end. He fell flat, his body was covered by a wave, and then appeared on the surface for a few seconds for the last time before disappearing forever under the water.

Near the spot where he fell, a boat tied to the ship's hull was still dragging along, and inside it, curled up and still alive, lay the man I had shot from above before he tried to climb onto the deck.

"Leo, finish him off," I said. "Just in case."

Taking aim, Leo fired a short burst, then another.

"I think that's enough, Chief."

"I think so too. Now shoot the engine."

Leo had to reload the magazine and emptied half of the next one into the heavy outboard motor to disable it.

Meanwhile, Marcos attempted to detach the anchor hook caught on the leash, which was dragging the boat. He couldn't manage it because the boat was too heavy. There was no tool to cut the yellow nylon rope, so he used his automatic rifle to fire several shots at it, aiming to cut the fibers. Once freed, the boat rapidly drifted away, helplessly bobbing on the waves and gradually shrinking in size.

"Now follow me, let's check the superstructure!" I repeated. We moved from deck to deck until we reached the engine room. There was no one else on the ship. Under the bridge, two of our comrades were fighting the fire with fire extinguishers. However, there was much more smoke than fire, and the damage, except for the captain's cabin, was minor. Only then did we notice that the antenna had been knocked down and the radar was out of order. One of the grenade launcher shots from the trawler, aimed at the wheelhouse, went significantly higher and hit the mast, damaging all the radio equipment there.

The captain was on the bridge. Surprisingly, although none of us was wounded, the captain's face was covered with blood from glass shards. In fact, he was our only casualty. I reported on the situation, not omitting the sad fate of the villains found on the deck and the clearing of the premises.

By this point, the entire crew, except for the two guys busy with the fire, had gathered on the bridge. "Good. Taking these bastards prisoner would be inconvenient. Are there any wounded?" He occasionally wiped blood from his face. No, he was the only one. "Good job, guys." He handed the wheel to the helmsman who had just joined us.

"Set course for Calabar, thirty-two degrees. The radar isn't working, and we can't send a Mayday call. Leo, stay on the bridge. Your job is to watch the starboard side in case of another attack. Marcos, do the same on the port side. Guys, reload your weapons and keep them ready. I doubt there will be another attack, but it's better to be safe than sorry. I don't see Victor. Where is he?"

Yes, Victor was not with us. Steve and I went down to make sure that he wasn't with our firefighters under the bridge. The fire had been extinguished, but the acrid smoke of the burnt wiring and plastic still hung heavily in the air. He was not there, and his cabin was empty too. It was strange. John, who was with him on the foredeck after they fired at the pirates boarding the stern, saw Victor running from the foredeck toward the stern and assumed that he might be somewhere there, while he himself moved to the starboard side to help to fend off the attacking trawler. After that, no one saw Victor.

However, he was not at the stern either. We moved down to the main deck, where spent shell casings were scattered and rolling near the hatch door. Leo was guarding the area there. As we walked along the starboard side, we headed toward the bow superstructure. It wasn't far. Victor was lying behind the second cargo hatch.

The hatch hid him; that is why we could not see him from the bridge or the bow superstructure. He was dead. In place of his right eye was a gaping hole from which blood flooded the entire right side of his face. The bullet had hit him directly in the eye, passed through his head, and exited the back of his skull leaving a large gory wound. Blood flooded his automatic rifle, which was pressed tightly against his body as if he did not want to let it go. A pool of blood mixed with brains spread around his head and had only just begun to coagulate. Death was instantaneous.

This was our only loss and sacrifice. Steve, who was standing nearby, crossed himself and muttered a few words from a prayer he remembered. Then some other members of the crew joined us.

We took him into an empty, air-conditioned room in the aft superstructure and laid him on a table, covering his body with a sheet.

The entire crew, free from their duties, gathered around. Everyone was silent. No one wanted to speak, there was nothing to say...

There were no more attacks. Maybe the attack was just a coincidence, or the attackers reported what happened and chose not to take any more chances. Who knows?

The whole attack actually took only a few minutes. But it seemed like several hours had passed.

A few hours later, we entered Nigerian territorial waters. As expected and contrary to what had been promised, there was no coast guard vessel to meet and escort us further to the port. However, there was no longer any particular need for this. Soon, the wide channel of the Cross River opened up, and we reached Oron, where we took a pilot on board. He was not particularly bothered by the sight of our smoke-filled wheelhouse after the attack; apparently, he had seen worse. He was much more concerned about the lack of communication on board, which was understandable.

Traffic on the Cross river and higher by the Calabar River was quite heavy, so we had to lose half a day anchored on the raid until we were provided with temporary radio communication before we could move on. The mouth soon began to narrow, although the width of the river was impressive even after entering the Calabar River itself. The murky, calm waters of the river and the banks covered with jungle under the scorching southern sun contrasted with our untidy appearance.

Tankers of all sizes and calibers were encountered on the route to the port, some waiting in the roadstead for their turn, while others, sitting low with full tanks, slowly moved down the river.

The captain called the port service, which in turn contacted the police department and the Nigerian Navy Reference Hospital to arrange receiving Victor's body. An ambulance was already waiting for us when we moored in the Old Harbor. Negotiations with the Russian consulate in Lagos were much more difficult as well as much less productive.

The consulate knew about our arrival but was more focused on the condition of the cargo than the attack and the death of the Russian citizen. Its reaction was completely predictable. Having spent my entire life on the Atlantic and seen ports in countries and states you can't even find on a map, with names I can't keep track of, I can say one thing: aside from the problems for us, the sailors, we could expect nothing else from the Russian diplomats. It was ridiculous and naïve to even expect any help from them.

After promising they would send a representative to Calabar and arrange for the body to be sent to Russia, without specifying a date or time, the conversation on this topic was quickly cut off by an overly enthusiastic consulate employee.

After mooring, unloading began almost right away. We never found out what was in those containers. The only thing that surprised us was that a detachment of Nigerian military police was present during unloading. However, the cargo was cleared up without any problems, quickly and, as it turned out, as a matter of priority, after which all interest in our ship was lost.

A little later, permanent communication was restored, and we did our best to clean up the damaged and burned rooms.

A couple of days later, the captain and I visited the hospital to ensure that Victor's body had been cared for and properly preserved for subsequent transportation to Russia.

I did not know if he had any relatives, let alone any addresses. That was a business of our company's personnel department, which, for some reason, kept a mysterious silence. The hospital, by the way, made a good impression, as did its staff.

The body was in the hospital morgue. A police detective was waiting for us there to clarify some details about the attack. However, upon arrival at the port, after the captain reported the attack, a police escort and a representative from the insurance company had already boarded the ship to take statements and assess the damage.

We didn't have to wait for long. After entering the room with refrigerators where the bodies were kept, we were shown Victor's body one last time. Strangely, he did not look like the man we knew in life, even though his body had been washed and changed. His face was badly disfigured, with a large black hole where his eye had been, filled with dried blood. His face, which had sunk in, was the same color as the gray sheet covering it.

"I'm sorry, my friend," said the captain, touching his hand. "Rest in peace, old vagabond..."

He turned and walked away. I stood next to him for a moment, then turned and followed the captain.

After giving my statement to the detective, I was surprised by what he said. "Guys, if everyone acted like you did, this mess would have ended long ago. Starting with sea, then we could clean up the country of this scum." Then he paused and, as if apologizing for his naivety, added: "It's just a pity that it will never happen."

"Detective, where's the nearest bar? My friend and I need a drink or two to commemorate our comrade. Care to join us?", the captain took initiative.

I expected that, like in all detective movies and books, the policeman would say he was on duty and so on, but in real life things flow a little differently - he nodded and momentarily agreed. We would surely find a better place in the port to unwind, but our good detective took us to some backwater hotel with a small bar-restaurant, flooded with sunlight and cheerful staff completely unsuited to our mood.

The day was drawing to a close. The concept of impaired driving, the matter of pride of all civilize world, had not yet reached that corner of the Gulf of Guinea, and after we had paid tribute to Victor's memory, the representative of the law kindly offered to give us a ride to the port, where the captain and I decided to continue in a more appropriate atmosphere in the port tavern. We spoke a little, mostly kept silent, and drank more than usual.

We boarded the ship closer to midnight, and a few days later, after taking on board cages with oil equipment bound for repair in Norway, we headed north to Stavanger.

Upon our return to Murmansk, I was informed that, due to a lack of information about his relatives, the company had decided not to bring Victor's body back to Russia and had buried him in a Christian cemetery in Kalabar. I'm not sure that what they said about the lack of relatives was true; most likely, they didn't want any unnecessary expenses or problems. And who really cared about him or us in our Motherland? We sailed under a dubious flag; the crew was a group of wanderers from all over the world. They paid us what had been promised, and we were supposed to be happy. The other problems are supposed to be ours and nobody else's.

The Motherland only owes you what is outlined in the contract, and even that, within reasonable limits. It's fair, and everyone is responsible for themselves. Perhaps that's the way it should be… Did you know him for a long time?" Igor asked me.

"Since childhood. We attended the same school."

"Yeah, I see," he said, "and have you seen each other recently?"

"I don't remember the last time I saw him... It's been a long time ago... He went to sea, then I left Russia. So, we pretty much lost touch. We exchanged emails for a while, but then that stopped, too. Time takes its toll, you know..."

We sat in silence for a while. It was getting late, and it was time to go. My plane was departing early the next morning, and I didn't want to wake up with a hangover. But Igor insisted on staying a while.

"Let's head to the bar to drink to his memory. He was a good guy. If only he knew he'd end up in some godforsaken place like Calabar," Igor sighed sadly. "Where is that bloody Calabar? Who's even heard of it? That's how it is..."

"When are you sailing out?" I asked.

"The day after tomorrow. Tomorrow we'll start getting ready. Back to Africa. Not too far away this time, to Dakar. And then, who knows where."

The last shot of screech.

" Thanks for coming. I wanted to share this with someone who knew him. With you..."

We shook hands. Then we exchanged a few empty phrases, promising to keep in touch and maybe to meet up the next time he is in Canada. We both knew it would never happen, but etiquette demanded that we go through the motions.

We left the restaurant and walked to the closest intersection. The cold wind was strong and gusty, and the weather was turning bad. I called a cab. We only had to wait for a few minutes.

"Are you going to the port? I will give you a ride," I offered.

"Thanks. I wouldn't mind. The weather's awful," he nodded toward the port.

We got to the port quickly. Several ships were moored along the pier, and a few more were a little further out in the bay.

"All right, Oleg. Thanks again for coming. All the best to you, and see you", Igor said.

We shook hands. I got back to the car, and we drove off. I glanced back. Igor, pulling his hood up and bending slightly against the gusts of wind, was walking quickly toward his freighter.

The car sped up, and after a few seconds, I could barely see his figure through the foggy rear window".

The potatoes had long since run out, and we sat by the fireplace finishing our second bottle of port. Alexander didn't interrupt me, listening with interest. The logs were burning and cracking in the fireplace.

"Yes, it's interesting how everything turned out. They turned out to be not too far from each other, Victor in Nigeria, Yuriy in Central Africa... Want some more?" he stretched his hand to the bottle.

"No, buddy. That's enough for today. Port wine, for sure, sobers me up, but it is giving me a headache no worse than vodka. We've already brought the battle with alcohol to a new level by cleaning out your supplies."

"Don't worry. I've got enough supplies to last a long siege. Maybe I should tell you another story about Andrey. Remember him?"

"What, Andrey? Arbenin?"

"Of course. Who else is? But not today. Today we've already inflicted a blow to the world alcoholism and in return received a blow to our livers. Maybe tomorrow. Yes. Let's do it tomorrow. You're not flying back to sunny Canada yet, are you?"

Then we broke up. But we didn't manage to meet up the next day, or the day after. Work, my schedule, and Alexander's schedule refused to cooperate, so we kept pushing off our meeting until, finally, the day of departure approached. It was our last night in the glorious city located on a fast and muddy Missouri River. But on that last evening, our schedules had coincided.

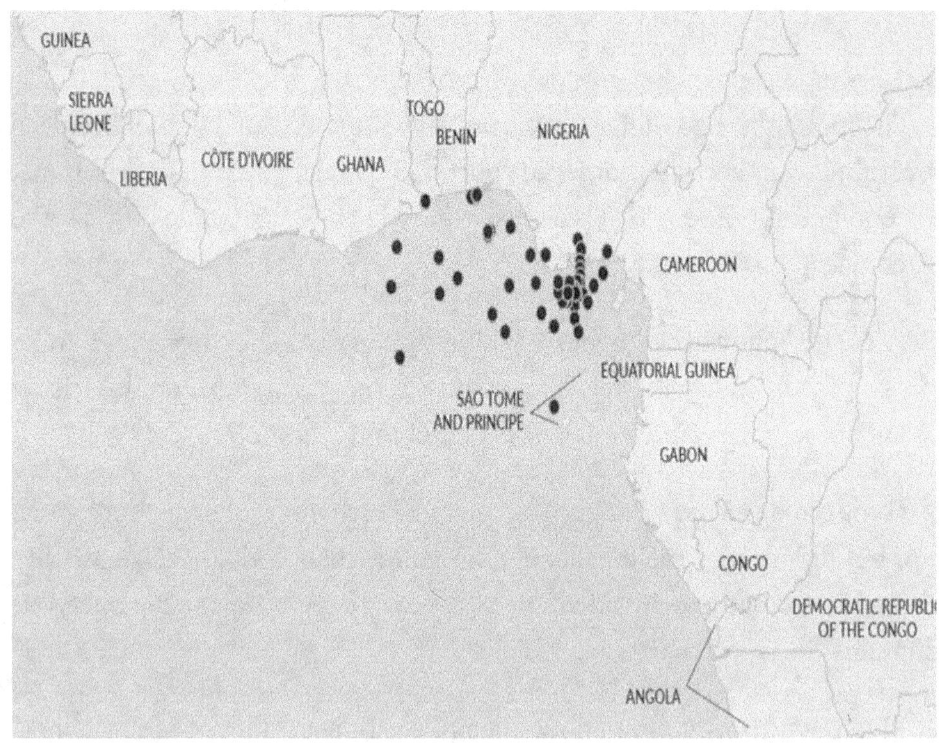

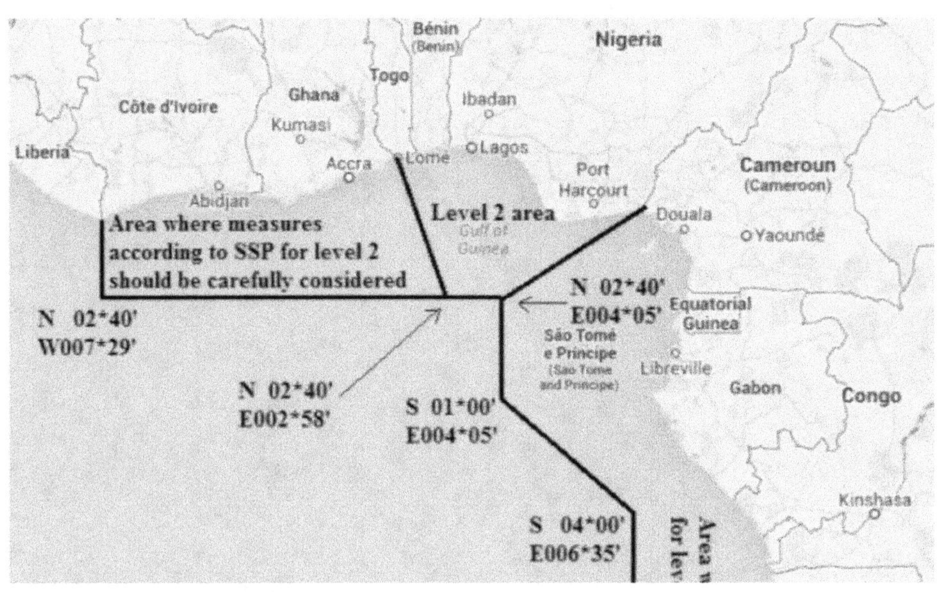

Bénin
(Benin)
Nigeria
Togo
Ghana
Côte d'Ivoire
Kumasi
Ibadan
Liberia
Accra
Lome
Lagos
Port
Harcourt
Cameroun
(Cameroon)
Abidjan
Douala
Yaoundé
Level 2 area
Gulf of
Guinea
Area where measures
according to SSP for level 2
should be carefully considered
N 02*40'
E004*05'
Equatorial
Guinea
N 02*40'
W007*29'
São Tomé
e Principe
(Sao Tome
and Principe)
Libreville
Gabon
Congo
N 02*40'
E002*58'
S 01*00'
E004*05'
Kinshasa
S 04*00'
E006*35'
Area
for lev

Chapter 3

Debt Repayment

Gordon Lonsdale

We remembered Andrey from our school time. He was a good student, but, unlike us, he wasn't romanticized by the sea and blue abyss; however, he did have another equally dangerous affliction — a desire to join the army. As far as we knew, he saw himself as nothing other than an officer, and after eighth grade, he tried to enroll in the Suvorov Military School. It didn't work out… His eyesight wasn't great, and he was rejected at the preliminary medical examination at the regional military commissariat. However, his enthusiasm did not wane, and he began to prepare for admission to the artillery school.

That time went better than before: we enrolled in our technical university, which was located a block away, and he entered his military school.

"Yes, we had a great time when he came home on vacation. What am I telling you? Remember?" Alexander began his story.

"Of course I do. I even remember how we got drunk and went to the theater to see Irka, who was performing there after graduating from theater college. I remember you fell asleep in the parterre."

"We drank a lot of beer back then. We drank in a café opposite the Sea Garden. By the way, what's on the menu today?"

Alexander thought for a moment. "Let me check."

"What do you have to drink?"

"Brother, I have everything that the soul of the most hopeless drunkard or intellectual alcoholic could desire."

"Well, if that's the case, let's have some wine. Today's theme will be military, as I understand it, which means no sweet wines. No Muscat, Vidal or port, and certainly no Rhine Rieslings would be appropriate for discussing such a serious subject."

"Really? Do you think so? Then what would be appropriate?" Alexander was somewhat confused.

"For an occasion like this, only pure alcohol would be appropriate, or at the very least, vodka. But we're not going to reconstruct a life in the Russian Army in such detail, are we? So, let's stick with what we started with – claret. You must have some claret, right?" I asked.

"Like any decent and high morale person, Andrey, I have enough claret to satisfy not only a writer of the Romanticism epoch, but also any French impressionist."

"Hm, well then, for the glory of God, get it out and pour full glasses!"

From the basement, so as not to go down again, he brought three bottles of claret, although they were different, apparently so that the story would not be tedious and dull, like a row of identical wine bottles, but bright, interesting, and instructive.

"As you probably remember, after artillery school, he was sent to serve somewhere in the north, and then to Chechnya, where he spent the entire second Chechen campaign. He volunteered to go there, by the way."

"Wait," I interrupted him, "how do you even know about him?"

"What do you mean, how do I know his story? He told me himself. We had a great time together in Vegas once."

"In Vegas?" I asked in surprise. "How did he end up in that den of sin and debauchery?"

"Ah, my friend, then you don't know anything about him," Alexander said. "He's been here in the States for a long time. He lives a quiet life in Hartford, Connecticut, working for Trane, some kind of HVAC manager. He forgot about his guns and howitzers long ago, but he hasn't lost his good habits. He's always ready for a drink, anywhere, anytime, without asking questions."

"What?!" I didn't expect that. "Why didn't you tell me right away?"

"How was I supposed to know? You didn't ask, so I didn't tell you."

"How did he get to the States?"

"That's what I intended to tell you. I won't discuss his service—I don't want to bore you. If you hadn't interrupted me, disrupted my train of thoughts, and had just sat quietly drinking your claret without asking questions, I would have shared the entire story with you, plainly, fairly and without exaggeration".

"Well, I'm sorry, I'm sorry, but it's all your claret's fault. If it had been a port, everything would have been clear and understandable, instructive and enlightening."

"Anyway, everything I'm about to tell you, I learned from him. He told me himself. He was very nervous at that time, very excited and eloquent, and we drank even more, so if I've missed anything or got something wrong, you understand - time and vodka are a dangerous combination, promising nothing but trouble, so I'll tell you what I remember. His story went something like this:

"After graduating from the artillery academy, I was sent to serve in Kaliningrad. By that time, the 11th Army, which had been based there before being disbanded and its units were transferred to the Baltic Fleet, had effectively made me a Navy officer. I won't bore you with all the details of my service; I'll just say that serving in the area separated from Russia by Lithuania, Belarus, and the sea turned out to be much easier than all my previous positions. Kaliningrad is, of course, a relatively small city, nothing special. There was practically nothing left of German architecture and Prussian glory, and what remained had been remodeled and disfigured beyond recognition. The only pleasant things were the proximity to the West and European civilization, besides the region's unusually beautiful nature. Overall, it was not bad to serve there.

Fleet command also assigned me an apartment. It was a separate, one-room apartment, but so shabby that it would rather fit a client of the Salvation Army. It was located in one of the houses built haphazardly during the Khrushchev era; the people who lived there, with the exception of a few officers' families, were ideally matched to that environment. At that time, there were hardly any jobs available in the poor region, and everyone I knew, if they worked at all, worked in trade.

However, in general, life in the region was not so bad. Military service in peacetime, in the region separated from the Russian mainland, was nothing compared to the combat life in Chechnya. Meaningless inspections and checks, reports, and memos followed one after another without leading to any changes, let alone improvements. Everyone understood this, diligently continuing to play the same game, trying to gain self-importance and impress the others with self-significance and useless work.

In the artillery chief's department, relations with the officers were not bad, as they were with the other officers from the combat support departments. But the relations with my immediate superior, who was grooming his protégé for the position I had been assigned to after graduating from the academy, were not very good. However, my immediate boss had no choice but to bite his tongue and wait for the right moment to somehow correct what he considered to be an error.

By that time, I had traveled all over the region, getting to know the units that had once threatened all of Eastern European neighbors from that most militarized region of Europe. However, at that time, the region could hardly be considered a threat to anyone. The state of the troops left much to be desired, and the materiel base was so dilapidated and impoverished that the former glory had faded to the point of being barely discernible. The ships based in Baltiysk, the main base of the Baltic Fleet, were in the same condition. With peeling paint, shamelessly revealing old rust, they stood at the piers preparing for another Navy parade or to test their engines.

It was funny that the officers who were retiring or quitting the service had no desire to leave the region and return to mainland Russia. The proximity to Europe, which was just a stone's throw away, had an effect even on the most die-hard patriots, who dreamed of the opportunity to travel to Poland or Germany after their retirement. Some succeeded, and some lucky ones managed to get jobs in the mayor's office or in the regional government organizations, where the salary and conditions were incomparably better, and the responsibilities were significantly less.

By that time, the Baltic Fleet headquarters had wisely chosen not to burden itself with combat training and all the associated military hustle and bustle, limiting its activities to preparing ships for the next ordinary celebration with proper fanfare and cameras from regional and federal TV channels. Meanwhile, it focused on paperwork and loud statements about strengthening, expanding, and increasing whatever could be expanded and increased, while sitting in the warm offices of the historic fleet headquarters building, which had once housed the Postal Service during the Reich era.

The bloated, lazy, and useless admirals, raised on political indoctrination and party directives, no doubt still remembering the speeches of Andropov and Chernenko from their cadet days, slogans and calls of party bureaucrats and ideologues, very clearly defined their own circle of unburdened tasks in blessed idleness and leisure, serving out their last years before retirement while building cottages on the beautiful Baltic dunes of Yantarny, Svetlogorsk, or Zelenogradsk.

Since my time at military school, I have disliked political classes as well as fat admirals, and even more those responsible for the catastrophe in this region, who were none other than Marshal Vasilevsky and Marshal Baghramyan. They successfully turned the beautiful city of Königsberg into an ugly, ordinary provincial settlement where I now had to live and serve.

I was not too concerned about my career prospects, because of my personal plans, the implementation of which was already looming on the horizon, that pushed all other plans into the background or simply made them meaningless.

The geographical proximity of the West influenced most of my comrades, but hardly anybody, with tiny exception, was moved to consider emigration or even a temporary departure abroad. Thus, a certain circle of my good acquaintances formed, who were also entertaining such thoughts. The assistant to the head of the armored service, a major, Andrei, a simple and kind guy, who had acquaintances in Germany, had not yet come to the decision to leave permanently, but was already in the throes of agonizing doubts, torn between his overwhelming desire to leave everything behind and his wife's unwillingness to risk of changing their established life. One way or another, his doubts had to be resolved somehow, but before his decision was put off, his wife, in order to support her arguments, gathered around her a circle of indignant patriotic wives of his colleague officers with whom she shared her husband's plans.

Another man was a captain and deputy commander of a repair and restoration battalion, who already had relatives in the Czech Republic, a foreign passport, and no doubts and hesitations to change his profession, region and country. He was the first to be detained, and soon he found himself next door to the Baltic Fleet headquarters, though in less comfortable surroundings. If the Fleet headquarters building had once been the Main Post Office of East Prussia and was later rebuilt and adapted for military use by the Soviet and later Russian state, the neighboring building had neither been destroyed nor modified and still matched its original purpose, serving as a prison since the time of the Imperial Germany and continuing to do so today.

I did not know what had triggered the captain's arrest, but the questions I was soon asked about his case at the military prosecutor's office concerned not only his desire to emigrate, but also his alleged systematic attempts to gather military information through his contacts at the Fleet headquarters. Whether it was true or not, I could not say, having big doubts about so heavy accusations.

The prosecutors pulled up the entire chain of his confidants, friends, acquaintances and whoever could fit a picture, and the captain, as expected, dragged everyone down with him. Then it was our turn, namely the tank major and me.

The mayor's outspoken wife cheerfully assisted her husband in entering the prosecutor's office by her patriotic reprimands shared with the wives of other officers. Our discussions about emigration quickly became public knowledge beyond what was intended, and while the tank officer was not detained, he was swiftly reassigned to a position far from Germany but very close to the Chinese border, greatly minimizing any chance of his departure to Western countries.

Then my 'criminal' talks about immigration were exposed as quickly as the unreliable winter ice on the Pregol River, and I followed his thorn path in the same eastern direction. The garrison prosecutor's office started investigating my relatives in Western Europe. Surprisingly, they were looking for them in wrong direction, while they should be looking in the US, although I was smart enough not to tell anyone about that. It's hard to say why Europe attracted their attention; they were probably shooting in the dark, hoping that something suspicious would be revealed by my interrogation. The FSB has its own reasons and methods of gathering information, and rumors in their games play a significant role. Eventually they will find out about my American relative but a little later, although perhaps too late for their taste.

So, I faced the same prospects as the tank officer before me. A delay with my transfer was caused by the FSB, which tried to pressure my wife into testifying against me, and when that didn't work, they threatened her with problems with her parents in Saratov. However, I did have a stroke of luck in this unpleasant affair: when my armored vehicle comrade's foreign passport was found during a search at his apartment, mine was not. To be honest, it would not be easy to find it, as it was kept at my parents' home in Astrakhan, and the FSB did not go that far.

Incidentally, I had obtained the passport shortly before these events, having had it issued by the Astrakhan OVIR (passport office) using false documents presented in my name as a civilian and supplemented with a persuasive number of US dollars. That charming mischief was not uncovered, though I woke up in a cold sweat many nights after the search in our apartment, expecting the omnipresent FSB would uncover this unsavory fact of my biography. However, this did not happen, and soon after, I was transferred to Borzya in cold and inhospitable Transbaikal region.

Having exchanged the frivolous European Kaliningrad region for the backwoods of the vast country, I lost all doubts, if I had any, about leaving Russia, and was solely consumed by worries of the oncoming results of our application to the American consulate for family reunification. The thing was that my wife's American uncle had agreed to sponsor our move to New York, where I could transform my knowledge of an artilleryman into more peaceful administrative or technical skills in his company, which consisted of several tire fitting shops. It was a gift from heaven, and very soon we received an invitation to an interview at the consulate, after which, a few months later, we were issued coveted emigration visas.

It is not difficult to imagine how things would have ended for me if information about my American uncle and my newly acquired passport had fallen into the hands of the FSB. However, as I said before, I had enough brains to keep this information to myself.

I knew that the FSB was skilled at loosening tongues. This knowledge was not unique; many people knew about it, and the authorities themselves had enjoyed the pleasure of reminding the Russian citizens about their talent, boasting of their abilities left and right since the days of Felix Dzerzhinsky. The unsophisticated officers of the special department in distant Transbaikalia would have been horrified to learn that I had such an overseas relative. But they were blessed by their own ignorance and spared from that knowledge. When they found out about my wife's uncle, it was only after we had already had the pleasure of sharing our memories in my wife's uncle's favorite Italian restaurant on West Merrick Road in the Big Apple.

Meanwhile, everything was going well in my new place of service, when my wife and I had already begun discussing the details of our departure and the submission of my report for dismissal from the armed forces, when my humble person had attracted the unwelcome attention of an officer of the regiment's special department. Soon FSB in Chita joined his efforts. For the regional FSB office, the 370 kilometers between Chita and Borzya were not an obstacle to start pulling me in for questioning on the same subject, related to the unfortunate artillery captain in Kaliningrad, who was at that time already awaiting trial in the detention center. It was obvious that FSB was trying to link these two cases, but it was not clear whether they were doing so on their own initiative, or it had been initiated and driven from Kaliningrad. The subsequent invitations soon led me to believe that their next step would be to place me under house arrest, and I decided to preempt the circumstances, even though there was some risk involved.

The Transbaikal hills are the subject of local epics. A barren, windswept land where it is bitterly cold in winter and hot in summer, where nothing grows and there is nothing to catch the eye, a desolate place, although it does have a certain charm. It is difficult to live there, but easy to die without losing anything and with nothing to regret about. November in Borzya is not the best month. In the middle of the month, the temperature is already consistently below zero, and the constantly blown winds freeze all desires and drives for great achievements, significantly increasing the treasury's profits for vodka sales.

However, the vodka remedy for Transbaikalia is not limited to November, where and when a life without vodka is impossible, but also to all other months. In general, November is not the best month for long journeys or fun vacations, as it is not the friendliest month in Russia as a whole. That's why only hopeless losers ask for a vacation in November, which is what I decided to do, because nothing else could make a fool happier than showing him that you are more stupid than he is. Flatter him, encourage his self-esteem, and you will not find a better supporter in any of your endeavors. This lemma has been known since ancient times, and that is why I thought that it would be too rude to deny them this pleasure.

I am not a hero and have never claimed to be one, leaving this noble role to other brave, fearless, or equally foolish people. My only desire was to leave my beloved homeland as quickly as possible, regardless of the cost. There was also a bit of generosity on my part, as I willingly stepped aside from the heroic role of a revolutionary for those interested in it. Meanwhile, I had to act quickly before it was too late.

At that time, I had not yet received the expected subpoena for another interrogation as a witness in captain's case, so I had to take my vacation and leave as soon as I could, without waiting for further gifts from my ungrateful fate.

My wife and I decided to leave right after my vacation request was approved; hers and mine were approved in no time without asking any questions, although there were traces of puzzlement on the faces of those who signed it. Without saying a word to anybody, giving any hints and leaving all our belongings behind, I bought a train ticket to Astrakhan, but on route, we decided to make a small detour and get off the train a little bit earlier to avoid possible, but unwelcome attention of FSB, so that instead of Astrakhan we could visit my wife's relatives in Saratov for just one day, and from there to make our way to America. It was done with a single purpose, not to be tracked or captured for further inquiries in Astrakhan.

Get to America! It's not as easy as it sounds, especially when you're expecting another visit from the FSB investigator. So, I didn't tell my parents about the upcoming vacation, as there was no need to, since I already had my passport and American visa in my hands at that point, and I didn't want to involve them in the details of our adventure.

I wanted, desperately wanted, to see them and my Astrakhan one last time, knowing that I would never come back, to say a final "Goodbye." But the old city was tired. Four centuries had worn down the provincial city, and it had ceased to be surprised by anything, looking down at the flow of recent events from the height of its centuries with deep indifference. Its old merchant buildings had fallen into disrepair, and the new ones, with their tastelessness and provincial kitsch, spoiled what was left of the once beautiful city on the Volga River. It was no longer interested in anything. The city was gradually returning to its roots, slowly covering itself with a Muslim veil - the Jews had already left it for their historical homeland, and now it was apparently the turn of the

Russians, many of whom had already left it in search of the greener pastures in Moscow and St. Petersburg and settled there, while I had to make a bigger step, jumping across the ocean. Astrakhan won't notice my departure, just as it didn't notice the departure of all my predecessors, nor will it notice those who will follow. It was wearied...

We essentially repeated the same deception with my wife's parents, telling them we planned to spend the rest of our vacation in St. Petersburg, while in reality, we headed for Ukraine. Why Ukraine? Because flying to America from Russia was extremely risky, if not outright foolish. At the border, agents would stop us and thoroughly examine our passports, not to mention our American visas, which would raise genuine interest and suspicion. They might find something dubious or doubtful in our travel to US, and even if they don't, they would suspect something anyway. Questions like: Where did you get your passport? How? When? Where did you obtain your visa? What is your occupation? Do you owe any debts? No? Do you have a criminal record? No? Let's check.

No, that option was dangerous and not practical. We had to flee through the third country that did not require a visa, and there were several such countries. I could have flown to the United States via Kazakhstan or Uzbekistan, or via Ukraine, which was much closer to the West. But here was another very important reason to use Ukraine.

The newly elected president of Ukraine, Viktor Yushchenko, had launched a powerful campaign to recognize the Holodomor, rehabilitate the UPA, and initiate a series of criminal cases against former leaders of the USSR and their accomplices. Relations with Putin, as a staunch adherent of the USSR inheritance, began to deteriorate sharply, which gave hope that the Ukrainian border guard corps would not express excessive zeal to cooperate with the Russian partners, which in turn gave us hope that Ukrainians would not be very interested in where Russian citizens were traveling through their territory. That is exactly what happened.

From Saratov via Voronezh, we reached Kiev without any problems or avoiding unnecessary attention. After spending a couple of days there and buying a ticket to New York via Frankfurt, we ended up straight in the strong and hot American embrace of my wife's uncle.

Overall, that marked the end of my epic journey out of Russia. From America, we informed our parents where we were, unfortunately exposing them to visits and interrogations by the local FSB. That was expected, and following our advice, they denied knowing about our departure, so the security service couldn't charge them with helping our escape. Eventually, after interrogating them, local FSB authorities couldn't do more than issue empty threats, and that was the end of that chapter.

A quiet American life began. If anyone sighs quietly about the difficult fate of immigrants, it cannot be applied to my case. The most basic start of our life in a cheap apartment in Valley Stream was already incomparably better than all the other places I had served at, from Kandalaksha to Borzya. The job I got was fine for a start and not too burdensome: first with Uncle Mike, and later on my own in the towns and cities of free America in Missouri and Michigan, working as a maintenance tech at an injection molding plant and later as a manufacturing engineer until I settled down as a decent and respectable burgher in Hartford, Connecticut, becoming a manager at Trane HVAC company. But it was a long road, long but not difficult, where the only regret was that we hadn't left earlier, much earlier.

Of course, there were problems; where would we be without them? One of the issues was getting my diploma recognized, a problem that has remained unresolved. Instead of banging my head against a brick wall, I chose the path of least resistance and finished college, which I did successfully.

However, more out of interest than of practical considerations, I did not lose hope of somehow achieving recognition of my academic diploma. Here, simple logic dictated that it would make sense to turn my attention to the famous West Point, an institution with a long reverential history and a heroic past. It was the right decision. It didn't cost me anything, and I had plenty of time, since I didn't yet have a house, and living in an apartment doesn't require much housekeeping. So, without further ado, I picked up a pen and started writing letters asking for an evaluation of my artillery academic diploma.

At first, things proceeded slowly, not showing much progress, although I was in no hurry either, but I still wanted to get some kind of response. And finally, I got it. The answer was rather laconic, but it left me with some hope that the West Point military scholars would still be interested in my application. Soon, I received a letter requesting information about my academy, the curriculum, departments, and so on. Mr. Erwin K., who agreed to help me in this matter, spoke Russian quite well and had even served in the office of the American military attaché in Moscow at one time. We began corresponding, and everything proceeded well and in my dreams I already saw that soon I would be able to adorn my office with a piece of fancy paper decorated with an eagle and Old Glory flag, impressing my employer and, among other things, giving me hope for career advancement as well as a pay raise, which in a capitalistic and immoral world of profit and interest is no less important than in the Russia I left behind.

Long ago, I noticed that an easy start in any endeavor leads to unpredictable and usually less brilliant results than were originally planned, and vice versa.

Having already begun my correspondence with West Point, I caught myself thinking that everything was going too well and smoothly to end up with a result that would be insignificant and not worth the effort and time. My premonitions did not deceive me. That's pretty much how it ended when, suddenly, all correspondence stopped, and I stopped receiving replies to my letters. I wrote again and again until I finally received a sad letter saying that my supervisor had passed away. May God rest his soul! He seemed like a good man and wanted to help me. The letter I received neither indicated that I would have a new supervisor nor provided any hint about the progress of my case. That was the end of it.

I received no more letters from West Point, but I did get a new job and all the incentives of American life, and I gave up the efforts I had started, getting caught up in the petty routine of everyday life. Time flew by quickly. We bought a house in Hartford, and over time, I began to forget all the turmoil of our departure from Russia.

By that time, FSB had shaken up all our parents but left them with nothing. The only fond memory they left to our parents was the threat that we would never see each other again because my wife and I would never be allowed to return to Russia, and our parents would never be allowed to leave. To expect anything else from FSB would be naïve, and we did not build illusions from the beginning. Having lived in Russia for so many years, it wasn't hard to predict the petty tactics of the security services, not capable of suppressing their revenge.

And then one day, a few years later, I suddenly received a message that my application to West Point had been revived, and I was asked to call back the number provided to discuss the further process of evaluating my academic qualifications. The caller was the academy instructor who had come across my application file.

If anyone expects to hear that I was thrilled to receive such a message, I will have to disappoint them. I wasn't thrilled, but I was definitely puzzled. So much time had passed since I had sent my application, and even when I first applied for it, I didn't really need it, as I already had a decent job and had no hope of finding a use for my academic diploma in American life. Even then, it was just a fun game; my outrageous cramp was caused by temporary idleness or spring vitamin deficiency. And then suddenly, it was this call.

Well, since the bottle was open, it had to be finished, and I was somewhat amused by the opportunity to chat with a representative of the famous American military school. It was late April, and New England was waking up from a snowy winter, shaking off the uncertainty of March and unpredictability of April weather, the slush and rain of the East Coast. I had no particular plans, so I decided that returning a call to the lieutenant colonel, I wouldn't risk anything and wouldn't need to commit myself to anything, as I wasn't particularly used to committing myself and always had an inclination to live by my rules as independently as possible, well fed and drunk, having my way and following my desires.

So, I called at the appointed time and heard on the other end of the line the voice of a man devoid of emotion and life, reminding me of a typical army officer clerk from the drill department, mired in the routine of orders, instructions, and directives. People of this type have always inspired me with aversion and were out of any interest to me, reminding me of honey without sugar, and I quickly lost interest in answering his routine questions, the answers to which, if he were familiar with my file, he should have known by heart.

The conversation was clearly dragging on, and I began to feel that I had made a mistake in agreeing to talk to such a boring and dull lieutenant colonel or whoever he was. Only my sympathy for the American cadets kept me fighting off sleep while I was answering his questions, which were asked in a boring and melancholic voice. I began to tire, and only a glass of wine gave me the strength to remain courteous and pleasant to that tedious defender of the Fatherland. I have a deep belief that all true defenders of their corresponding fatherlands must be very boring, completely devoid of humor, and as predictable as traffic lights so as not to bring confusion and disorder to such a responsible task as defending their desks and papers.

Exhausted beyond measure and having lost interest, I had to apologize, citing some alleged event that I was supposedly to attend. Surprisingly, this had some effect, and the lieutenant colonel suddenly woke up from his slumbering state, into which he also had been successfully lulling me, and suddenly suggested that I should meet one of his associates on Friday evening in downtown Hartford at a bar on Pratt Street.

Yes, I thought then, this lieutenant colonel must be a good psychologist and not yet lost to good society as I had initially thought, because the idea of interviewing in a bar could only come from the mind of a worthy and respectable citizen of his country, especially when the subject of the discussion was a matter of state security. Naturally, I agreed right away. What else could I do? I even forgot to ask him why and what for I needed to meet in person if we could discuss everything over the phone, or maybe I just didn't want to provoke the situation and, waving the white flag, immediately surrendered to his conditions.

This was becoming interesting. If they want to meet with me, why not meet me at West Point, and why, all of a sudden, in such pleasant surroundings, also perfectly suited to my schedule? Where is this sudden interest coming from? Naturally, such attention implied some kind of offer, although it was unclear to me of what kind. I had left Russia quite some time ago, where changes took place under the influence of the avalanche of money that had fallen on Russia with high oil prices, which was being shouted about by all the Russian news on TV and the internet. But in my opinion, if anyone was suddenly interested in any information regarding the Russian Army, then that was hopelessly outdated. Then what information could I possess that they didn't know? Given the level of Russian corruption, there is no need for the CIA or similar organizations to steal meticulously guarded military secrets; it would suffice to pay a humble amount of money to acquire them easily, safely, and without trouble, and there would be no shortage of sellers.

On the other hand, aside from the "debt" to my former homeland, which long ago became a crazy stepmother evil, neglected, and dirty poking into everyone's affairs that shouldn't concern her, secretly loathing all her children, and running around her house with a lit torch, ready to set fire to her own house as well as the neighboring homes, I had no other obligations. My old homeland, with its wild ways, had long since frightened away and scattered most of its good children, who fled around the world but still demanded filial love and religious devotion from those who remained. I turned that page and didn't worry about her troubles, trying to forget my Russian life and feeling no sympathy for her actions.

That's what I thought, not seeing in that any apostasy or deviation from the basic logic or common sense.

On Friday evening, as agreed, at six o'clock, I was already on Pratt Street, leaving myself extra time in the rush hour to park my car in the vicinity of the restaurant.

Car parking there isn't a fun business, and on Friday evening, it's getting even worse, so after driving around the blocks, I found a spot a block away. Now I had to find Major James Howe, with his nondescript American first and equally typical American last names. However, I reasoned that if they called for this meeting and I was an invitee, since they were the ones who had arranged it, then they should take trouble to look for me and not the other way around. It was a wise decision, and with confidence, I entered the restaurant and headed for the bar.

An interview in a bar is the ideal place for a casual interview. It's a shame that the HR departments of all the companies I worked for never realized this simple truth, and probably because of that, the personnel turnover in those companies was higher than average. In this regard, the military was far ahead of civilian organizations, and I was very grateful to them for that.

Sitting in the bar shuffling papers and leafing through résumés would have been awkward, so I had no intention of embarrassing the bartender and fair clients with such a bizarre activity. That is why I had no papers or résumés with me, only a pen and a sheet of standard paper folded in four. To lighten the mood, I ordered some red wine and began to wait, furtively watching the approaches to the bar. However, I did not have to wait for long before a balding gentleman of about forty approached me and called my name. I introduced myself, we shook hands, and the Army major, without hesitation, ordered himself some wine as well.

By doing that, I recognized him as an experienced and intelligent officer with whom it would be pleasant to do business. The only thing that surprised me was that there were several people sitting at the bar, but for some reason, he came straight over to me. His firm handshake, direct gaze, and pleasant smile, combined with the ordered glass of wine, clearly endeared me to this man.

After a few meaningless questions and phrases that were difficult to hear over the loud music, he suggested having supper at the back of the restaurant, away from the bar, as it was not very comfortable to talk in such a cacophony of sounds. I liked his suggestion, and we moved towards the entrance to the restaurant to order a table.

The major turned out to be a friendly, cheerful man who was a pleasure to talk to. He asked questions and listened with obvious interest to my answers and stories without interrupting, laughing at my jokes, and nodding with approval. I had already answered the questions I was asked a couple of years ago, but perhaps it was all new and interesting to him as a new curator, so his interest was quite understandable.

After briefly recounting my service records from the Russian north to Lermontov's Chechnya and from the Kaliningrad region to Transbaikalia, we moved on to questions about military training at the school and the academy. As a teacher, he found this particularly interesting. In addition, it turned out that he had once served in Hawaii, far from the mainland, so questions about life and service in the enclave of the Kaliningrad region were both interesting and understandable to him.

Time flew by unnoticed, and the wine and bourbon we later switched to flowed freely. It turned out that he was originally from Wichita, Kansas, had always aspired to be a military man, came from a good family, had graduated from West Point, had never participated in military conflicts or wars, and had eventually gone into teaching. He knew how to listen without interrupting, sometimes interjecting intelligent and witty comments, and listened with attention, with moderate, not exaggerated reactions, responding to the ups and downs of my military service, emigration, and escape from the country. Everything about him was likable, and it was clear from the beginning who would be paying for the party. However, that didn't matter, as the pleasure was mutual.

By his words, he had some business in Boston. He intended to leave the next day after spending the night at the nearby Goodwin Hotel, which awakened my childhood memories of "The Wizard of the Emerald City," shamelessly plagiarized by Volkov from Baum's "The Wizard of Oz." As we parted, he shook my hand a bit longer than necessary, promising to call back without mentioning a date. I did not properly respond to that revelation of his emotions, having my thoughts turning around on what time to leave home tomorrow to pick up my car, since driving home in its current state would not be advisable.

That was the end of our evening, to our mutual satisfaction, and it was only the next day when, suddenly, it dawned on me what the purpose of our meeting was. I received a call from West Point a few years after my case had been closed, and then they arranged a meeting at a restaurant, entertained me, and pleased me with a good wine, hardly trying to find anything new, having already been very familiar with all aspects of my biography. It was a little strange, though pleasant, and I soon forgot about this amusing incident until one evening, a couple of weeks later, James called me again and said that he was passing through Hartford again and asked if we could meet.

Having a rough idea of how such a meeting would turn out, I naturally didn't resist, didn't look for excuses to decline, and didn't pretend that sudden sickness had overcome me, so without wasting his or my time, I agreed to meet in the same place.

We met like old friends, ordered dinner without wasting time at the bar counter, and continued our pleasant conversation. The dinner was wonderful, although we drank much less and finished with cannoli and éclairs, with solemnity and all appropriate respectability that might impress even Her Majesty's court. That time, everything revolved around my escape from Russia and the likelihood of my possible arrest, and who and how could have betrayed all our Kaliningrad Carbonari society, and how could we have avoided FSB attention? The questions were interesting but staying so far from artillery and military service matters that at times I began to wonder if I was talking to a psychologist, although his genuine interest and mirroring of my movements, which for some reason caught my eye, sobered my attitude toward the current conversation. I decided not to push my luck and just observe the flow of our bizarre conversation before jumping to conclusions. The conversation covered a wide variety of topics: from the Napoleonic Wars to the Normandy invasion, and from wine preferences to the historical sights of Rome.

However, there was a way to test such an upskilled and cultivated "teacher." It seemed that James knew much more about me than he was trying to show, at least judging by the topics he brought up, which were very familiar and understandable to me. However, there was also something in the conversation that he could not know. It was that in my leisure time in years past, I had been interested in neurolinguistic programming, had read a bit on the subject, and had, though with interchangeable success, tried to apply my knowledge to some of my former bosses as well as to pleasant ladies at work. I'm not sure if my endeavors had some effect, but I must have learned something from those wise and thick books, and some of it even stuck deep in my memory, so I furrowed my brows and racked my brain to try to remember what I had read in the past.

He asked many questions, but he also talked a lot. I remembered that a reaction to a statement usually contains more information than a direct question, and if he had truly been interested in the topic, he would have responded to my clear and concise statement with a lengthy counterargument. I tried once, but there was no reaction. I tried again on another topic, and the result was the same. It became clear that he wasn't interested in the topics I suggested but rather in my reaction or, perhaps, in my way of presenting the subjects.

He also joked a lot, and his jokes were sharp and made me laugh. It is well known that people's personalities are best revealed by what they find funny. He was clearly observing me, and I began to find it amusing. Of course, he was not just an ordinary teacher from the military academy. He had other goals, but I couldn't comprehend them. What did he want to find out about me? What could I tell him that he didn't already know? Recruit me? But he knew my biography as well as I did, and therefore he knew that I couldn't go to Russia under any circumstances. What did he want then? It didn't look like "a direct recruitment"; maybe it will happen later under a different pretext, judging by the fact that he pretends to be an army officer, but he definitely wasn't one, though he was quite familiar with military service. Or will it be a case of "step-by-step recruitment," when he will later reveal his true intentions? I did not doubt that he wanted to involve me in something, but it seemed that he was in no hurry with his offer, stalling for time, waiting for something, trying to understand me better, or quietly forcing me to suggest my services to him, helping him to carry out the "reverse" version of recruitment. Or was it all just my imagination?

He appeared to notice my distraction as I tried to understand his point and asked what I was thinking. I avoided the question by saying I was having issues with my boss that were slowly escalating into a conflict, which was a reasonable and convincing explanation.

He fell silent and sat quietly staring at me. Here it is! Here is the moment when it is not difficult to determine a person's will and desire. I clearly recalled what I needed to do now and stared straight at him, not taking my eyes off his. If he were just making conversation, then after such a simple and banal explanation, he would look away, as if embarrassed. If, however, he was trying to establish some kind of contact with me for future work, then he would have to sustain my gaze like of a subordinate; otherwise, he would not be suitable for the role of leader with me.

I kept looking at him as he calmly held my gaze, sitting quietly and not looking away. That's it! Now I was sure that behind the facade of a joker and a bon vivant, there was something much bigger, more serious, and probably dangerous.

And I decided to go on the offensive, even though it was a bit ahead and risky.

"Listen, James, you don't seem like a bad guy, but I'm a little lost... What are you getting at? It seems to me that you know me better than I know myself, and I have some doubts about your artillery background. We're not here to just chat and shoot the breeze, are we? It's getting late; there's no time to beat around the bush. Can you tell me straight what you want?"

"What are you talking about? I don't understand," the officer said, genuinely surprised. He held himself well and confidently. Maybe I was wrong after all? The same thought pierced me again, and I tried to push it away. They came to me, which means they needed me, not the other way around, and if that's the case, then I can afford to be a little more daring. I decided to go for broke.

"You know what I mean, James. Okay, there's no point in continuing this game, and it's getting late. If you want to talk, give me a call; otherwise, I have other plans for today."

I stood up and extended my hand to him. He didn't move; he sat and stared at me intently, just as he had before.

"See you and have a good time," I said, and already started to turn away when he changed his tone and spoke in a firmer voice.

"Sit down! I can see you're not that simple either. All right, you want to talk; let's talk."

I was still standing. "Correction, James, it's not I; it's you who wants to talk, so let's keep that in mind, okay?"

His face changed. The friendliness that had lit up his face just seconds ago disappeared. Sitting in front of me was a completely different person, with a serious look and clearly not in the mood for jokes. I sat down. He pushed his plate away and pulled his wine glass closer.

"Let's have a drink, Andre. We'll talk later." He raised his glass. "Cheers!"

"Cheers! Just let's skip the other bullshit you fed me before."

"Agreed." At that point, I knew that I had won. I myself, not him on his own will, had forced him to get straight to the business if he wanted to talk to me. I showed him that it was he, not me, who was interested in continuing the conversation. It was a psychological victory, and although I didn't see any emotion on his face, I knew clearly that he understood that I had the upper hand. It was also important for me to emphasize my independence from him, whoever he was.

I don't like being dependent on anyone. Even when I was in the army, I drew a mental line between my military service and personal life, contrary to the famous Soviet song that claimed army officers were one close-knit family. Even here in the United States, I couldn't bring myself to wear a jacket or shirt with the company's logo. I could easily wear a jacket with the logo of any other company where I had worked before or had never worked at all, but never the one I work for now. Strangely enough, it reminded me of a factory brand burned into a horse's neck to indicate that it is the property of a certain stud farm. So, I was an incorrigible maverick and dissenter, and I wanted my counterpart to understand this plainly and unequivocally, and I knew that there was no way he could like it. And I didn't want to give him the initiative; if they needed me, then let them play, if not by my rules, then at least keep them in mind.

So, I didn't rush, continuing to sip my wine and surveying him. He wasn't rushing to answer either, apparently not knowing how to restart the broken conversation and trying to regain ground. Fine, let him do it. But I didn't want to aggravate the situation and decided to help him.

"My wine is running out, James, and when it's gone, there will be nothing left to talk about."

"There will be a wine. There will be so much wine that the two of us won't be able to drink it all. Okay? You probably already understand that we need your help."

"Who are 'we'?"

"What difference does it make? The United States, if you wish."

"Oh, so my taxes aren't enough anymore to keep the States afloat. I'll lend you some money if it helps."

"That's funny... Listen, I understand that you still owe Russia something?"

"I? Owe?" I was taken aback.

" Owe. Owe. For not letting you go to the West, for all the troubles you and your family have faced with the FSB. For the fact that your friend, who wanted to leave Russia just like you had, is now rotting in jail."

James was apparently well aware of my idée fixe and also knew my weak spot. And what kind of special agent would refuse to deal with somebody who has a weak spot?

"Listen, James, don't try to advocate for my old dreams. I was fed up with the Soviet Union and Russia, and I dreamed of repaying the debt you're mentioning now even before I left the country. Just don't take me for a fool. If you want me to help you with something, even if I'm unsure what it is, I'll be happy to do so. However, I won't work in the dark without a clear understanding of the task. First of all, I want to know who you are. Second, if I realize that you are bullshitting me, I will immediately jump off this train, and believe me, you will not have a second chance to convince me to work for you. I want this to be clear and understandable. And if that's okay with you, let's get down to business; I'm not in the mood today after your clever approaches, and it's already late."

"Okay. This is a deal."

James seemed quite satisfied with this outcome.

"I hope this conversation stays between us. I will be obliged if it will. I'll call you, and we'll discuss everything next time."

"Agreed."

James paid the bill, just like last time, even though I offered to do it myself. We shook hands and parted ways.

All the way home, I thought about our conversation. It seemed like it didn't go as they had planned. If this was serious, then I had no doubt that our conversation had been recorded. That meant they would need time to listen to the recording, analyze it, discuss it, make a decision, and then decide whether to proceed further or drop the case. Consequently, I wouldn't hear from them for several days, maybe even weeks. That suited me just fine.

At the same time, I was definitely flattered that the Americans, the people of the country that had taken me in and become my home and homeland, asked me to do this. However, deep down, I knew that if Mongolia or Vanuatu had asked me to do the same, I would have agreed just as easily. I felt no doubts or guilt, nor could I have. If Russia had confidently driven itself into that mess since the late 1990s then it was a problem of the Russian people. To the quicksand into which they had confidently and successfully driven themselves and which they continued to sink into even over the following decades, only they were responsible, and I had nothing to do with it. I made my own choice, followed my own path, and they have to follow theirs.

I was in no hurry, and I declared my consent to work with them without even being asked; they can take credit for that "reverse recruitment," and so all that remained for me was to wait, although I was extremely eager to repay my "debt" to Russia and I didn't want to miss such an opportunity at all, though I didn't want to show my new friends my excessive zeal. Otherwise, they would get spoiled, and that's like spoiling a good contractor; under no circumstances should you praise or give leniency to the latter, because it will cost you more in the end.

That's pretty much how it happened. I didn't hear from James for couple of weeks, and I began to forget about our meetings. And why not? And just when I was planning my vacation, as it happens in some dramas and in all vaudevilles, the phone rang. The ID didn't show up, as it does with regular spam calls, and I was about to ignore the call when the thought of a possible rendezvous with James flashed through my mind. And, of course, it was him. This time, he didn't tell me about his occasional travelling through Hartford or his business in Boston but asked directly about next meeting. Well, it seemed that my remarks about empty chatter and wasted time had not been in vain, and he had gotten my message, which made me happy. By all means, it did.

Everything happened just like last time, only this time the location was different, much closer to my work, which suited me better. And again, it was Friday. Why Friday? Isn't it because even on the most miserable Fridays, when the sky is covered with gray, impenetrable clouds brought by cold winds from the Atlantic and a nasty, fine November rain drizzles down, or even when Friday falls on the thirteenth day of the month, someone's soul is still full of hopes and sweet dreams of the coming weekend? On any Friday, a person's good-natured mindset lifts him into a positive mood, regardless of whether he is preparing for a fun weekend or attending a funeral. You don't believe me? Imagine going to a bar on the best Monday evening and compare it to the most miserable Friday. The worst Friday is always better than the sunniest Monday, and that makes it much easier to handle people.

We met in East Hartford, not far from the airport. This time, James was already waiting for me at a table at the back of the restaurant, which was quite quiet despite the large number of visitors. James greeted me without his usual enthusiasm; his former good humor was gone, and he looked more serious and focused. Besides, he was not alone. With him was another gentleman named Ian, even more serious and even less talkative than today's James. We placed our orders and, while waiting for them, got down to business.

"Andre, I would like to ask you for a small favor that you could have done for me, if you don't mind, of course." James got straight to the point while his companion watched me silently.

I had no answer to such a vague question, although I noticed that James, while being in company, avoided using the word "we" and spoke on his own behalf instead. This is also a common technique used to downplay the importance of the party being referred to and not to scare off a potential client.

"What, do you want to hire me as a part-time Bond?" I asked with a touch of irony.

"Come on now. What are you talking about? I just want to ask you for a favor, a small one, nothing hard, and maybe you'll even find it rewarding too. What do you think?"

I sat silent, and after a pause, James continued, "As far as I know from your previous military service in the Kaliningrad region, you were acquainted with Vyacheslav Butusov, weren't you?"

I must admit I was pretty surprised by their knowledge, but I tried my best not to show it, although I'm not sure whether I succeeded. Nevertheless, I answered in the affirmative, since the latter served in the Baltic Fleet headquarters in the operational section, and we were quite well acquainted.

"I don't know if you know that Butusov now works in the Department of Construction and Road Maintenance of the Kaliningrad Regional Government."

I didn't know that, but I wasn't surprised because Vyacheslav was born and raised in Kaliningrad, had connections there, loved cars, and sometimes brought vehicles from Germany to sell through his friends at some shady dealerships, so I just nodded silently, raising my eyebrows in surprise.

"I see you're well informed; you know much more than I do," I said sarcastically.

They ignored my sarcasm and continued.

"Could you help me get in touch with him? Don't worry," James continued smoothly, "I am not asking you to travel to Russia. What I request from you isn't very complicated or dangerous. I'm even sure it's much simpler than you think," he emphasized the last word, smiled coquettishly, and glanced at his gloomy companion, who had remained silent until then.

"We won't ask much of you, believe me, and I'll pay for your travel and accommodation in one of the European countries. You can even earn some money for your troubles and time. How does that sound?" Ian spoke for the first time.

"You know, gentlemen, if you hadn't been beating around the bush, you would have saved a lot of your time and mine also. I understand that you need my help, and I am glad that you will cover my travel expenses. But you don't need to pay me anything above. As you said, James, "I have an old debt." That's true, and I will gladly repay it to my "historical homeland". If you explain the details to me, I will do everything in my power."

"Here we go! We didn't expect anything else from you. Thank you. Let's do this: I'll call you during the week, and we'll meet in a quieter place to discuss the details."

"All right. I would like to do this 'without interruption from production,' as they used to say in Russia."

" That's no problem. How about Saturday?"

"Excellent."

James raised his glass. "Let's drink to our business!"

"For Good luck!" repeated his friend and me. We clinked glasses.

"Yes, by the way, Andre," Ian spoke again, "we certainly trust you, but according to the protocol, wouldn't you mind taking a lie detector test? You can refuse, of course, but I would ask you to take it."

"I can even swear on the Bible if you like."

"Well, I think that's unnecessary. The 'detector' will suit us just fine," Ian said with a knowing smile, his first of the evening.

After that, the conversation picked up, and dinner ended on a high note. For some reason, I sensed they had doubts about whether I agreed or not, and my more-than-willing consent seemed to bring them clear relief.

Dinner was over, we shook hands, and James reminded me again that he would call me and we would arrange our next meeting. We went to the parking lot. It turned out that our cars were parked side by side.

"That's a good sign," James said loudly, beaming like a new penny, waving at me, and pointing to our cars. They got into their Toyota and, without warming up the engine, slowly drove out of the parking lot. I stayed in my car a little longer, trying to organize everything in my mind. Frankly, I was very happy that, without much effort, I got a chance I had been waiting for years. A long time ago, when I had just arrived in the United States and was lying in bed at night, I thought about possible ways to get revenge on all those who had tried to put obstacles in my way, preventing me from leaving Russia and trying to ruin my life. Why were they doing this? For another star on their epaulets? It's unlikely that they would have been awarded one for that particular incident. For gratitude for their service? Was it really worth it? I don't know... But now I had a real chance. I didn't know what was expected of me, but I was ready for anything. Damn it! If only James knew, I would have been willing to pay for such a chance. Although it's quite possible he guessed so... Well, 'strike while the iron is hot,' as they used to say in old times.

The week went by quickly, filled with thoughts and doubts. I had no information about what they were seeking in Kaliningrad or how I could assist them. Still, I could infer some things from open sources. In fact, the Russian websites and news agencies were shouting about recent events so loudly that they could wake the dead.

The headlines were full of news about Poland and the deployment of American missile defense systems on its eastern borders, which caused a lot of outrage and threats from Russia. This was understandable. At the market, when a poor buyer discovers that his wallet is missing, the thief himself is the first one to shout, "Catch the thief!" All the news revolved around the most heavily armed region in Europe, the Kaliningrad area, which was trying to present itself as the righteous victim, shouting louder than anyone else and threatening to deploy its medium-range missile complexes that remained in its neglected and dilapidated arsenals on the mainland.

There was no need to go to a clairvoyant and stare into a crystal ball until you lose your mind; everything was clear and understandable, straightforward and intelligible. Russia was clearly going to deploy medium-range missiles that once were already conveniently located there, and apparently, this affair was necessary to determine Russian intentions, capabilities, and plans. This did not require recruiting generals and admirals who had swollen on government salaries and become dull from prolonged idleness, who had forgotten what the Navy is, and were only capable of making straight and serious countenances at the pompous military parades in bright uniforms reminding Latin American colonels.

For this purpose, clerks and pretty secretaries from the local city hall departments of construction, education, social welfare, or the tax service were quite suitable, and Comrade Butusov was the perfect candidate for this role, given his love of money and German vehicles, whose liver would not be difficult to tickle. And what spy would miss such a lucky chance to tickle his opponent's liver, or even kick it? Preferably by his foot… So, in principle, without any revelations from my hosts, and they were, of course, my hosts, questioning whom would make no sense and would have been a waste of time; the picture was more or less clear. But it was not clear what exactly they wanted from me. Should I bribe Butusov for some terribly secret information? That's too banal and primitive, and what kind of secrets could he possibly possess in his department?

Is it that I pass something on to him or receive something from him? Hardly… They didn't need me for such trivial schemes, and they could have executed the transfer using technical means without anyone's help. So why did they need me? They couldn't entrust an outsider with any serious task, which was clear from their doubts and their suggestion that I take a polygraph test. All I could do was wait. But time went on, and no one called me, no one sent secret messages or mysterious notes, no one tried to lure or poison me, and no one attempted to kidnap me on the street or from my office. I began to feel ashamed and hurt by this lack of attention to my humble person.

American life is rich and diverse, and offers ample opportunities for both productive activities and equally effective ways to spend one's earnings. Therefore, without further deliberation or waiting for the weather to change, we decided to take a long weekend trip to Quebec City, a place I had a surprising affinity for.

For a while, I entertained myself with the thought that by immersing myself in the foggy and confusing labyrinth of communication with representatives of that government profession, I would be able to repay my debt and emerge in time from the whirlpool that was beginning to sweep me away and to which I had so recklessly and easily succumbed. I was also amused by the fact that, apparently due to some incredible misunderstanding, they suspected me of being privy to a multitude of secrets that I certainly did not possess. All that remained for me was to wait and see how events would unfold and whether my communication with their organization would bring me any unpleasant surprises.

Time flew by as it usually does on a good vacation (if, of course, there are such things as bad ones), and no one bothered me again until, finally, one day after work, James called and suggested a meeting in the DoubleTree Hotel, which was not the most impressive but far from the cheapest. "Damn, how predictable and understandable everything is in this world of cloaks and daggers," I thought, entering the modern lobby of an equally modern hotel. Without delay, I went straight to the elevator to go up to the third floor to the room where my meeting was scheduled. I knocked, and almost immediately, James opened the door. It was obvious that they were already waiting for me, even though I was three minutes early. Ian was sitting at the table by the window. When I entered, he stood up to shake my hand. A smile appeared on his face, quite obviously forced and feigning some pleasure at meeting me. There was a bottle of water and three glasses on the table.

James pointed to a chair next to him and sat down. "I don't think I need to repeat that what we discuss must remain between us," he said, pushing a sheet of paper already on the table toward me and turning it over, inviting me to read and sign it.

Needless to say, this was a condition of non-disclosure of the information I had received. What was interesting was that the non-disclosure had a time limit, which I had never seen before. I read and signed the document. Ian, who had been sitting silently until then, fidgeted in his chair.

With a mysterious look that must be typical of all intelligence agencies and trendy spy series, he began to let me in on the secrets of the upcoming mission, apparently hoping to captivate and enthrall my imagination.

"Andre, you probably already understand that we need to establish contact with Butusov to..." He hesitated slightly, "obtain some assistance from him. We won't burden you with details, but there are a few things we'd like to share. As an intelligent person, you presumably already realize, or at least have some idea, of what might interest us in the Kaliningrad region. As you know, the United States is planning to deploy a missile defense system in Poland aimed at countries with unstable regimes, such as Iran, which could already threaten the security of European nations and American interests in Europe.

The Kaliningrad region holds a key strategic position; unfortunately, due to Russia's irresponsible policies, there is a risk of derailing the planned measures or even provoking regional confrontation, which could disrupt these efforts. Perhaps Mr. Butusov could provide valuable help by sharing some information from his department. Interestingly, the information itself isn't classified, but it could be very useful to us. We've learned that Vyacheslav is currently facing some serious financial difficulties that we might help him resolve. The problem is we have no access to him, but you do. If you could help us get in touch with him, we'd be very grateful. Are you willing to assist us?"

I listened silently to what Ian was explaining to me. In principle, I understood what they wanted, and the logic of his reasonable and concise explanation was clear to me. I was quite satisfied with the offer. The only thing that was unclear was how they intended to arrange everything. However, I didn't have to wait long before Ian put everything in place.

"We would like to ask you to contact your acquaintances in Kaliningrad through emails and introduce yourself as a successful businessman with a network of dealerships selling new cars. Your business is performing exceptionally well, and you are now targeting Eastern Europe, with a potential focus on the Kaliningrad region, where you plan to establish your dealership. Butusov could possibly be a candidate to head your office in Kaliningrad and later in Gdansk, whose port, located not far from Kaliningrad, will naturally be the destination for American cars arriving by sea. How do you like that story? Do you like cars?" Although it was a rhetorical question, Ian was clearly waiting for my answer.

"Cars? Of course, I do like them, though no more than donkeys or horses if I need to get from point A to point B. I especially like both in small forms and sizes; they require fewer oats."

"I see. You're a joker, Andre. It is good. It's even better than you think or we expected," he said, looking at me thoughtfully with what seemed to me to be a mocking smile, and added, "But we'll still arrange a little consultation for you on how to run this kind of business, if that's okay with you, of course."

He continued, "In addition, what can you tell us about him that we don't know? Maybe about his preferences? Or his habits? Does he like money?"

"Do you know anyone who doesn't?" I asked. "Would you acquaint me?"

"Well, you know what I mean," he continued. "Maybe he likes women? Or does he prefer young guys?"

Apparently, my face reflected what I was thinking about the latter question, and before I had time to answer, he had corrected himself: "Well, that's just an example, so to speak."

"Yeah... Not a very good example, to be honest," I said slowly, looking away.

"Well, you know... Maybe he's a collector? He loves cars, after all. Maybe there's something else. Think about it. Any information would be useful. Okay?"

I paused for a moment. Then I added, "You're right about his love for cars. I don't remember him showing any sympathy for the West other than for Western cars, preferably German, but I do remember that his main weakness was money. But I can't say how easy or difficult it would be to satisfy that weakness, or how much it would cost. However, it's probably within the price range of a car. Something like that. But it all will depend on what you want from him and how much risk he is willing to take."

"Is he a risky person?

"It is hard to say for certain. I didn't know him well enough to give you an accurate answer; it probably depends on what is at stake and how high the risk is."

"Well, that's what we thought. Okay. If you recall anything or get any ideas, let us know. We still have time."

I had nothing to add and nodded silently like a horse that needed more oats.

"In the meantime, you will contact those who know Vyacheslav and indirectly pass through them the information about your business and your interest in expanding it to the Kaliningrad region to him with a request that if he is interested in your business, he contacts you. Most likely, that's what will happen. You will tell him that you are going to Poland to take care of your business and that it would be nice to meet him on Polish territory in Ketchyn, for example, where you are going to visit the museum Hitler's headquarters in Wolf's Lair, which is about sixty kilometers from Bagrationovsk, if I'm not mistaken. Once you were planning to go there anyway, weren't you? There you will meet him, take him to a nice restaurant, sit down, and make him relax and drink up to an acceptable level, and start bringing him up to speed on your business. As you understand, it would be awkward for us to approach him ourselves; it might scare him, and any doubts on his side could ruin this undertaking. We'll discuss all the details later, including the restaurant, the hotel, and how you'll introduce me to him. The sequence of your conversation will be important, even what you eat and drink. I'll join you a little later when the "client is ripe," he said, the last two words in good Russian, albeit with a noticeable accent.

Finishing his sentence, he looked at me with a smile, waiting for my reaction. The first thing that struck me was his awareness that I had been thinking about visiting Ketshin and the museum of Hitler's headquarters for a long time.

Later, I thought long and hard about how they could have found out about it, but I couldn't come up with an answer. I couldn't remember mentioning my plans to anyone in my correspondence.

I decided that whoever was going to be at the meeting would have to speak Russian, but the sudden switch from English to Russian clearly caught me off guard, which definitely amused Ian. But I still couldn't suspect him of being the one. He gave the impression of a man devoid of humor, a kind of human machine, suitable for the role of a recruiter, as I was for the role of a ballerina.

I didn't come across this type of person very often, if at all, except for one instance when I was already working at Trane HVAC. Our regional manager, Murray Zane, was exactly of that type. The company's old-timers said that someone had heard him joking and laughing once. For any official meeting, the company couldn't find a more representative manager with a stonier face and charm akin to Lenin's mummy.

As the company's official, he might play the role of the company's face, as unshakable as a pier and as straightforward as the Pennsylvania Railroad Station platform. Talking to him amused me as much as Livingstone's communications with representatives of the M'bomou tribe must have amused him, from a purely scientific point of view, and resembled my communication with a robot at the Exhibition of Achievements of the National Economy in Moscow, selling tickets to the pavilion. He showed no more emotion than a provincial morgue attendant, and talking to him was an indescribable pleasure for any researcher and an irresistible delight for any artist, which I considered myself to be to some extent.

Of course, he was the best among the managers in our company. I am more than sure that he never skipped class or shot birds and streetlamps with a slingshot like we did in our childhood. Even when drunk, he never crossed the street at the wrong place, let alone at a red light. The company's rules were his law, and I would be very surprised to learn that he drove his truck while intoxicated. But how can one trust a man who doesn't drive his truck after being intoxicated?

That was exactly the impression I had of Ian, and it seemed unthinkable and incredible to me that a man like him would be able to charm and recruit someone as cunning as Butusov, who was not easily fooled. Ian was undoubtedly an intelligent man, albeit completely devoid of a sense of humor and any hint of basic charm. I am sure it would not be easy to find a person who will be willing to take a risk after talking to machine.

Apparently, the people in his organization understood this too, because at our next and final meeting, he was no longer there, and Alex took his place. He asked us to call him Alexei, and even in James's presence, our communication was exclusively in Russian. At that point Ian's role remained unclear to me.

Alexei was still a fairly young man, cheerful and very easy to talk to. Working with him was easy and pleasant.

By the time of our meeting, events were already in full swing: I made several calls and sent a few emails to my old acquaintances in Kaliningrad, and very soon, I received an email from Butusov. The email was short, exciting and noncommittal. Vyacheslav was happy to hear about me and was asking general questions that anyone would ask someone he hadn't seen for a long time and with whom he had lost his originally not so strong connections. However, his email also had different meanings. He was clearly intrigued by the information he had heard about me from third parties, and his email was an invitation to further communication. That was what we had been waiting for. We exchanged a few emails. My replies were full of stories about my life, world traveling, and, of course, my car dealership business.

At that time, I had taken a short course in managing a car dealership at our college and had been armed with some basic information about that business. I showered him with details about the structure of my non-existent business.

My business's website confirmed my success and growth and captivated the imagination of my opponent, who already saw himself as the manager of American dealership on Russian soil. But I had my doubts. My emails were full of doubts and a lack of understanding of how business works in Russia, which fueled his heated imagination when he started to convince me that he would be the ideal candidate for that sort of business. I reluctantly agreed, although there was a catch - I couldn't go to Russia because of the possibility of my arrest due to my sudden departure from the Army and the country.

Yes, it was inconvenient, but that was no obstacle for Vyacheslav, and after all, he himself suggested that we meet in Poland. It was a success! This perfectly matched the alternative that we had already discussed with Ian and James about my excursion to Hitler's Eastern Headquarters in East Prussia, near Ketshin, and also suited Vyacheslav. So, we agreed to meet, and I booked rooms for him and myself at Ketchin's hotel Koch and asked Vyacheslav not to worry about any expenses, which could not but have made him even more excited.

So, Alexei would play the role of my junior business partner and join us at the restaurant after a hearty, drunken dinner, when Vyacheslav would be better prepared for further discussions and proposals. Alexei didn't say so, but it was clear from what needed to be done to recruit Butusov with minimal effort. When I asked Alexei whether I should call him when Vyacheslav was in the required state, he just waved his hand and said he would show up at the right moment. That was enough for me and led me to believe that someone else might be in the room, most likely nearby, who would let him know.

All that remained for me was to figure out the details of the trip. Unfortunately, my vacation could not be extended simply on the basis of "service to the Fatherland," and I had to use only the vacation days I had. Round-trip to Warsaw, hotel rentals, a Mercedes SUV, and all other expenses of my "vacation," plus the remaining days that I spent at my discretion, were covered by James' organization, and all I had to do was to play my part.

Butusov and I discussed the details once more, and I was ready to start my Polish vacation. Two weeks wasn't quite enough notice for my boss, who frowned and grumbled a little to support his status of authority and importance before approving my vacation request, but he eventually gave in to my charm and blessed the request. All that was left was to wait for my vacation to start and for my mission in Poland to begin.

The LOT plane was already at the terminal gate, but there were still forty minutes left before boarding. What does a normal individual do at the airport before boarding a long flight across the ocean? Indeed, he looks for a decent table with a view of the tarmac so that he can dispel his doubts and sorrows and strengthen his spirit with a couple of glasses of decent wine to give his soul an angelic lightness and raise it to the cruising altitude of his transatlantic flight. It was a wise and time-tested practice, and having strengthened my spirit, I was ready for my adventurous tour to Eastern Europe. Boarding was complete when the deep black night had already descended over JFK airport. Outside the window, the darkness was pierced by a sea of countless multicolored twinkling lights intended either to mark the runways and taxiways or to disorient anxious passengers and inside the terminal crowds of people were in permanent motion similar to Brownian movement to complete a picture of the organized airport chaos.

After a few intricate turns, the plane finally rolled out onto the runway, the lights in the cabin went out, the engines roared, and the sky airliner, vibrating and roaring, rushed forward with its wheels drumming a familiar tattoo over the uneven concrete runway to get up there where my soul was already waiting for it after the wine I had drunk at the airport bar. At an altitude of twelve thousand meters, the plane carrying my mortal body met my immortal soul, floating in the heavens among the fluffy night clouds after a few glasses of wine, after which I fell asleep, only to be awakened by the commotion preceding the late celestial supper.

We flew not long enough to enjoy the dubious delicacies of the heavenly cuisine and too long to be served by the terrible wine that is usually served on all planes flying over the black night-shrouded ocean. My seat was not by the window, although it was not in the middle row, so there was nothing to distract me. The passengers began to drift off into a post-supper sleep, casting aside their doubts and worries. The lights in the plane were switched to standby mode, and only my neighbor and I could not fall asleep.

The late instructions and advice rushed through my head, along with memories of the proposed "lie detector" test, which I never got the chance to try, but that didn't upset me at all. Apparently, they wanted to test my reaction. Was that why Ian was present at all interviews? It was clear what they wanted from Butusov, but will he agree? From my army experience, I knew that most officers of the Russian army had a delicate affection for money; every second one was willing to take a certain risk to earn more, but not many were willing to take a gamble at higher stakes.

Everything was determined by the old, tried and tested formula: supply and demand, or price and quality, depending on your point of view. Butusov, like everyone else, belonged to the first category, fully corresponded to the second, and was no stranger to the latter. If my assumptions were true, then the only question left to resolve was about the price. If they only wanted to use him once, then my "business" would easily and simply play its role and cost nothing, but if they wanted to use him for a prolonged time, which was more likely, then my "business" over time would become unnecessary, and they would most likely have to simply buy him lock, stock, and barrel, which should not be difficult at all. The question would then be slightly modified depending on the value of the information provided and how much he will be willing to accept to match the associated risk.

I didn't know why my neighbor was awake or what he was thinking, and I didn't bother to find out, but we both started asking for another glass of the disgusting wine from the lovely stewardess. Under combined pressure, or maybe because of my Russian or his Polish charm, after resisting for a few seconds, she eventually gave in, and the celestial being brought us two glasses of airplane swill. This was enough for now, and we, like good neighbors, began to share what lay ahead.

As is well known, the first half of the journey is usually spent talking about what one has left behind, and the second half about what lies ahead. So, they say, but we violated a common rule and, without delay, moved to what had been waiting for us ahead, and why we had left New York and America. He was traveling from Chicago to his relatives in Warsaw, while I was planning to open a business selling American cars in Gdansk. Time flew by as we talked, and only somewhere south of Greenland, when our wine ran out, could we follow the positive example of our wiser neighbors, who had long since then found a much more useful use for their time on the long voyage, stretch our legs, and catch at least a couple of hours of sleep.

Warsaw's Chopin Airport is very nice and convenient. It is small, clean, and more than practical. It lacks the hubbub of Amsterdam and the transport intricacies of Heathrow, the crowds of exotic nations in Brussels, and the chaos of Paris's Charles de Gaulle. Everything is clear, orderly, measured, and balanced. Everything except the car rental offices. It is much more complicated there. They require things that American offices of the same kind aren't even aware of. In Chopin airport, they slowly and meticulously study licenses and insurance policies, credit cards, and itineraries. They examine everyone with a piercing gaze, like an X-ray, who wants to get their hands on the coveted car that, for some reason, is not available at the moment. They offer you something you don't need at all until you finally explain to the responsible employee that neither his cars nor his service are of any interest to you anymore. You find what you need at his competitor's counter steps away. It helps. It is a convincing tool, and after some hesitation and consultation with the manager, you will be rewarded with a car with an automatic transmission that suddenly appears like a rabbit out of a magician's hat. That's pretty much how it was at that time.

My Mercedes was much larger than I needed and didn't meet my personal standards. Having lived in America for many years, I never learned to love big cars, especially SUVs, and I couldn't stand trucks. My vehicles have always been small, nimble, and economical, requiring minimal maintenance, attracting minimal attention, and being easy to replace with similar models if needed, rather than costly repairs. So, when I got behind the wheel of this shiny silver beast, I just sighed sadly, accepting the temporary inconvenience of adopting a James Bond persona. However, I didn't have a hat, black sunglasses, or even a silly fake beard, so I failed to make even the slightest image of a most lousy spy.

The GPS in my Mercedes confidently guided me north, and after a bit of wandering through the streets of Warsaw and, of course, getting lost by turning where the smart German electronic navigator told me not to, I finally made my way out of Warsaw and gradually headed north, toward former East Prussia. I wasn't short of funds, and soon, having accepted the massive size of my amazing SUV, I set off like a true tourist to meet my former acquaintance who was eager to get a job at my imaginary company.

Time flew by unnoticed, and after lunch at a local trattoria in the old town of Pultusk, where I enjoyed delicious but straightforward Polish cuisine, I continued my journey.

The wooded countryside, the lack of traffic, and European architecture evoked a poetic melancholy and memories, accompanied by the invigorating patriotic polonaise of Ogiński and the quiet melody of Chopin's nocturne. Passing the Masurian Voivodeship I was greeted with austere but charming German architecture.

There could have been more strict but so dear to me after service in former Konigsberg, German architecture, but the war had erased and destroyed the most beautiful buildings, although credit must be given to the Poles who restored what they could, sticking to the old Prussian style, which, contrary to them, had been so methodically and ruthlessly destroyed in the Kaliningrad region.

I definitely needed a smaller car. Driving this German vehicle, the dream of many of my acquaintances and friends, made me unintentionally speed up and deprive myself of the pleasure of watching the peaceful and quiet views of Masuria, so richly watered with blood at both world wars. I turned off the radio so as not to be distracted, inadvertently trying to understand individual words in Polish that had certain similarities to Russian. Beyond Mragowo, the magnificent two-lane road transformed into a municipal road, reminiscent of the state of New York, lined with trees and dotted with scattered farmhouses and farm buildings. Here and there, a light haze began to rise above individual houses, transforming the sprawling landscape into a pastoral scene of the artists of the Hudson River School. The slightly rugged terrain was interspersed with small lakes and was pleasing to the eye.

Unfortunately, the golden autumn was already over, the leaves had fallen, and the bare branches, barely swaying in the wind, did not add much joy to a lone traveler deprived of the country's simple but magnificent beauty.

However, all roads come to an end, and so did mine. The sky was overcast with clouds, and evening was approaching. Although it was warm in the car, the cold outside was clearly noticeable. A drizzle started, and the wind picked up, blowing the withered leaves off the roadside, when a charming little town appeared before me, surprisingly spared by the last war. The 591st road, with hardly any twists and turns, led me through several roundabouts, which are so popular in Eastern Europe, straight to a hotel with a German name that perfectly suited the atmosphere of the old Teutonic town.

After checking in, I took a large room on the second floor and, after dinner with a bottle of Tokaji wine, decided to go to bed. My meeting with Butusov was scheduled for tomorrow, and I rightly suspected that he was not yet at the hotel. In any case, there was no point in meeting him earlier than at the appointed time, and I didn't particularly want to see him more than I needed to. We were supposed to meet tomorrow at four o'clock in the hotel lobby, but what I was interested in knowing was whether Alex had already arrived or not. I assumed that he would arrive earlier and most likely not alone. Perhaps someone would be assigned to provide support for him before and during the meeting.

Additionally, I was certain that I would be under surveillance, as would my meeting with Butusov. I was advised not to meet with Alex or try to meet him before meeting our client, which again confirmed my belief that my arrival at the hotel would be noticed. It was for this purpose that I ordered dinner at the hotel, to show those who were interested that I am in and to familiarize myself with the layout of the restaurant and find out the table where I would invite Butusov, even though I already had a map of the restaurant. Alex took care of this shortly before my departure.

I decided not to waste time and spent the next day in the town. After wandering through the streets of the old, once German city, I dedicated the rest of my time to the medieval castle of astonishing grandeur with equally astonishingly poor exhibits. There were few visitors, and I was able to calmly explore room by room, admiring the ancient medieval architecture under the watchful eye of old female attendants who looked at everyone passing through the rooms entrusted to them with undisguised suspicion. At first, I felt a little uncomfortable under the suspicious glances of these zealous guards and their police protection, but then I stopped paying attention to them and tried to immerse myself in the depths of past centuries.

However, I did not succeed and continued to be amused by the thought of who might be that villain risking stealing these humble artifacts from the castle's poor collection. Nevertheless, I walked through the galleries and halls of the medieval castle, where the masters of former times haughtily looked down on me from the ancient portraits framed in heavy golden frames. None of them manifested their sympathy to me.

Their condescending, arrogant glances clearly made me feel out of place. What made the situation worse was that my modest attire did not match their ceremonial uniforms decorated with scarves and stars, and their powdered wigs. I had neither one nor the other, and my journey through time could not dispel my disappointment. Only a faint hope, as faint as the light of a distant and unknown star, glimmered in my soul that perhaps, for my merits on Polish soil, one of those stars from the American firmament would one day fall and land on my chest. However, I resisted and shook off the sweet fog of unfulfilled dreams and headed for the exit.

Time was running out, and it was time to grab a before going to meet Butusov.

After having a simple lunch at a bar in the old town and not drinking a single glass of wine, which certainly did not improve my mood and deeply upset my feelings, I consoled myself with the thought that the sacrifice I was now making would be for the good of the United States and serve the cause of world peace. I told myself that one day my name would be immortalized in the annals of history if, before that, I didn't stumble on the slippery parquet floor of my secret mission.

After taking a shower, I came down to the lobby, which was decorated with a large glass chandelier sparkling with all the colors of the rainbow. There was no one at the reception desk or in the lobby, except for two or three people sitting on a sofa and engaged in lively conversation.

The windows of the lobby were covered with streaks of rain, behind which no one was visible, and only dreary, cold rain reigned over the deserted and gray streets of this lovely little town. It wasn't time yet; there were still a few minutes left before the appointed hour, but I began to have certain doubts about my client's punctuality.

I could think over the details of our upcoming meeting one more time. It had been several years since we had last seen each other. Something could have changed in him and in me. True, not too many things might change my attitude towards Russia over my time being in the US. I could only guess how time had affected Vyacheslav.

His position in the regional municipality gave him some opportunities to replenish his pockets with city funds. All Russian municipalities are identical, their employees are the same, and to expect something different from Kaliningrad's servants would be naïve. That's how all Russian municipalities and government bodies work, and there are no exceptions. However, he apparently wanted more, which is why he was interested in my offer.

But I had to be careful. Excessive initiative and excitement on my side would only do harm. Rushing into things is never a good idea, so a dose of skepticism wouldn't hurt. The initiative must come from him and not the other way around. I will have to show great potential of my 'business' while doubting his ability to organize and manage it, at the same time, not to promise anything to him until he finally surrenders and makes me believe in his proficiency. I will have to be skeptical, while my 'partner' will have to come across as a simple, good-natured American guy who immediately takes a liking to Vyacheslav. Alex must become a positive character, as he will have to work with Vyacheslav in the future.

The time came, but Butusov still was not in the lobby, which didn't surprise me at all, remembering from my experience how the military staff work was done and what could really be expected from its former employees.

The evening, smeared on the wet windows of the Polish hotel with a German name, did not match the temper of Chopin's waltzes, but evoked Schopenhauer's gloomy mood.

After waiting for another ten minutes, succumbing to the mood of the "Philosopher of Pessimism," I returned back to my room, still hoping that his delay was the result of the usual carelessness of a former Russian officer, and not the result of his doubts.

Soon, as I had expected, my hopes were fulfilled, and I received a call from the reception desk informing me that Mr. Butusov was waiting for me there. I had no desire to go back downstairs to meet him, but rather invite him to my room, but I had no choice, the meeting had to take place in plain sight so that those who were watching us, although I didn't know who they were, would understand that everything was going according to the plan, albeit with a slight delay. Duty called me downstairs so that I could play my role and perhaps even earn a big shiny medal to adorn my formal attire and inspire admiration from all my colleagues at Trane.

I went downstairs, where Butusov was waiting for me, restlessly turning his head. He had changed, gained a little weight but hadn't lost any of the sparkle in his eyes or the lively attitude that seemed to come from his ancestors from Kuban valleys and the foothills of the Caucasus Mountains.

When he noticed me, he broke into a big smile and moved toward me with his hand already outstretched for a handshake. His face glowed with genuine good nature, just as it had in years past during his inspections of artillery units, where he was a member of commissions with a single goal: to remove or replace a unit commander. Kindness and good nature, the real value of which I knew well, shone on his face, expressing genuine delight at seeing me. To make a picture complete I also smiled in response, but immediately pulled myself together, suddenly remembering the seriousness of the moment and the responsibility of my mission, and decided to behave according to the rules long adopted by the Russians, that is, in a completely Russian manner, putting on a mask of solemn seriousness more befitting a funeral than a meeting with an old comrade.

My first thought, even before we shook hands firmly, was that not only would I not hire him for my imaginary company, but I wouldn't even invite him to a job interview at Trane. This was not so much because he was late as because of his shoes with pointed toes that stuck out far beyond the hem of his trousers. That was enough to cast a shadow over the beginning of our meeting. But mindful of the importance of the moment, I had to restrain a surge of indignation and emotion.

"Andrey, wow! I can't recognize you! Great to see you!" He grabbed my hand and shook it vigorously.

"Hi, Vyacheslav! How was your trip?" I asked because I had to ask something. "Have you settled in yet?"

"No. I just got here. There's a traffic jam at the border; the border guards were rummaging through every vehicle. How about you? Listen, I can't recognize you."

"Okay, okay. Come on, go to your room, drop your stuff, relax, and then we will talk. What time is it? It's a quarter to five. Come on, take your time, we'll meet here in the lobby at six for supper. Don't be late. Come on, get your stuff and go to your room." I patted him on the shoulder and nudged him toward the stairs.

"No, listen, Andrey, tell me how you are? How are you?"

"Vyacheslav, we have the whole evening ahead of us. Get settled, you've had a long day, we'll talk over supper," I hurried to get rid of his greetings because the long toes of his shoes bothered me and began to greatly annoy me.

At six o'clock, I was already in the lobby to meet Butusov, but, as I expected, he wasn't there yet. There was no one at the reception desk, nor was there anyone in the lobby, and his carelessness was beginning to irritate me no less than his shoes. Actually, there was nothing surprising about it - such behavior of a typical Russian, and to make it worth, a "servant of the people", cannot be different. But damn it, who is the supplicant here, and why the hell is he acting like a chooser?!

Finally, five minutes later, he emerged from the elevator, naturally wearing the same shoes, the toes of which seemed to have grown even longer.

No, of course, those who needed my services should give me the brightest medal, at least for spending this evening with such an unpunctual adherent to the fashion I find so ridiculous, which I regret having had to hide. But one can expect only so much from a human being…

"You could have been more punctual, Vyacheslav. I've been waiting here for five minutes, and believe me, I don't have that much time."

I should have put him in his place right away and made it clear that the favor I was doing him had its price.

"Sorry, Andrey, I had to sort out some things, so I'm a little late." He changed his tone slightly, which was good and soothed me a bit. "How did you end up here, anyway? Why not Elbląg or Gdańsk? They seem more decent places."

I looked at him but didn't reply. There was no point in explaining that I would much rather spend time at the historical site "Wolfsschaze" than with him, and I didn't want to waste my effort explaining my interests and preferences; he probably wouldn't have appreciated them anyway.

"Okay. How was your trip?" I asked him, although this question should rather have been directed at me, who crossed the ocean, but Butusov was hardly interested in such details. I pointed to the bar. "Let's get a drink, and you can tell me there."

It was time to begin my mission of bringing my unpunctual client to the required condition.

We went to the bar, where there were already several people.

"What would you like to drink?" I asked, trying to lighten the mood and dispel my irritation. "Wine, cognac?"

"Yes, cognac would be nice in this weather."

"I think it would be just as good in any other weather," I thought to myself, but I was happy with his choice.

"Great. I see they have Hennessy, Courvoisier, and Remy Martin. Which one would you like?"

"Hennessy. It's a good cognac."

"Yes, it's good, but Remy Martin is better. Shall I order it?"

"Yes? Go ahead, Remy will do, or whatever its name."

"Martin," I added, "you won't regret it. I'll have some wine, if you wouldn't mind."

"Yeah," he drawled, "you've changed. You're not the man I remember you."

But what was more important was that it was exactly how I remember him. I ignored his comment while ordering from the tall waiter. I avoided speaking Russian with anyone in Poland, preferring English instead. The explanation for this was quite logical—the younger generation wisely chose not to learn Russian, while the older generation preferred to forget it. Well, they had good reasons to do it…

"Okay, tell me, how's life, how's the family? How is your business?"

I wasn't very interested in answering the first part of the question, and I already provided him with the answers to the second part, so I decided to focus more on the questions that interested me, but not before he matures to the required condition to start that part of the conversation.

The first shot of cognac was followed by a second, and Butusov, quickly realizing who was paying for the banquet, visibly relaxed. I didn't expect anything different, just as I wasn't surprised to see how the Russian drinks cognac. He consumed it the same way everyone in the world drinks vodka. He drank it like an orchestra conductor – throwing his head back in ecstasy, in the moment when a curtain falls. This fashion he might as well have been drinking moonshine at a village wedding…

We drank some more, reminiscing old friends, mutual acquaintances, commanders, and army brass, and then I suggested going to a restaurant for supper.

Butusov visibly relaxed but talked incessantly, constantly slipping into stories about which of his former commanders had built a house or cottage, bought an apartment, or moved to Moscow to do the same in the bigger scale. It was obvious that the welfare of our mutual acquaintances was weighing heavily on Vyacheslav's mind, and without directly mentioning the possibility of his getting a job in 'my company', he was waiting for me to bring up the subject.

Meanwhile, dinner was served. East Prussia had been famous for fish farming since the days of the Empire, and I, having no doubt about the achievements of German ichthyology, paid tribute to the freshwater fish of the local restaurant. Nevertheless, I was in no hurry to move on to the topic that interested us both. The time had not come yet, we hadn't drunk enough, and perfectly baked fish had not yet been eaten.

"Vyacheslav, don't be shy, order whatever you'd like and don't worry about the cost. It's all taken care of," and here I wasn't lying, "as long as business is going the way it is, we can afford this little banquet. And I hope it won't be the last one. By the way, how are things with you? A lot of work?"

"Yes, enough. Construction is going on, although, as always, there's not enough money. When was there ever enough? By the time the order reaches the contractor, half of it has already gone 'to the side'. Well, you know how it works. So, by the time it reaches us, there's not too much left. The work itself isn't dirty, but one can't get very far on one salary, you understand, don't you?"

We often cannot comprehend the motives behind many human actions and deeds, whether they are influenced by the circumstances or deviated consciousness, cannot understand what drives and compels a person to commit a despicable act or perform an unprecedented feat. Still, with Vyacheslav, everything was completely different. Good cognac is considered good for a reason. It did its job as well as Freud or Festinger could have done, and Butusov revealed himself as a beautiful tea rose bud revealing its petals in the morning sun.

It also became clear and caused a holy indignation that blatant injustice he had been subjected to, state allocations for road construction and repair were being divided up at the level of his department head and above, leaving clerks like Butusov with only 'bones and tendons'.

"They lost conscience. It looks like we're doing one thing, but all we get is the leftovers from the master's table."

He was right. It looked like the teamwork of his department was suffering under atrocious injustice. Vyacheslav's Catonian honesty made him a credit, and his genuine appearance harmonized perfectly with his black-and-striped tie. And indeed, such injustice could not be tolerated, and to fix it, we have appeared before Vyacheslav in white robes and rays of glory.

I was simply delighted: with a client like that, Alexei and Ian could work without any stress. My sweet Tokaji wine also had a beneficial effect on me, and its warmth, nurtured in the valleys of Carpathian Mountains, not only revived me and made me forget about his pointed shoes, but also cheered me up.

"Well, that's fixable. If you take on a couple of my dealerships", I didn't want to be petty with just one dealership and decided to start with two, "then I don't think you'll regret it, and if you get control of the other in Gdansk, then there will be a significant remuneration."

Vyacheslav's eyes lit up. They were already shining, demonstrating the beneficial effects of the good cognac, and the waiter couldn't keep up pouring fast enough. I had no doubt that the American taxpayers had overpaid for Butusov's cognac; he was ready to sell himself as whole, with or without the entire Kaliningrad region to the Devil himself, for a much lower price.

I periodically scanned the room, waiting for the 'heavy artillery' in the form of Alexei to arrive. The tables around us were gradually filling up, it was getting noisier and more cheerful, and Vyacheslav was already quite ready for certain proposals and negotiations. Remy Martin can work wonders, no worse than a well-aged port wine.

"Until opening of a representative office in your area..."

"In 'your area," he interrupted mockingly, "come on, 'in your area'! Have you forgotten how we used to get our hands dirty together at the training ground?"

I wasn't quite sure what training ground he was talking about where we had 'our hands dirty' together, but I smiled, generously agreed, and continued, "Roads, roads, my friend, dirt roads and highways, concrete and the regular asphalt roads, that's what you need to know before you start delivering cars to your customers. You understand that if there are good roads, then there will be good, fast and expensive cars available; and if there aren't, then you can't sell anything better than a horse carts. So, I need to know if you're building them or not, and if so, where, how long, and for what purpose, do you understand?"

"I understand." Vyacheslav nodded his head, though not very convincingly. "Listen, what do you drive yourself, huh? What? What do you drive? Come on, show me what you drove here in!"

Then I suddenly remembered I had completely forgotten about my fancy SUV, which I would gladly trade for a Renault Scenic and should show to Butusov when I get the chance. Oh God, how can a tin box on four wheels be so interesting? That seditious thought flashed through my mind, which I immediately dismissed, overwhelmed by a sense of responsibility that had come from nowhere. This sense is undoubtedly part of me, but sometimes it gets lost, and it takes time to find it again.

"Well, come on, I'll show you my 'bicycle'. Do you smoke?"

"I do. Oh, you Americans don't smoke, do you? You have a sober lifestyle. But we don't. We smoke. And we drink too."

"That's good, as long as you build roads."

"Roads? Yeah, we're building roads, or rather, they're building roads for us. Our contractors. So, where's your 'carriage'"?

The cold drizzle had stopped, but turned into a mist that, according to the professors of the Department of Weapons of Mass Destruction, was ideal for the use of neuroparalytic gas. This amazing and life-affirming thought suddenly fluttered through my head like a butterfly on a hot summer day and, fortunately, quickly flew away from such gloomy subject. Where did it come from? Probably from the Academy where, on the staff training, my anti-tank regiment lost thirty per cent of its personnel after crossing the affected area in similar weather. What a stupid association; maybe the wine was not good?

My silver horse, washed by rain, stood where I left it in the hotel parking lot. It couldn't sparkle in the twilight of the fading day, but it did a good job of enchanting and stirring the feelings of a retired Russian lieutenant colonel, whose eyes widened with delight, although this may be because of the lack of lighting.

"Well, Andrey, you're the man! This is a 'carriage'! A real 'carriage'! Yes! Could you ever have dreamed of such a thing when we were in the Army?!"

"Don't worry. Work with us and you'll have one like this."

Here I paused. "With us." Words like "us," "with us," and other plural terms should never be used in such cases to avoid causing alarm or even fear. One should only speak for himself, and to defuse the tension, I immediately added: "My partner has one just like this and now I'd like to know where the hell he is."

Butusov was still moving slowly along the car, walking around my clumsy Mercedes, smoothly running his hand over its wet hood.

"Okay, Vyacheslav. Let's go inside, I don't want to get chilled by the fog like Esenin in his 'Anna Snegina', besides Alexei should be here by now."

Vyacheslav finished his tour and slowly walked toward the entrance. The cognac had done its job, but Butusov wasn't staggering, but his gait was clearly unsteady.

Two Polish gentlemen were standing in front of the hotel entrance, arguing about something. One of them, a grenadier man holding a cigarette, was talking animatedly to his companion, waving his arm vigorously. As he passed by, Butusov slightly swayed at the very moment when the Pole turned halfway toward him, not noticing Vyacheslav passing by, who caught the Pole's left arm with his hand. Neither of them apologized, as is common in the US. The Pole muttered something under his breath, while Butusov cursed, as is usual in his homeland.

"Spojrzn a to Rosyjski pijana"

Neither he nor I knew Polish, but from the intonation and circumstances, it was very clear what was said.

"What are you muttering about, you!" Butusov stared at the Pole, who grabbed Butusov's right hand with his left hand while Butusov regained his balance. A conflict was brewing that could ruin everything. To complete a full picture, what we needed was a good fight and police on the scene.

I literally jumped next to the Pole, whose advantage over Butusov was obvious.

"Excuse me, sir. I am very sorry. My buddy is a bit tired and regrets what happened."

The Pole looked at me blankly. His face was expressionless. Then his friend approached him and whispered something in his ear. Meanwhile, Butusov pulled his wrist out of the Pole's hand and took a step back, muttering something through his clenched teeth.

At that very moment, the concierge ran out of the lobby and began to explain something loudly and quickly to the Poles. Behind him was Alexei, who followed the concierge and quickly approached Butusov, standing between him and the Pole, and pushed Vyacheslav toward the entrance rapidly.

"It's okay, sir. Everything is fine," I waved goodbye to the Pole when I noticed that he was also quite inebriated, just like his partner. However, they were no longer paying attention to us. The concierge was still talking quickly, holding both Poles at the hotel entrance, apparently to prevent them from following us. We went to our table, Alexei in front, followed by Vyacheslav, and I brought up the rear, closing the glorious procession.

Butusov continued to swear until Alexei, in a few short but meaningful words, told him to shut up and sit down at the table.

"What's the matter, buddy, have you lost your senses?! Do you want to deal with the police?! They can ban you from entering Europe. Do you realize it?" Alexei, not even bothering to introduce himself, was already attacking Butusov. "I see you guys have had a good time here without me! Fucking clowns! By the way, I'm Alexei." I hope Andrey has already told you about me. "

It was very good and, most importantly, a timely introduction. Alexei quickly changed the subject, reaching across the table to shake Butusov's hand.

The latter continued to mumble something about the Pole, obviously forgetting the purpose of his visit. For me, it looked like the right moment to start playing my role. "Yes, Vyacheslav, we're not going to get anywhere like this. Listen, if you can't control your emotions, then it's probably too early for you to work for me. I do not think I can let you work with our customers. Let's wait a year, then we will talk!"

Butusov looked at me sullenly, biting his lips and saying nothing.

"Andrey, wait, don't rush things. Vyacheslav doesn't seem like a bad guy; he just got carried away a little, but that might happen to everyone. Look how he jumped on him! Wait, I think he has potential". Then waiting for while, he continued addressing Butusov more than me. "Look, the Russian dealership is not established yet. Let him learn a bit about business and understand what's going on in the region. Give him a chance", Alexei chimed in, suddenly taking a liking to Vyacheslav's escapades.

Butusov's eyes gradually lit up as he listened to my "partner's" heartfelt speech.

"Listen, Vyacheslav, there's a lot of money at stake, and I can't risk it or the business," I replied, looking at my plate and picking at what remained of the fish. "I want fish. I need to order more," I said, looking around for the waiter and pausing for a long moment so that Alex could continue his speech as a master defender, and he seized the moment.

"Andrey, I believe he'll do well. I liked him immediately. Let him begin collecting information about the ro..." he paused and quickly corrected himself, "about the car market, and we'll cover his expenses from our reserve fund to see how it progresses".

"Guys, listen, give it a try, I'll manage it, I will do what you say," Butusov had completely forgotten about the incident, and the talk of quick payment cleared his head better than any breath of fresh air. Then he suddenly hiccupped, as if to emphasize and punctuate his statement.

"Well, I don't know," I continued to express my skepticism, giving Alexei the opportunity to develop his proposal into something more concrete.

Alex continued, "Vyacheslav, let's do this. There is no dealership in the region yet." Then, turning toward Butusov, he continued, "We'll hire you and see what you're capable of, plus during that time you'll learn and understand how business works. I need to know everything about the prospects for road construction in the region, their current condition, and future development plans for asphalt, concrete, gravel, and their intended use. This information will help me justify and create a business case to get a loan to open and build the dealership. In the meantime, I'll pay you on a sliding scale even before the dealership opens. If you can handle it, the job is yours. How do you feel about that?"

Butusov poured the rest of the cognac into his glass, forgetting to pour our glasses. It was clear that he was ready to accept the offer without discussing further details. The reflection of American dollars danced in his pupils, and it looked like he was ready to embrace and kiss Alex right at the table.

"Guys, I'll do everything. You'll see. This is my department. I'll get everything you need, exactly and on time."

"Well, you see, Andrey, everything will work out," Alex's face couldn't express more good nature. "We'll discuss the details tomorrow. I'll tell you exactly what you need to provide, and then we'll start spinning the story," he continued, turning to Butusov. " Just don't spread it around too much. We don't need any competition. And most importantly, don't screw things up from the start, or it'll all be for nothing, agreed?"

Butusov put his hand on Alex's shoulder and looked into his eyes with dog-like devotion.

"Well, that's great. Now let's continue the party, because I haven't eaten anything yet. And you, Vyacheslav, I think you've had enough," he nodded at the empty bottle of cognac, "otherwise I doubt you'll be good for anything tomorrow." Alex logically ended the conversation, trying to save Butusov's drunken head for tomorrow's work and trying not to overdo it with his obligations.

We continued our dinner with wine, while Butusov pondered his dreams of easy money that had so readily and quickly come into his possession. Alex ordered his meal, and we switched to less sensitive subjects. The fish was delicious, and the Tokaji did its part, and I, feeling full of wine and good spirits, was thankful to Alex for steering the conversation away from the asphalt and highway roads of Kaliningrad to a more cheerful, though not entirely decent topic.

The evening passed wonderfully. Butusov was drunk, I was also well pumped with wine, as the instructions and circumstances demanded, which happily coincided with my desire to relax after my transatlantic journey. It remained to hope that the drunk Vyacheslav would remember at least something in the morning about today's conversation.

We agreed to meet at nine o'clock here for coffee, after which the drunk Butusov was escorted to his room and carefully left on the bed.

"If he remembers anything tomorrow, I'll be extremely surprised," I remarked pessimistically.

"Then we'll repeat the lesson over coffee. Don't put any more pressure on him; he's ripe. He'll be in touch with me as his junior 'partner,' and you'll be too busy to deal with him, as we discussed. By the way, when are you leaving?"

"Tomorrow. Tomorrow I'm going to the Wolfsschaze Museum, and then to Lithuania for several days."

"Great. See you tomorrow, then. It looks like you are well-oiled also."

"Well, I did it as was ordered, didn't I?" I replied and walked down the corridor to my room.

That was how, so banally and simply, months of preparation came to an end. In the morning, of course, Butusov didn't show up on time. He wasn't in the lobby or the restaurant, and we had to wake him up in his room, where we had to restore him to proper shape by nasty coffee from the room coffee machine, and went through the same briefing as yesterday. Alex left him his phone number and email address, instructing him not to share his prospects or his activities.

In the end, of course, Butusov realized what was required of him and that there was no company and no dealership, but he was paid, which didn't contradict his goal of earning some extra income. He was quite satisfied with all he so easily got, and he had no objections but to continue working for Alex. Both sides were quite satisfied with the success of their venture, and there were no mutual complaints or disagreements.

However, he did not have to work for long, and a year later, when the passion for missile defense subsided, Butusov was transferred to the reserve and ordered to sit quietly and wait for further call. I found out about this a year later when, following a similar pattern, I was asked to hold a meeting with the Captain Third Class from the main base of the Baltic Fleet in Baltiysk, but this time in Lithuania.

The candidate from the Fuel and Lubricants Service turned out to be so malleable and quick-witted that he didn't even need to get drunk; he understood everything right away. As it turned out, finding candidates for easy money in the Kaliningrad region was not just easy, but very easy. The snakes of betrayal had long since made their nest in the Kaliningrad region, although, in all honesty, they were hardly ahead of Moscow and other Russian cities and towns and were ready to sell themselves with all their guts combined with all available sensitive and classified materials for a reasonable price without any fuss, so that zeal in recruitment proved unnecessary and no virtuoso tricks were required.

The Captain Third Class was a true military man and nothing less than an excellent student of combat and political training, as straight as a pole and as frank as John the Theologian, and had no need for Chinese ceremonies in preparation for exchanging American banknotes for the required information. He had plenty of fuel, gasoline, and diesel, plenty of oil and lubricants, but he didn't have a good car to utilize the possessed treasure, but his superiors had both. And he wanted to remedy that injustice. It was difficult to challenge his logic and impossible to dispute his argumentation. Under the weight and pressure of indisputable facts, we had no choice but to give in. The remaining problem was the price, but we resolved that fairly quickly, honestly and without haggling, at least at the initial stage. I don't know how the process went after that, but I completed my second mission smoothly and with less effort than the first one, also without medical consequences for my liver from excessive alcohol consumption. It would be tedious and boring to recount that affair in all details, so I will describe it briefly.

I contacted him, then an officer in the rear service of the Baltic fleet based in Baltiysk, and suggested a meeting in Lithuania, since he was prohibited from traveling to Poland as a military man. He was also forbidden to go to Lithuania, but on my advice, he requested a passport to drive through Lithuania to allied Belarus to sell his car. And he sold it. He sold it without much haggling and without doubt underpriced, but he had no regrets or hard feelings because the one-time compensation for the unsuccessful sale was enough for him to buy a much newer Audi.

In order to avoid the narrow two-lane A16 road connecting the Kaliningrad region with Grodno in Belarus, I arranged a meeting in the charming and quiet provincial town of Alytus, thirty kilometers south of the A16 highway and located not too far away from Augustów in Poland, which was comfortably located on my route from Warsaw to Vilnius.

We held a meeting in a small hotel, Vaidila, as there are no large hotels there. We spent a quiet and civilized evening, without any incidents or aggressive Poles, without shouting, drunkenness, or fighting, and finished dinner with a bottle of Armenian brandy in Alex's room. The only inconvenience was parking our client's car, which we left on a bystreet in that quiet town so as not to attract too much attention to his Russian car license plates had he parked it at the hotel parking lot.

That's pretty much how both of my trips to Eastern Europe went. I don't want to bore you with more details, since it's probably a bit early to talk about, so let's just leave it at that point. I didn't learn anything about the results of the work with the Captain Third Class, nor did I try. Everything went well with Butusov, although it only lasted a little over a year. He did his job honestly, providing all information for existing and planned roads, including roads leading to potential missile sites and some additional data as a bonus, using what he had received from his contacts and army friends. He died a few years later, quietly and peacefully, as an honest citizen and family man of the Russian Federation.

I combined my trips to Poland and Lithuania, covered by Alex's employer, with my personal trips around Lithuania and Poland, without taking for myself a single cent from my friends or American taxpayers, fulfilling my old promise to repay my debt to my historical homeland. It is not for me to judge how successful I was, although I hope that I did return something not so pleasant for their taste, though I would have liked to do more, putting myself to the service of my friends and my new homeland.

I was very disappointed by the Russian military, represented by the young naval officer who was deprived of any artistry and romanticism in doing that business. My genuine grief lay in the banality and simplicity of the recruitment of both guys, which required no grace and adroitness and turned out to be akin to milking cows, where the better the silage, the higher the yield. In the latter case, the captain turned out to be almost a teetotaler, who, by definition, is a person who nurtures something dark and antisocial deep in his soul, completely untrustworthy, as well as being as straight as a telegraph pole. Both were interested only in money, and there was no place in either of them for poetry or innovations. Even drinking with them was uninteresting and boring, because one soon got drunk like a pig, while the other drank practically nothing, and looking at them, I could barely contain my nausea and repulsion. A gray shroud of disappointment enveloped me as I watched those two poor creatures so routinely selling classified information. With them, I felt immensely lonely, tired, and broken when all my hopes for interesting cooperation with such seemingly decent people miserably failed, turning out to be devoid of any signs of expressiveness. Cooperation with so primitive personalities reminded me of buying used tires at the car market in Kaliningrad…

But what could I do? Life is full of disappointments and unfulfilled hopes. One must be prepared for this, develop resilience, and be capable of enduring adversity while adopting a philosophical outlook to unpredictable events. This involves learning lessons from one's own experiences and those of others, drawing wisdom from past thinkers like Montaigne and his essays such as "On Vanity" or "On Bad Means for Good Purposes." That is why I highly recommend everyone read Montaigne; you'll gain a lot of insight into this chaotic world, which might be extremely beneficial.

I know for sure what you want to ask me, so I'll answer your question in advance. No, I never had any doubts or regrets about what I did, because I wanted to do it at the first opportunity. The moral side of this matter was not and is not a problem for me. For me, it would have been more immoral to forget or ignore all the troubles that were created in Russia for me and mine and for those who wanted to follow the same path. I simply had to do what I did, and if I hadn't, I would have found another opportunity and a different means to achieve it. Debts must be paid, although I must admit that sometimes it happens with a long delay.

But that's a sacrifice one must be prepared to bring to altar following this twisted path."

Alexander finished his story, and we sat silently staring at the dying fire in the fireplace. We didn't know what to say or how to comment. Empty wine bottles sat under the table, as is common in Russia, and we should have gone for another one to logically conclude the story and end the evening, which had already turned into the early hours of the morning.

"Well, shall we continue?" Alexander asked uncertainly, nodding toward the pile of empty bottles.

"Maybe a little bit, in memory of our friends, living and dead," I replied. And then I added, "But what a good collection of people they were!"

"Well said, and most importantly, very life, life-affirming," he stumbled over the awkward word, "life-affirming. "Yes, just like that," after which he walked unsteadily to the basement for another bottle of wine.

In the morning, I left. My head hurt, and I continued to suffer from headache the entire flight home. My thoughts were confused. Chechnya and Africa, Venezuela and the Gulf of Guinea, along with Lithuania and Poland, were mixed together into one big boiling mess that spilled over the edges of a smoky cauldron, which I tried unsuccessfully to cover up with the lid of my excited imagination. But the mess spilled over, and I landed and took a cab to get home to sort out what I had learned about my friends, living and dead, maimed and healthy, in my sick head.

Maybe when I sort through all these memories, I'll put my recollections down on paper, so that one day I can read them and recall the years that have passed long ago, meet, at least on the pages, my old friends, and the events that, I hope, did not pass without a trace and left a deep mark on my memory. Maybe, maybe...

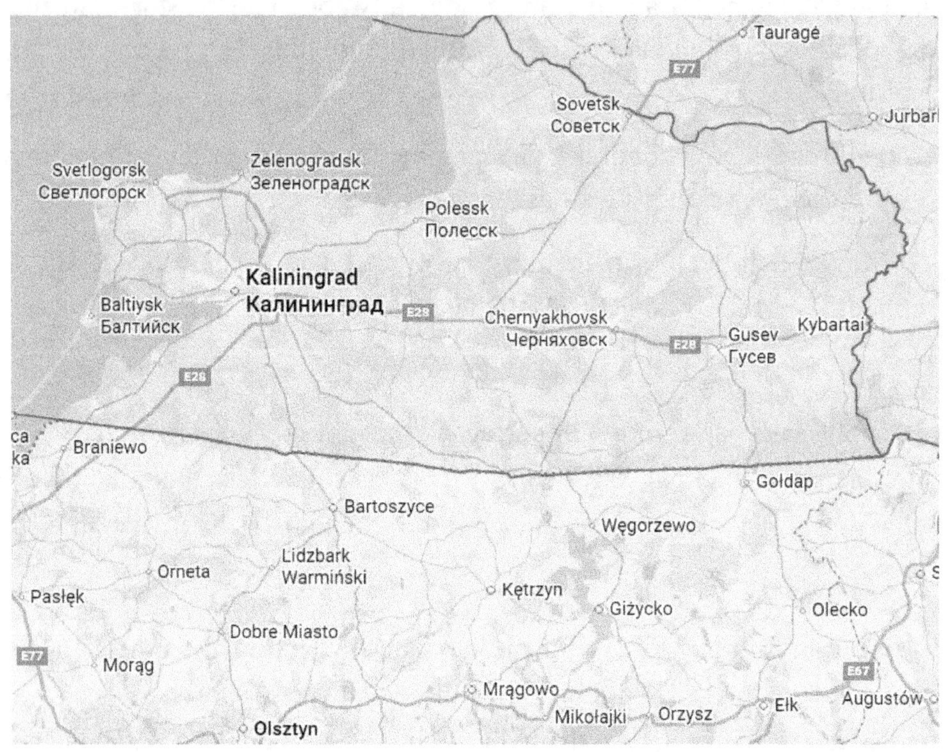

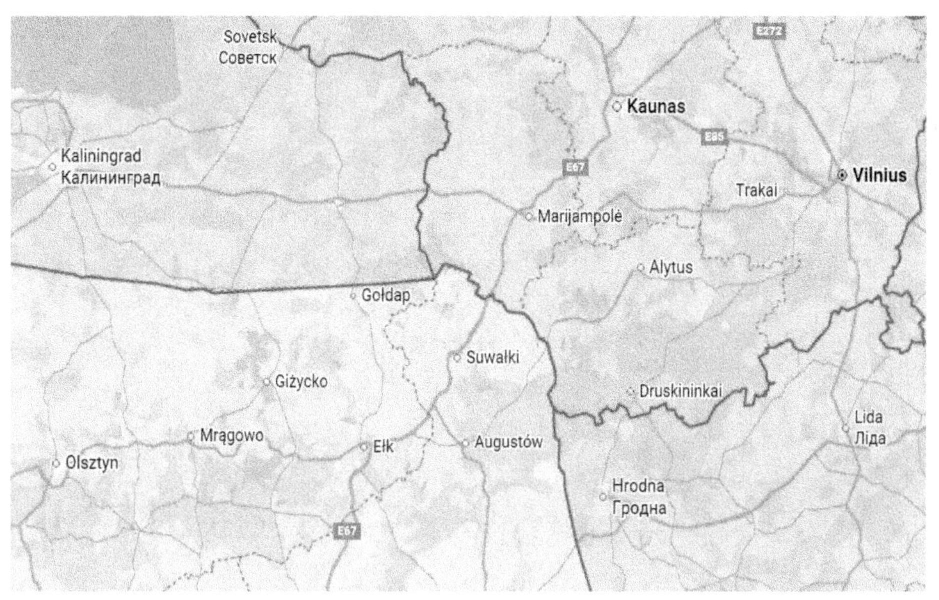

Sovetsk
Советск
Kaliningrad
Калининград
Kaunas
E272
E85
E67
Trakai
Vilnius
Marijampolė
Alytus
Gołdap
Suwałki
Druskininkai
Giżycko
Lida
Ліда
Mrągowo
Ełk
Augustów
Olsztyn
Hrodna
Гродна
E67